SOME THINGS DARK AND DANGEROUS

selection

"A delightful potpourri of mysteries. Most are by older writers, including Sheridan Le Fanu, Algernon Blackwood, William H. Prescott, F. Marion Crawford, and Dorothy Sayers. Newer writers include John Collier, Q. Patrick, Lewis Padgett. Evelyn Waugh sets the chilling temperature with the first story, his classic, 'Mr. Loveday's Little Outing.'"
Library Journal

"[The author] has turned her attention to younger readers for the first time and come up with . . . stories . . . that should cause the reader to take a few quick and cautious looks over his shoulder when he finishes them."
New York Times Book Review

Other Avon Flare Books Edited by
Joan Kahn

SOME THINGS FIERCE AND FATAL
SOME THINGS STRANGE AND SINISTER

SOME THINGS DARK AND DANGEROUS

EDITED BY JOAN KAHN

AN AVON FLARE BOOK

For my nephews and their typewriters

Grateful acknowledgment is made as follows for the copyrighted material reprinted in this collection:
"Mr. Loveday's Little Outing," by Evelyn Waugh. Copyright 1936, 1942, 1943, 1947, 1953, 1954 by Evelyn Waugh. Reprinted from *Tactical Exercise* by Evelyn Waugh, by permission of Little, Brown and Company and A. D. Peters Co. "The Murder of Dr. Burdell," by Edmund Pearson. Reprinted by permission: Copyright 1935, 1963, The New Yorker Magazine, Inc. Reprinted by permission of Mrs. Mary S. Pearson. "The Destruction of Smith," by Algernon Blackwood. Reprinted from *Tales of the Mysterious and Macabre* by Algernon Blackwood, by permission of the Public Trustee and Paul Hamlyn Ltd. "Wet Saturday," by John Collier. Copyright 1938, 1965 by John Collier. Reprinted by permission of Harold Matson Company, Inc. Originally appeared in *The New Yorker.* "The Fantastic Horror of the Cat in the Bag," by Dorothy L. Sayers. Reprinted from *Lord Peter Views the Body* (1928), by Dorothy L. Sayers, by permission of Harper & Row, Publishers, Inc., and David Higham Associates, Ltd. "Portrait of a Murderer," by Q. Patrick. Copyright 1942 by Harper's Magazine, Inc. Reprinted by permission of Curtis Brown, Ltd. "Boy Hunt," by John Bartlow Martin. Copyright 1944 by Harper & Brothers. Reprinted by permission of Harold Ober Associates Incorporated. "Calling All Stars (Intercepted Radio Message Broadcast From the Planet Cybernetica)," by Leo Szilard. Copyright © 1961 by Leo Szilard. Reprinted from *The Voice of the Dolphins* by Leo Szilard, by permission of Simon and Schuster, Inc. " 'These Terrible Men, the Harpes!' " by Robert M. Coates. Copyright 1930 by Robert M. Coates. Reprinted by permission of Harold Ober Associates Incorporated. "When the Bough Breaks," by Lewis Padgett. Copyright 1944 by Street & Smith Publications, Inc. in the U.S.A. and Great Britain. Reprinted from *Astounding Science Fiction,* by permission of Harold Matson Co., Inc.

AVON BOOKS
A division of
The Hearst Corporation
959 Eighth Avenue
New York, New York 10019

Copyright © 1970 by Joan Kahn
Published by arrangement with Harper and Row Publishers, Inc.
Library of Congress Catalog Card Number 82-45465
ISBN: 0-380-01556-0

Library of Congress Cataloging in Publication Data
Main entry under title:

Some things dark and dangerous.

(An Avon/Flare book)
1. Detective and mystery stories, American. 2. Detective and mystery stories, English. 3. Horror tales, American. 4. Horror tales, English. I. Kahn, Joan.
PS648.D4S58   1982   813'.0872'08   82-45465
ISBN 0-380-01556-0 (pbk.)   AACR2

First Avon Printing, April, 1974
First Flare Printing, October, 1982

FLARE BOOKS TRADEMARK REG. U.S. PAT. OFF. AND IN OTHER COUNTRIES, MARCA REGISTRADA, HECHO EN U.S.A.

Printed in the U.S.A.

WFH 10 9 8 7 6 5 4

Contents

Introduction

Being frightened or mystified on paper is the best way to be frightened or mystified. Stories that scare you and mystify you can be splendidly entertaining.

I grew up in a house with lots of books by authors who were not only superb storytellers but were able to chill your blood and widen your eyes—and make you jump whenever a floorboard creaked behind you.

So, naturally, I wound up editing suspense novels, Harper Novels of Suspense. I've done that for a long time now. Most of the writers I have worked with are English or American, and they are a varied group—professors, lawyers, a jockey and a judge and a prisoner among them.

In between working with authors who were creating books for today, and perhaps tomorrow, I started thinking about all the splendid stories that had been written and were sitting, largely unnoticed, on somebody's bookshelf. I felt that the best way to reintroduce these good but forgotten stories was to collect them in an anthology—and that's what I did (after I disinterred them, of course).

The first collection I did was called *The Edge of the Chair* and enough people enjoyed reading it for me to do a second anthology, *Hanging by a Thread*. It's amazing how much good material has sunk out of sight in how many places (some of the places rather dusty, to be sure). The more things I found, the more I realized how much there was still to be found.

So, here's a third anthology—this time for young readers.

All the entries herein are, I think, exciting. Some are fiction, some are fact. Included you'll find Mr. Loveday, who had committed a murder, but who seemed like such a nice old fellow now. Evelyn Waugh introduces him. Dorothy Sayers presents a noted nobleman, that marvelous detective Lord Peter Wimsey, in a strange case of mistaken luggage. And Howard Pyle, whose books about pirates once delighted me, frightens me now (and, I trust, will frighten you) and an eerie story set in Florence about a young man and a magician.

There are stories of today and stories from the past and stories about other worlds as well. All of them, I hope, will keep you reading happily—and, perhaps, jumping whenever a floorboard creaks.

JOAN KAHN
April 3, 1970

Mr. Loveday's Little Outing

by Evelyn Waugh

fiction

*As a young man Mr. Loveday had killed some-
body; however he seemed perfectly harmless
now.*

1

"You will not find your father greatly changed," remarked Lady Moping, as the car turned into the gates
of the County Asylum.

"Will he be wearing a uniform?" asked Angela.

"No, dear, of course not. He is receiving the very best
attention."

It was Angela's first visit and it was being made at her
own suggestion.

Ten years had passed since the showery day in late summer when Lord Moping had been taken away; a day of
confused but bitter memories for her; the day of Lady
Moping's annual garden party, always bitter, confused that
day by the caprice of the weather which, remaining clear
and brilliant with promise until the arrival of the first
guests, had suddenly blackened into a squall. There had
been a scuttle for cover; the marquee had capsized; a
frantic carrying of cushions and chairs; a table-cloth lofted
to the boughs of the monkey-puzzler, fluttering in the rain;
a bright period and the cautious emergence of guests on to
the soggy lawns; another squall; another twenty minutes of
sunshine. It had been an abominable afternoon, culminat-
ing at about six o'clock in her father's attempted suicide.

Lord Moping habitually threatened suicide on the occasion of the garden party; that year he had been found
black in the face, hanging by his braces in the orangery;

some neighbours, who were sheltering there from the rain, set him on his feet again, and before dinner a van had called for him. Since then Lady Moping had paid seasonal calls at the asylum and returned in time for tea, rather reticent of her experience.

Many of her neighbours were inclined to be critical of Lord Moping's accommodation. He was not, of course, an ordinary inmate. He lived in a separate wing of the asylum, specially devoted to the segregation of wealthier lunatics. These were given every consideration which their foibles permitted. They might choose their own clothes (many indulged in the liveliest fancies), smoke the most expensive brands of cigars and, on the anniversaries of their certification entertain any other inmates for whom they had an attachment to private dinner parties.

The fact remained, however, that it was far from being the most expensive kind of institution; the uncompromising address, "COUNTY HOME FOR MENTAL DEFECTIVES" stamped across the notepaper, worked on the uniforms of their attendants, painted, even, upon a prominent hoarding at the main entrance, suggested the lowest associations. From time to time, with less or more tact, her friends attempted to bring to Lady Moping's notice particulars of seaside nursing homes, of "qualified practitioners with large private grounds suitable for the charge of nervous or difficult cases," but she accepted them lightly; when her son came of age he might make any changes that he thought fit; meanwhile she felt no inclination to relax her economical régime; her husband had betrayed her basely on the one day in the year when she looked for loyal support, and was far better off than he deserved.

A few lonely figures in great-coats were shuffling and loping about the park.

"Those are the lower class lunatics," observed Lady Moping. "There is a very nice little flower garden for people like your father. I sent them some cuttings last year."

They drove past the blank, yellow brick façade to the doctor's private entrance and were received by him in the "visitors room," set aside for interviews of this kind. The window was protected on the inside by bars and wire netting; there was no fireplace; when Angela nervously attempted to move her chair further from the radiator, she found that it was screwed to the floor.

"Lord Moping is quite ready to see you," said the doctor.

"How is he?"

"Oh, very well, very well indeed, I'm glad to say. He had rather a nasty cold some time ago, but apart from that his condition is excellent. He spends a lot of his time in writing."

They heard a shuffling, skipping sound approaching along the flagged passage. Outside the door a high peevish voice, which Angela recognized as her father's, said: "I haven't the time, I tell you. Let them come back later."

A gentler tone, with a slight rural burr, replied, "Now come along. It is a purely formal audience. You need stay no longer than you like."

Then the door was pushed open (it had no lock or fastening) and Lord Moping came into the room. He was attended by an elderly little man with full white hair and an expression of great kindness.

"That is Mr. Loveday who acts as Lord Moping's attendant."

"Secretary," said Lord Moping. He moved with a jogging gait and shook hands with his wife.

"This is Angela. You remember Angela, don't you?"

"No, I can't say that I do. What does she want?"

"We just came to see you."

"Well, you have come at an exceedingly inconvenient time. I am very busy. Have you typed out that letter to the Pope yet, Loveday?"

"No, my lord. If you remember, you asked me to look up the figures about the Newfoundland fisheries first?"

"So I did. Well, it is fortunate, as I think the whole letter will have to be redrafted. A great deal of new information has come to light since luncheon. A great deal ... You see, my dear, I am fully occupied." He turned his restless, quizzical eyes upon Angela. "I suppose you have come about the Danube. Well, you must come again later. Tell them it will be all right, quite all right, but I have not had time to give my full attention to it. Tell them that."

"Very well, Papa."

"Anyway," said Lord Moping rather petulantly, "it is a matter of secondary importance. There is the Elbe and the Amazon and the Tigris to be dealt with first, eh, Loveday? ... Danube indeed. Nasty little river. I'd only call it a stream myself. Well, can't stop, nice of you to come. I

would do more for you if I could, but you see how I'm
fixed. Write to me about it. That's it. *Put it in black and
white.*"

And with that he left the room.

"You see," said the doctor, "he is in excellent condition.
He is putting on weight, eating and sleeping excellently. In
fact, the whole tone of his system is above reproach."

The door opened again and Loveday returned.

"Forgive my coming back, sir, but I was afraid that the
young lady might be upset at his Lordship's not knowing
her. You mustn't mind him, miss. Next time he'll be very
pleased to see you. It's only to-day he's put out on account
of being behindhand with his work. You see, sir, all this
week I've been helping in the library and I haven't been
able to get all his Lordship's reports typed out. And he's
got muddled with his card index. That's all it is. He
doesn't mean any harm."

"What a nice man," said Angela, when Loveday had
gone back to his charge.

"Yes. I don't know what we should do without old
Loveday. Everybody loves him, staff and patients alike."

"I remember him well. It's a great comfort to know
that you are able to get such good warders," said Lady
Moping; "people who don't know, say such foolish things
about asylums."

"Oh, but Loveday isn't a warder," said the doctor.

"You don't mean he's cuckoo, too?" said Angela.

The doctor corrected her.

"He is an *inmate.* It is rather an interesting case. He has
been here for thirty-five years."

"But I've never seen anyone saner," said Angela.

"He certainly has that air," said the doctor, "and in the
last twenty years we have treated him as such. He is the
life and soul of the place. Of course he is not one of the
private patients, but we allow him to mix freely with
them. He plays billiards excellently, does conjuring tricks
at the concert, mends their gramophones, valets them,
helps them in their crossword puzzles and various—er—
hobbies. We allow them to give him small tips for services
rendered, and he must by now have amassed quite a little
fortune. He has a way with even the most troublesome of
them. An invaluable man about the place."

"Yes, but why is he here?"

"Well, it is rather sad. When he was a very young man

he killed somebody—a young woman quite unknown to him, whom he knocked off her bicycle and then throttled. He gave himself up immediately afterwards and has been here ever since."

"But surely he is perfectly safe now. Why is he not let out?"

"Well, I suppose if it was to anyone's interest, he would be. He has no relatives except a step-sister who lives in Plymouth. She used to visit him at one time, but she hasn't been for years now. He's perfectly happy here and I can assure you *we* aren't going to take the first steps in turning him out. He's far too useful to us."

"But it doesn't seem fair," said Angela.

"Look at your father," said the doctor. "He'd be quite lost without Loveday to act as his secretary."

"It doesn't seem fair."

2

Angela left the asylum, oppressed by a sense of injustice. Her mother was unsympathetic.

"Think of being locked up in a looney bin all one's life."

"He attempted to hang himself in the orangery," replied Lady Moping, "*in front of the Chester-Martins.*"

"I don't mean Papa. I mean Mr. Loveday."

"I don't think I know him."

"Yes, the looney they have put to look after Papa."

"Your father's secretary. A very decent sort of man, I thought, and eminently suited to his work."

Angela left the question for the time, but returned to it again at luncheon on the following day.

"Mums, what does one have to do to get people out of the bin?"

"The bin? Good gracious, child, I hope that you do not anticipate your father's return *here.*"

"No, no. Mr. Loveday."

"Angela, you seem to me to be totally bemused. I see it was a mistake to take you with me on our little visit yesterday."

After luncheon Angela disappeared to the library and was soon immersed in the lunacy laws as represented in the encyclopædia.

She did not re-open the subject with her mother, but a

fortnight later, when there was a question of taking some pheasants over to her father for his eleventh Certification Party she showed an unusual willingness to run over with them. Her mother was occupied with other interests and noticed nothing suspicious.

Angela drove her small car to the asylum, and after delivering the game, asked for Mr. Loveday. He was busy at the time making a crown for one of his companions who expected hourly to be anointed Emperor of Brazil, but he left his work and enjoyed several minutes' conversation with her. They spoke about her father's health and spirits. After a time Angela remarked, "Don't you ever want to get away?"

Mr. Loveday looked at her with his gentle, blue-grey eyes. "I've got very well used to the life, miss. I'm fond of the poor people here, and I think that several of them are quite fond of me. At least, I think they would miss me if I were to go."

"But don't you ever think of being free again?"

"Oh yes, miss, I think of it—almost all the time I think of it."

"What would you do if you got out? There must be *something* you would sooner do than stay here."

The old man fidgeted uneasily. "Well, miss, it sounds ungrateful, but I can't deny I should welcome a little outing, once, before I get too old to enjoy it. I expect we all have our secret ambitions, and there *is* one thing I often wish I could do. You mustn't ask me what. . . . It wouldn't take long. But I do feel that if I had done it, just for a day, an afternoon even, then I would die quiet. I could settle down again easier, and devote myself to the poor crazed people here with a better heart. Yes, I do feel that."

There were tears in Angela's eyes that afternoon as she drove away. "He *shall* have his little outing, bless him," she said.

3

From that day onwards for many weeks Angela had a new purpose in life. She moved about the ordinary routine of her home with an abstracted air and an unfamiliar, reserved courtesy which greatly disconcerted Lady Moping.

"I believe the child's in love. I only pray that it isn't that uncouth Egbertson boy."

Angela read a great deal in the library, she cross-examined any guests who had pretensions to legal or medical knowledge, she showed extreme good will to old Sir Roderick Lane-Foscote, their Member. The names "alienist," "barrister" or "government official" now had for her the glamour that formerly surrounded film actors and professional wrestlers. She was a woman with a cause, and before the end of the hunting season she had triumphed. Mr. Loveday achieved his liberty.

The doctor at the asylum showed reluctance but no real opposition. Sir Roderick wrote to the Home Office. The necessary papers were signed, and at last the day came when Mr. Loveday took leave of the home where he had spent such long and useful years.

His departure was marked by some ceremony. Angela and Sir Roderick Lane-Foscote sat with the doctors on the stage of the gymnasium. Below them were assembled everyone in the institution who was thought to be stable enough to endure the excitement.

Lord Moping, with a few suitable expressions of regret, presented Mr. Loveday on behalf of the wealthier lunatics with a gold cigarette case; those who supposed themselves to be emperors showered him with decorations and titles of honour. The warders gave him a silver watch and many of the non-paying inmates were in tears on the day of the presentation.

The doctor made the main speech of the afternoon. "Remember," he remarked, "that you leave behind you nothing but our warmest good wishes. You are bound to us by ties that none will forget. Time will only deepen our sense of debt to you. If at any time in the future you should grow tired of your life in the world, there will always be a welcome for you here. Your post will be open."

A dozen or so variously afflicted lunatics hopped and skipped after him down the drive until the iron gates opened and Mr. Loveday stepped into his freedom. His small trunk had already gone to the station; he elected to walk. He had been reticent about his plans, but he was well provided with money, and the general impression was that he would go to London and enjoy himself a little before visiting his step-sister in Plymouth.

It was to the surprise of all that he returned within two

hours of his liberation. He was smiling whimsically, a gentle, self-regarding smile of reminiscence.

"I have come back," he informed the doctor. "I think that now I shall be here for good."

"But, Loveday, what a short holiday. I'm afraid that you have hardly enjoyed yourself at all."

"Oh yes, sir, thank you, sir, I've enjoyed myself *very much*. I'd been promising myself one little treat, all these years. It was short, sir, but *most* enjoyable. Now I shall be able to settle down again to my work here without any regrets."

Half a mile up the road from the asylum gates, they later discovered an abandoned bicycle. It was a lady's machine of some antiquity. Quite near it in the ditch lay the strangled body of a young woman, who, riding home to her tea, had chanced to overtake Mr. Loveday, as he strode along, musing on his opportunities.

The White Cat of Drumgunniol

by J. Sheridan Le Fanu

fiction

*The white cat was sitting in its old place on the
dead man's breast.*

There is a famous story of a white cat, with which we
all become acquainted in the nursery. I am going to tell a
story of a white cat very different from the amiable and
enchanted princess who took that disguise for a season.
The white cat of which I speak was a more sinister animal.

The traveller from Limerick toward Dublin, after passing the hills of Killaloe upon the left, as Keeper Mountain rises high in view, finds himself gradually hemmed in,
up the right, by a range of lower hills. An undulating plain
that dips gradually to a lower level than that of the road
interposes, and some scattered hedgerows relieve its somewhat wild and melancholy character.

One of the few human habitations that send up their
films of turf-smoke from that lonely plain, is the loosely-
thatched, earth-built dwelling of a "strong farmer," as the
more prosperous of the tenant-farming classes are termed
in Munster. It stands in a clump of trees near the edge of
a wandering stream, about halfway between the mountains
and the Dublin road, and had been for generations tenant-
ed by people named Donovan.

In a distant place, desirous of studying some Irish records which had fallen into my hands, and inquiring for a
teacher capable of instructing me in the Irish language, a
Mr. Donovan, dreamy, harmless, and learned, was recom-
mended to me for the purpose.

I found that he had been educated as a Sizar in Trinity College, Dublin. He now supported himself by teaching, and the special direction of my studies, I suppose, flattered his national partialities, for he unbosomed himself of much of his long-reserved thoughts, and recollections about his country and his early days. It was he who told me this story, and I mean to repeat it, as nearly as I can, in his own words.

I have myself seen the old farm-house, with its orchard of huge mossgrown apple trees. I have looked round on the peculiar landscape; the roofless, ivied tower, that two hundred years before had afforded a refuge from raid and rapparee, and which still occupies its old place in the angle of the haggard; the bush-grown "liss," that scarcely a hundred and fifty steps away records the labours of a bygone race; the dark and towering outline of old Keeper in the background; and the lonely range of furze and heath-clad hills that form a nearer barrier, with many a line of grey rock and clump of dwarf oak or birch. The pervading sense of loneliness made it a scene not unsuited for a wild and unearthly story. And I could quite fancy how, seen in the grey of a wintry morning, shrouded far and wide in snow, or in the melancholy glory of an autumnal sunset, or in the chill splendour of a moonlight night, it might have helped to tone a dreamy mind like honest Dan Donovan's to superstition and a proneness to the illusions of fancy. It is certain, however, that I never anywhere met with a more simple-minded creature, or one on whose good faith I could more entirely rely.

When I was a boy, said he, living at home at Drumgunniol, I used to take my Goldsmith's *Roman History* in my hand and go down to my favourite seat, the flat stone, sheltered by a hawthorn tree beside the little lough, a large and deep pool, such as I have heard called a tarn in England. It lay in the gentle hollow of a field that is overhung toward the north by the old orchard, and being a deserted place was favourable to my studious quietude.

One day reading here, as usual, I wearied at last, and began to look about me, thinking of the heroic scenes I had just been reading. I was as wide awake as I am at this moment, and I saw a woman appear at the corner of the orchard and walk down the slope. She wore a long, light grey dress, so long that it seemed to sweep the grass behind her, and so singular was her appearance in a part of the world where female attire is so inflexibly fixed by custom, that I could not take my eyes off her. Her course lay diagonally from corner to corner of the field, which was a large one, and she pursued it without swerving.

When she came near I could see that her feet were bare, and that she seemed to be looking steadfastly upon some remote object for guidance. Her route would have crossed me—had the tarn not interposed—about ten or twelve yards below the point at which I was sitting. But instead of arresting her course at the margin of the lough, as I had expected, she went on without seeming conscious of its existence, and I saw her, as plainly as I see you, sir, walk across the surface of the water, and pass, without seeming to see me, at about the distance I had calculated.

I was ready to faint from sheer terror. I was only thirteen years old then, and I remember every particular as if it had happened this hour.

The figure passed through the gap at the far corner of the field, and there I lost sight of it. I had hardly strength to walk home, and was so nervous, and ultimately so ill, that for three weeks I was confined to the house, and could not bear to be alone for a moment. I never entered that field again, such was the horror with which from that moment every object in it was clothed. Even at this distance of time I should not like to pass through it.

This apparition I connected with a mysterious event; and, also, with a singular liability, that has for nearly eight years distinguished, or rather afflicted, our family. It is no fancy. Everybody in that part of the country knows all about it. Everybody connected what I had seen with it.

I will tell it all to you as well as I can.

When I was about fourteen years old—that is about a year after the sight I had seen in the lough field—we were one night expecting my father home from the fair of Killaloe. My mother sat up to welcome him home, and I with her, for I liked nothing better than such a vigil. My brothers and sisters, and the farm servants, except the men who were driving home the cattle from the fair, were asleep in their beds. My mother and I were sitting in the chimney corner chatting together, and watching my father's supper, which was kept hot over the fire. We knew that he would return before the men who were driving home the cattle, for he was riding, and told us that he would only wait to see them fairly on the road, and then push homeward.

At length we heard his voice and the knocking of his loaded whip at the door, and my mother let him in. I don't think I ever saw my father drunk, which is more than most men of my age, from the same part of the country, could say of theirs. But he could drink his glass of whisky as well as another, and he usually came home from fair or market a little merry and mellow, and with a jolly flush in his cheeks.

To-night he looked sunken, pale and sad. He entered with the saddle and bridle in his hand, and he dropped them against the wall, near the door, and put his arms round his wife's neck, and kissed her kindly.

"Welcome home, Meehal," said she, kissing him heartily.

"God bless you, mavourneen," he answered.

And hugging her again, he turned to me, who was plucking him by the hand, jealous of his notice. I was little, and light of my age, and he lifted me up in his arms, and kissed me, and my arms being about his neck, he said to my mother:

"Draw the bolt, acushla."

She did so, and setting me down very dejectedly, he walked to the fire and sat down on a stool, and stretched his feet toward the glowing turf, leaning with his hands on his knees.

"Rouse up, Mick, darlin'," said my mother, who was growing anxious, "and tell me how did the cattle sell, and did everything go lucky at the fair, or is there anything wrong with the landlord, or what in the world is it that ails you, Mick, jewel?"

"Nothin', Molly. The cows sold well, thank God, and there's nothin' fell out between me an' the landlord, an' everything's the same way. There's no fault to find anywhere."

"Well, then, Mickey, since so it is, turn round to your hot supper, and ate it, and tell us is there anything new."

"I got my supper, Molly, on the way, and I can't ate a bit," he answered.

"Got your supper on the way, an' you knowin' 'twas waiting for you at home, an' your wife sittin' up an' all!" cried my mother, reproachfully.

"You're takin' a wrong meanin' out of what I say," said my father. "There's something happened that leaves me that I can't ate a mouthful, and I'll not be dark with you,

Molly, for, maybe, it ain't very long I have to be here, an' I'll tell you what it was. It's what I've seen, the white cat."

"The Lord between us and harm!" exclaimed my mother, in a moment as pale and as chap-fallen as my father; and then, trying to rally, with a laugh, she said: "Ha! 'tis only funnin' me you are. Sure a white rabbit was snared a Sunday last, in Grady's wood; an' Teigue seen a big white rat in the haggard yesterday."

" 'Twas neither rat nor rabbit was in it. Don't ye think but I'd know a rat or a rabbit from a big white cat, with green eyes as big as halfpennies, and its back riz up like a bridge, trottin' on and across me, and ready, if I dar' stop, to rub its sides against my shins, and maybe to make a jump and seize my throat, if that it's a cat, at all, an' not something worse?"

As he ended his description in a low tone, looking straight at the fire, my father drew his big hand across his forehead once or twice, his face being damp and shining with the moisture of fear, and he sighed, or rather groaned, heavily.

My mother had relapsed into panic, and was praying again in her fear. I, too, was terribly frightened, and on the point of crying, for I knew all about the white cat.

Clapping my father on the shoulder, by way of encouragement, my mother leaned over him, kissing him, and at last began to cry. He was wringing her hands in his, and seemed in great trouble.

"There was nothin' came into the house with me?" he asked, in a very low tone, turning to me.

"There was nothin', father," I said, "but the saddle and bridle that was in your hand."

"Nothin' white kem in at the doore wid me," he repeated.

"Nothin' at all," I answered.

"So best," said my father, and making the sign of the cross, he began mumbling to himself, and I knew he was saying his prayers.

Waiting for a while, to give him time for this exercise, my mother asked him where he first saw it.

"When I was riding up the bohereen,"—the Irish term meaning a little road, such as leads up to a farmhouse—"I bethought myself that the men was on the road with the cattle, and no one to look to the horse barrin' myself, so

I thought I might as well leave him in the crooked field below, an' I tuck him there, he bein' cool, and not a hair turned, for I rode him aisy all the way. It was when I turned, after lettin' him go—the saddle and bridle bein' in my hand—that I saw it, pushin' out o' the long grass at the side o' the path, an' it walked across it, in front of me, an' then back again, before me, the same way, an' sometimes at one side, an' then at the other, lookin' at me wid them shinin' eyes; and I consayted I heard it growlin' as it kep' beside me—as close as ever you see—till I kem up to the doore, here, an' knocked an' called, as ye heerd me."

Now, what was it, in so simple an incident, that agitated my father, my mother, myself, and finally, every member of this rustic household, with a terrible foreboding? It was this that we, one and all, believed that my father had received, in thus encountering the white cat, a warning of his approaching death.

The omen had never failed hitherto. It did not fail now. In a week after my father took the fever that was going, and before a month he was dead.

My honest friend, Dan Donovan, paused here; I could perceive that he was praying, for his lips were busy, and I concluded that it was for the repose of that departed soul.

In a little while he resumed.

It is eighty years now since that omen first attached to my family. Eighty years? Ay, is it. Ninety is nearer the mark. And I have spoken to many old people, in those earlier times, who had a distinct recollection of everything connected with it.

It happened in this way.

My grand-uncle, Connor Donovan, had the old farm of Drumgunniol in his day. He was richer than ever my father was, or my father's father either, for he took a short lease of Balraghan, and made money of it. But money won't soften a hard heart, and I'm afraid my grand-uncle was a cruel man—a profligate man he was, surely, and that is mostly a cruel man at heart. He drank his share, too, and cursed and swore, when he was vexed, more than was good for his soul, I'm afraid.

At that time there was a beautiful girl of the Colemans, up in the mountains, not far from Capper Cullen. I'm told that there are no Colemans there now at all, and that family has passed away. The famine years made great changes.

Ellen Coleman was her name. The Colemans were not rich. But, being such a beauty, she might have made a good match. Worse than she did for herself, poor thing, she could not.

Con Donovan—my grand-uncle, God forgive him!—sometimes in his rambles saw her at fairs or patterns, and he fell in love with her, as who might not?

He used her ill. He promised her marriage, and persuaded her to come away with him; and, after all, he broke his word. It was just the old story. He tired of her, and he wanted to push himself in the world; and he married a girl of the Collopys, that had a great fortune—twenty-four cows, seventy sheep, and a hundred and twenty goats.

He married this Mary Collopy, and grew richer than before; and Ellen Coleman died broken-hearted. But that did not trouble the strong farmer much.

He would have liked to have children, but he had none, and this was the only cross he had to bear, for everything else went much as he wished.

One night he was returning from the fair of Nenagh. A shallow stream at that time crossed the road—they have thrown a bridge over it, I am told, some time since—and its channel was often dry in summer weather. When it was so, as it passes close by the old farm-house of Drumgunniol, without a great deal of winding, it makes a sort of road, which people then used as a short cut to reach the house by. Into this dry channel, as there was plenty of light from the moon, my grand-uncle turned his horse, and when he had reached the two ash-trees at the meering of the farm he turned his horse short into the river-field, intending to ride through the gap at the other end, under the oak-tree, and so he would have been within a few hundred yards of his door.

As he approached the "gap" he saw, or thought he saw, with a slow motion, gliding along the ground toward the same point, and now and then with a soft bound, a white object, which he described as being no bigger than his hat, but what it was he could not see, as it moved along the hedge and disappeared at the point to which he was himself tending.

When he reached the gap the horse stopped short. He urged and coaxed it in vain. He got down to lead it through, but it recoiled, snorted, and fell into a wild trembling fit. He mounted it again. But its terror continued, and it obstinately resisted his caresses and his whip. It was bright moonlight, and my grand-uncle was chafed by the horse's resistance, and, seeing nothing to account for it, and being so near home, what little patience he possessed forsook him, and, plying his whip and spur in earnest, he broke into oaths and curses.

All on a sudden the horse sprang through, and Con Donovan, as he passed under the broad branch of the oak, saw clearly a woman standing on the bank beside him, her arm extended, with the hand of which, as he flew by, she struck him a blow upon the shoulders. It threw him forward upon the neck of the horse, which, in wild terror, reached the door at a gallop, and stood there quivering and steaming all over.

Less alive than dead, my grand-uncle got in. He told his story, at least, so much as he chose. His wife did not quite know what to think. But that something very bad had happened she could not doubt. He was very faint and ill, and begged that the priest should be sent for forthwith. When they were getting him to his bed they saw distinctly the marks of five fingerpoints on the flesh of his shoulder, where the spectral blow had fallen. These singular marks—which they said resembled in tint the hue of a body struck by lightning—remained imprinted on his flesh, and were buried with him.

When he had recovered sufficiently to talk with the people about him—speaking, like a man at his last hour, from a burdened heart, and troubled conscience—he repeated his story, but said he did not see, or, at all events, know, the face of the figure that stood in the gap. No one believed him. He told more about it to the priest than to others. He certainly had a secret to tell. He might as well have divulged it frankly, for the neighbours all knew well enough that it was the face of dead Ellen Coleman that he had seen.

From that moment my grand-uncle never raised his head. He was a scared, silent, broken-spirited man. It was early summer then, and at the fall of the leaf in the same year he died.

Of course there was a wake, such as beseemed a strong farmer so rich as he. For some reason the arrangements of this ceremonial were a little different from the usual routine.

The usual practice is to place the body in the great room, or kitchen, as it is called, of the house. In this particular case there was, as I told you, for some reason, an unusual arrangement. The body was placed in a small room that opened upon the greater one. The door of this, during the wake, stood open. There were candles about the bed, and pipes and tobacco on the table, and stools for such guests as chose to enter, the door standing open for their reception.

The body, having been laid out, was left alone, in this smaller room, during the preparations for the wake. After nightfall one of the women, approaching the bed to get a chair which she had left near it, rushed from the room with a scream, and, having recovered her speech at the further end of the "kitchen," and surrounded by a gaping audience, she said, at last:

"May I never sin, if his face bain't riz up again the back o' the bed, and he starin' down to the doore, wid eyes as big as pewter plates, that id be shinin' in the moon!"

"Arra, woman! Is it cracked you are?" said one of the farm boys as they are termed, being men of any age you please.

"Agh, Molly, don't be talkin', woman! 'Tis what ye consayted it, goin' into the dark room, out o' the light. Why didn't ye take a candle in your fingers, ye aumadhaun?" said one of her female companions.

"Candle, or no candle; I seen it," insisted Molly. "An' what's more, I could a'most tak' my oath I seen his arum, too, stretchin' out o' the bed along the flure, three times as long as it should be, to take hould o' me be the fut."

"Nansinse, ye fool, what id he want o' yer fut?" exclaimed one scornfully.

"Gi' me the candle, some o' yez—in the name o' God," said old Sal Doolan, that was straight and lean, and a woman that could pray like a priest almost.

"Give her a candle," agreed all.

But whatever they might say, there wasn't one among them that did not look pale and stern enough as they followed Mrs. Doolan, who was praying as fast as her lips could patter, and leading the van with a tallow candle, held like a taper, in her fingers.

The door was half open, as the panic-stricken girl had left it; and holding the candle on high the better to examine the room, she made a step or so into it.

If my grand-uncle's hand had been stretched along the floor, in the unnatural way described, he had drawn it back again under the sheet that covered him. And tall Mrs. Doolan was in no danger of tripping over his arm as she entered. But she had not gone more than a step or two with her candle aloft, when, with a drowning face, she suddenly stopped short, staring at the bed which was now fully in view.

"Lord, bless us, Mrs. Doolan, ma'am, come back," said the woman next her, who had fast hold of her dress, or her "coat," as they call it, and drawing her backwards with a frightened pluck, while a general recoil among her followers betokened the alarm which her hesitation had inspired.

"Whisht, will yez?" said the leader, peremptorily, "I can't hear my own ears wid the noise ye're makin', an' which iv yez let the cat in here, an' whose cat is it?" she asked, peering suspiciously at a white cat that was sitting on the breast of the corpse.

"Put it away, will yez?" she resumed, with horror at the profanation. "Many a corpse as I sthretched and crossed in the bed, the likes o' that I never seen yet. The man o' the house, wid a brute baste like that mounted on him, like a phooka, Lord forgi' me for namin' the like in this room. Dhrive it away, some o' yez! out o' that, this minute, I tell ye."

Each repeated the order, but no one seemed inclined to execute it. They were crossing themselves, and whispering their conjectures and misgivings as to the nature of the beast, which was no cat of that house, nor one that they had ever seen before. On a sudden, the white cat placed itself on the pillow over the head of the body, and having from that place glared for a time at them over the features of the corpse, it crept softly along the body towards them, growling low and fiercely as it drew near.

Out of the room they bounced, in dreadful confusion, shutting the door fast after them, and not for a good while did the hardiest venture to peep in again.

The white cat was sitting in its old place, on the dead man's breast, but this time it crept quietly down the side of the bed, and disappeared under it, the sheet which was spread like a coverlet, and hung down nearly to the floor, concealing it from view.

Praying, crossing themselves, and not forgetting a sprinkling of holy water, they peeped, and finally searched, poking spades, "wattles," pitchforks and such implements under the bed. But the cat was not to be found, and they concluded that it had made its escape among their feet as they stood near the threshold. So they secured the door carefully, with hasp and padlock.

But when the door was opened next morning they found the white cat sitting, as if it had never been disturbed, upon the breast of the dead man.

Again occurred very nearly the same scene with a like result, only that some said they saw the cat afterwards lurking under a big box in a corner of the outerroom, where my grand-uncle kept his leases and papers, and his prayer-book and beads.

Mrs. Doolan heard it growling at her heels wherever she went; and although she could not see it, she could hear it spring on the back of her chair when she sat down, and growl in her ear, so that she would bounce up with a scream and a prayer, fancying that it was on the point of taking her by the throat.

And the priest's boy, looking round the corner, under the branches of the old orchard, saw a white cat sitting under the little window of the room where my grand-uncle was laid out and looking up at the four small panes of glass as a cat will watch a bird.

The end of it was that the cat was found on the corpse again, when the room was visited, and do what they might, whenever the body was left alone, the cat was found again in the same ill-omened contiguity with the dead man. And this continued, to the scandal and fear of the neighbourhood, until the door was opened finally for the wake.

My grand-uncle being dead, and, with all due solemnities, buried, I have done with him. But not quite yet with the white cat. No banshee ever yet was more inalienably attached to a family than this ominous apparition is to mine. But there is this difference. The banshee seems to be animated with an affectionate sympathy with the bereaved family to whom it is hereditarily attached, whereas this thing has about it a suspicion of malice. It is the messenger simply of death. And its taking the shape of a cat—the coldest, and they say, the most vindictive of brutes—is indicative of the spirit of its visit.

When my grandfather's death was near, although he

seemed quite well at the time, it appeared not exactly, but very nearly in the same way in which I told you it showed itself to my father.

The day before my Uncle Teigue was killed by the bursting of his gun, it appeared to him in the evening, at twilight, by the lough, in the field where I saw the woman who walked across the water, as I told you. My uncle was washing the barrel of his gun in the lough. The grass is short there, and there is no cover near it. He did not know how it approached but the first he saw of it, the white cat was walking close round his feet, in the twilight, with an angry twist of its tail, and a green glare in its eyes, and do what he would, it continued walking round and round him, in larger or smaller circles, till he reached the orchard, and there he lost it.

My poor Aunt Peg—she married one of the O'Brians, near Oolah—came to Drumgunniol to go to the funeral of a cousin who died about a mile away. She died herself, poor woman, only a month after.

Coming from the wake, at two or three o'clock in the morning, as she got over the stile into the farm of Drumgunniol, she saw the white cat at her side, and it kept close beside her, she ready to faint all the time, till she reached the door of the house, where it made a spring up into the white-thorn tree that grows close by, and so it parted from her. And my little brother Jim saw it also, just three weeks before he died. Every member of our family who dies, or takes his death-sickness, at Drumgunniol, is sure to see the white cat, and no one of us who sees it need hope for long life after.

The Murder of Dr. Burdell

by Edmund Pearson

---

fact

Mrs. Cunningham's Select Boarding House for Gentlemen was a house one gentleman should have avoided.

Breakfast was brutally interrupted. This meal was usually a placid one at Mrs. Cunningham's Select Boarding House for Gentlemen. But even though the family, lingering over their buckwheat cakes, were being soothed by young Mr. Snodgrass, playing his banjo, no one could remain calm after Mary Donohue, the housemaid, burst into the room, screaming, "Oh, Mrs. Cunningham, come an' see! Somebody's been an' murdered Dr. Burdell! He's down there, an' he's all over the room, an' he's been murdered terrible, Mrs. Cunningham!"

This was true. When they rushed downstairs into the Doctor's apartments, it looked as if there had been a riot. Never was such an untidy murder. The "dastard or dastards," as the newspapers judicially described them, who had lain in wait for Dr. Burdell when he came in the night before had evidently started work with a lasso. For the Doctor's neck showed that strangulation or hanging had been attempted. Then they chased him round and round the room, upsetting the furniture, and prodding him with knives, poniards, and other edged tools, piercing his heart, severing a carotid artery, and inflicting thirteen other wounds—mostly fatal. The walls were splashed with blood, and the bloodstains afterward found in other parts of the house may—or may not—have been carried there as a result of this first inrush of spectators.

It was the last day of January, 1857. New York had not had a big, scandalous murder for a dozen years—nothing to which the newspapers of Philadelphia and Boston could point as cause for thanking God that *their* cities were pure. Policemen, reporters, coroners, and physicians came boiling into 31 Bond Street, Dr. Burdell's rather large and pretentious house, where he had kept the first floor for his dental office and sleeping quarters, and leased the rest to Emma Cunningham to take in boarders and lodgers.

Mrs. Cunningham had only glanced at what was left of the big, bumbling dentist, lying huddled in one corner. Then she had raised her arms and uttered a wail.

"Oh, my poor dear Doctor! Poor, darling Harvey! He is dead, and once more I am a widow!"

A widow! What the nation was this, asked everybody of everybody else. Why, Dr. Burdell and Mrs. Cunningham had fought like cats and dogs; the Doctor ate his meals at a Broadway hotel rather than at Mrs. Cunningham's table; they had sued and countersued each other; the lady had railed at the Doctor for what she described as "bringing females into the house for improper purposes"; and Dr. Burdell had told a friend, within the week, that the Cunningham lease would expire on May 1st, and he intended to throw the whole gang of 'em out, neck and crop. When and where and how had these cordial enemies been married?

They couldn't get any answer out of Mrs. Cunningham, who had swooned away. Or from her sixteen-year-old daughter, Helen, who also had fainted. But the other daughter, Augusta, who was eighteen, and all dressed up that morning, preparing to leave for a school at Saratoga, said that she knew about it.

"Mamma was married to Dr. Burdell last October. I was the only witness. It was at Dr. Marvine's house—the Reverend Dr. Uriah Marvine of the Dutch Reformed Church on Bleecker Street."

The people in the house looked at each other in discomfort. Exactly how much any of them knew is a mystery, but they realized that they soon must explain how it was possible for such a murder to occur without anybody hearing a sound. Poleaxing a bullock would be about as quiet: the Doctor was capable of a fine stentorian bellow, and the crime had turned his quarters "into a perfect shambles." (This valuable phrase probably originated at this time.) And there were ten other people in the house.

On the top floor, in addition to the two maid servants, had slept Mr. George V. Snodgrass, the banjo-player, who shared a room and a bed with the two youngest Cunninghams, Georgie and Willie. On the floor beneath, Mrs. Cunningham herself, dark-eyed, vivacious, and in her late thirties; the two Miss Cunninghams, the Hon. Daniel Ullmann, and Mr. John J. Eckel. How the people on this floor were bestowed when everyone was tucked in for the night was a matter over which reporters and detectives grew gray and bald, but the unanimous testimony of the three ladies was that on the night of the great slaughter, mother and daughters all slept together in one bed, because of Miss Augusta's proposed early departure. So Messrs. Ullmann and Eckel each lay in his own room.

Over Mr. Ullmann there never hung the faintest suspicion of any irregularity. Like Dr. Burdell, he ate his meals elsewhere, and so was not present at the interrupted breakfast. He was a Yale graduate and had been a Master in Chancery. If these things were not enough, he was now the Hon. Daniel, by virtue of being defeated for the governorship of New York (on the Know-Nothing ticket), and some years later he was to emerge from the Civil War a major general. His shirt was already a bit stuffed, and his testimony as to what he knew (appropriately, he knew nothing) was given with offended pomposity.

Mr. Eckel was surrounded by no such cloud of respectability. An associate and hanger-on of minor politicians, and a dealer in Hides and Fat, he started with nothing much in his favor. Besides, it was reported that one morning at breakfast, when the talk dwelt, as usual, upon the ogre of the household, Dr. Burdell, Mr. Eckel had said, "I'd like to help string up that old son-of-a-gun!" And that he was rewarded by handsome Widow Cunningham with a low, chuckling laugh, and the playful remark, "What things you *do* say, Mr. Eckel!"

The only real contribution which Mr. Eckel made to the higher life was unappreciated by the police. He kept seventeen canaries, which were distributed all over the house in ornamental cages. The two Miss Cunninghams often helped him with them in the mornings, for watering and rationing seventeen birds took no small amount of doing.

As for nineteen-year-old Mr. Snodgrass, he was the son

of a Presbyterian minister of Orange County; he was ad-
dicted to writing and reading poetry. Whether he was engaged in anything as innocent as banjo-playing was dis-
puted, since little Georgie Cunningham swore that at the
moment Mary Donohue came in with her dread news,
"Mr. Snodgrass was marking my sister's clothes."

However this may have been, when the reporters and
police turned the house upside down, they found the room
of Mr. Snodgrass full of "knickknacks" and feminine underwear. Whether the underwear, as one faction declared,
belonged to the Cunningham girls or whether, as others
asserted, it was the property of Mr. Snodgrass, whose peculiar pleasure it was to wear such fripperies, the young
man rapidly declined in public esteem.

Practically everyone from the house was hustled off to
the Tombs: Mrs. Cunningham, Eckel, and Snodgrass as
having constituted the lynching party, and the others—for
a day or two—as material witnesses. And the clergy of
New York, wishing appropriately to lecture their congre-
gations on the following Sunday, decided to talk about Sin
in general. It would have been hard to select any particular sin.

Some of the darkest suspicions arose because of the testimony of the Reverend Dr. Marvine. He came to the
house and looked at Mrs. Cunningham and Augusta. Then
he peered at Dr. Burdell, who was lying in a very elegant
rosewood coffin with two silver handles on either side. Augusta he recognized as one of the wedding party in October; of Mrs. Cunningham he was not very sure; and of
Dr. Burdell he was not sure at all. Since the dentist had
prospered and was supposed to be worth $100,000, it was
highly advantageous to seem to be his widow. And the
popular theory was that the bridegroom calling himself
Dr. Burdell had really been Mr. Eckel. With bushy hair
over his ears, and under his chin, and all over his face, the
boarder was equipped to impersonate the Doctor. His only
deficiency was in hair on the top of his head, and this, it
was asserted, had been repaired by the purchase of a tou-
pee at Cristadoro's wig shop, 6 Astor House. Mr. Cristadoro recalled the sale.

Mrs. Cunningham's career was unfavorably reported. As
Miss Emma Hempstead of a Brooklyn suburb, she had
been remarkable for "a well-developed, voluptuous form
and more than ordinary powers of fascination." She drew

within her unholy toils George D. Cunningham, who, for her sake, abandoned his "legal spouse." Mr. Cunningham, the joyous proprietor of a distillery, later made the mistake of going to California in search of better fortune, and returned to find his distillery had been ignominiously transformed into a sarsaparilla factory. He promptly died "in a fit," and Emma turned up with his $10,000 life-insurance policy and, to clinch her claim upon it, a certificate of marriage. She and the four little Cunninghams then carried on with the $10,000. It was said that in Saratoga, as well as in New York, she had been known in sporting circles as Mrs. Douglass and as Mrs. Garouse.

For the next eight months, her name was as notorious as any in the world. To the reek of scandal that went up from 31 Bond Street was devoted newspaper space which might have been allotted to Walker the filibuster, to the free-soil troubles in Kansas, and to the Dred Scott decision. On one day the *Tribune*, in reporting the Cunningham-Burdell mystery, used four full pages of such fine print that it would probably fill six pages in that paper today. To all the usual hokum of a murder case—whether or not Mrs. Cunningham was left-handed, and whether anyone had examined the retinas of the dead man's eyes for "last images"—were added innumerable complications.

Justice was befogged by an absurd inquest, which dragged on for two weeks in the Burdell parlor. The Coroner, "Dr." E. Downes Connery, a lame man with a rich brogue, flattered the powerful, insulted the humble, and allowed everyone to come and talk his head off. The Coroner himself helped illustrate the early use of a piece of slang. Mary Donohue testified that Dr. Burdell for the last month had stayed in his own quarters, neglected the lady who now said she was his bride, and abandoned her to the deplorable Eckel.

"I thought," said Mary, "that what was going on between Mr. Eckel an' Mrs. Cunningham was not proper; he sat every night in her bedroom, an' took up presents to her—birds an' things."

The Coroner: "Yes, he was a bird himself."

The suspicions against Mrs. Cunningham and Eckel strengthened when a man named John Farrell told his story. He had chosen to sit on the steps of 31 Bond Street that night, to repair his shoelace. Resting there, he had observed Dr. Burdell, heavily shrouded in a shawl, plodding down the street and entering the house. There was some mystery as to Dr. Burdell's doings between his five-o'clock dinner at the Metropolitan Hotel and his home-coming at about midnight. The belief was that he had been in Brooklyn and—like everyone who went to Brooklyn in those days—up to mischief.

Mr. Farrell heard Dr. Burdell's footsteps echo down the empty hall. Then he heard a muffled cry of "Murder!," a blow or two, a groan, and a choking sound. Mr. Farrell, too much an aesthete to be disturbed by matters like these, finished with his shoelace and continued to gaze upon the night and admire the fine effects of light and shadow upon Bond Street.

Finally somebody opened the door, put his head out, and said, "What you doing?"

Mr. Farrell murmured some polite trifle, whereupon the man—who was heavily bearded—remarked, "Well, get the hell outer here!"

And Mr. Farrell, sighing, went on his way. He was later taken to the Tombs, where, crouching on the floor in front of the prisoner Eckel (so as to get a view from beneath, looking up), he swore that this was the man. The trio of suspects were then all indicted for murder.

Meanwhile, Mrs. Cunningham's attorney, Henry L. Clinton, was convinced that the story of the marriage was true and that his client would do better to appear at her trial as the lawful Mrs. Burdell rather than a spurious claimant. So he got the question of the marriage before the Surrogate, asking that Mrs. Cunningham be appointed administratrix. He reminded Dr. Marvine that Dr. Burdell on his wedding night probably looked a little better than three months later, when he was thoroughly strangled and stabbed, and put into a rosewood coffin. Dr. Marvine admitted it, and added that, in his present opinion, it *was* the dentist and not the dealer in Hides and Fat who had married Mrs. Cunningham. Dr. Burdell's heirs, a brother and his family, had retained the eminent Samuel J. Tilden to represent them, but this astute lawyer seemed nearly to lose this first round. The Surrogate, however, reserved his decision.

In May, Mrs. Cunningham was tried for murder. Eckel's turn was to come. Mr. Snodgrass had been discharged; he had spent miserable weeks in the Tombs, where they deprived him of his banjo and restricted him as to lingerie.

Indignation had subsided. Burdell, an upstate New Yorker, had made a good many enemies in his forty-five years. True, he would be roaring in rage at some man or woman on Monday, and be quite chummy with the same person by Wednesday. But it was easy to imagine that he had foes outside his house who might be glad to come in and chop him up.

The State's case turned out to be weak. Mrs. Cunningham undoubtedly had motive, the circumstances were suspicious, and she was said to have threatened the Doctor's life. But the prosecutor, A. Oakley Hall (afterward Tweed's Mayor of New York), had to rely on oratory and abuse. He compared the prisoner to Messalina, to Lady Macbeth, to that Queen of Hungary "who bathed her feet in the blood of sixty-three knights."

The jury, looking at the widow as she sat in her black bombazine, flanked by her two pretty daughters, could not see the aptness of those comparisons. They were out only half an hour, and found her "not guilty." Mr. Eckel promptly went free.

The fatal witness, Farrell, never appeared at all. He had turned out to be an inveterate liar who hungered for notoriety. It will be interesting to people who are impressed by the "dying confessions" which follow notorious murders to learn that at later dates three, if not four, men, as they stood on the gallows for other murders, each confessed to exclusive guilt in the Burdell case.

In public opinion, Mrs. Cunningham was now a grievously-wronged woman, and her lawyer, Mr. Clinton, again besieged the Surrogate to grant his client permission to administer the Burdell estate. The household at 31 Bond Street was more or less restored, and interesting events were preparing.

The Surrogate seemed well disposed, but again postponed decision, allowing Mr. Clinton to depart for his summer holidays. When he returned, in August, it was to be horrified, disillusioned, and disgusted—feelings which he shared with Horace Greeley and many other New Yorkers. Mrs. Cunningham was in the Tombs again, and this time accompanied not by any of her boarders but by a bogus baby.

Before her acquittal, she had told the matron of the Tombs that the stork was hovering overhead. After her return to Bond Street, she let her physician, Dr. David Uhl, into the secret, and the Doctor for a time believed her. At last, one day, she remarked archly, "You know, Dr. Uhl, I'm not really going to have a baby."

"No?" queried the Doctor.

"No. But as I am Dr. Burdell's widow, it would be advantageous if he should have an heir. Could you use one thousand dollars, Doctor?"

The physician was cagy. He said he would think it over—and he went to the District Attorney, Mr. Hall. That officer, delighted at a chance to bring "the scheming Jezebel" to justice for something, told Dr. Uhl to go ahead and stage-manage an impressive childbirth.

Dr. Uhl and Mrs. Cunningham, during the warm days of July, laid their plans. The lady picked August 3rd for the day. It should take place, as a tribute to the late Dr. Burdell, in the room where he had lain in state. There was a Dr. Catlin, over in Brooklyn, who had presided over the fatal fit of Mr. Cunningham. He should be the accoucheur.

"I've got *him* right under my thumb," grimly remarked Mrs. Cunningham.

As for the leading personage—the baby—it was procured from a "California widow"; i.e., a lady whose husband's long absence in the gold fields had made the birth of a child biologically amazing.

On the night selected, the baby was fetched in a basket. Mrs. Cunningham lay in the room where once Dr. Burdell had rested in his silver-handled coffin. All the paraphernalia—to the last realistic detail—was ready. Among the mentionable items was a friend of Dr. Uhl, one Dr. Gilchrest, a pharmacist, who entered into the spirit of the occasion so heartily as to put on a nightcap, get into bed, and groan. The venal Dr. Catlin and a nurse stood by.

When, by orders of the District Attorney, the police rushed in, they found Mrs. Cunningham and the baby together. Dr. Gilchrest, the groaner, had done his stuff and withdrawn.

"Don't you touch my baby," said the lady in a tone of deep distress. "That is the child of Harvey Burdell."

But Dr. Uhl and the minions of the law had marked the

baby as if it were counterfeit money. It had a string about
its navel, and was touched under each ear and armpit with
lunar caustic.

Although the raid upon the Burdell estate was defeated,
for the Surrogate now decided that the widow had never
married the Doctor, District Attorney Hall was baffled to
the end. The statute under which Mrs. Cunningham was
supposed to be liable forbade the production of a baby for
fraudulent purposes. But it was not clear that she had "produced" a baby within the meaning of the act, since the financial part of the fraud had not been completed.

So Mrs. Cunningham was released on bail, and retired
to California, where she successfully cultivated a vineyard.
The bogus baby was rewarded with an engagement in Bar-
num's Museum at twenty-five dollars a week.

The Destruction of Smith

by Algernon Blackwood

fiction

Lurid it was, and in some way terrible.

Ten years ago, in the western States of America, I once met Smith. But he was no ordinary member of the clan: he was Ezekiel B. Smith of Smithville. He *was* Smithville, for he founded it and made it live.

It was in the oil region, where towns spring up on the map in a few days like mushrooms, and may be destroyed again in a single night by fire and earthquake. On a hunting expedition Smith stumbled upon a natural oil well, and instantly staked his claim; a few months later he was rich, grown into affluence as rapidly as that patch of wilderness grew into streets and houses where you could buy anything from an evening's gambling to a tin of Boston baked pork-and-beans. Smith was really a tremendous fellow, a sort of human dynamo of energy and pluck, with rare judgment in his great square head—the kind of judgment that in higher walks of life makes statesmen. His personality cut through the difficulties of life with the clean easy force of putting his whole life into anything he touched. "God's own luck," his comrades called it; but really it was sheer ability and character and personality. The man had power.

From the moment of that "oil find" his rise was very rapid, but while his brains went into a dozen other big enterprises, his heart remained in little Smithville, the flimsy mushroom town he had created. His own life was in it. It was his baby. He spoke tenderly of its hideousness. Smithville was an intimate expression of his very self.

Ezekiel B. Smith I saw once only, for a few minutes; but I have never forgotten him. It was the moment of his death. And we came across him on a shooting trip where the forests melt away towards the vast plains of the Arizona desert. The personality of the man was singularly impressive. I caught myself thinking of a mountain, or of some elemental force of Nature so sure of itself that hurry is never necessary. And his gentleness was like the gentleness of women. Great strength often—the greatest always—has tenderness in it, a depth of tenderness unknown to pettier life.

Our meeting was coincidence, for we were hunting in a region where distances are measured by hours and the chance of running across white men very rare. For many days our nightly camps were pitched in spots of beauty where the loneliness is akin to the loneliness of the Egyptian Desert. On one side the mountain slopes were smothered with dense forest, hiding wee meadows of sweet grass like English lawns; and on the other side, stretching for more miles than a man can count, ran the desolate alkali plains of Arizona where tufts of sagebrush are the only vegetation till you reach the lips of the Colorado Canyons. Our horses were tethered for the night beneath the stars. Two backwoodsmen were cooking dinner. The smell of bacon over a wood fire mingled with the keen and fragrant air—when, suddenly, the horses neighed, signalling the approach of one of their own kind. Indians, white men—probably another hunting party—were within scenting distance, though it was long before my city ears caught any sound, and still longer before the cause itself entered the circle of our firelight.

I saw a square-faced man, tanned like a redskin, in a hunting shirt and a big sombrero, climb down slowly from his horse and move towards us, keenly searching with his eyes; and at the same moment Hank, looking up from the frying-pan where the bacon and venison spluttered in a pool of pork-fat, exclaimed, "Why, it's Ezekiel B.!" The next words, addressed to Jake, who held the kettle, were below his breath: "And if he ain't all broke up! Jest look at the eyes on him!" I saw what he meant—the face of a human being distraught by some extraordinary emotion, a soul in violent distress, yet betrayal well kept under. Once, as a newspaper man, I had seen a murderer walk to the electric chair. The expression was similar. Death was *be-*

hind the eyes, not in them. Smith brought in with him—
terror.

In a dozen words we learned he had been hunting for
some weeks, but was now heading for Tranter, a "stop-
off" station where you could flag the daily train 140 miles
south-west. He was making for Smithville, the little town
that was the apple of his eye. Something "was wrong"
with Smithville. No one asked him what—it is the custom
to wait till information is volunteered. But Hank, helping
him presently to venison (which he hardly touched), said
casually, "Good hunting, Boss, your way?"; and the brief
reply told much, and proved how eager he was to relieve
his mind by speech. "I'm glad to locate your camp, boys,"
he said. "That's luck. There's something going wrong"—
and a catch came into his voice—"with Smithville." Behind the laconic statement emerged somehow the terror
the man experienced. For Smith to confess cowardice and
in the same breath admit mere "luck," was equivalent to
the hysteria that makes city people laugh or cry. It was
genuinely dramatic. I have seen nothing more impressive
by way of human tragedy—though hard to explain why—
than this square-jawed, dauntless man, sitting there with
the firelight on his rugged features, and saying this simple
thing. For how in the world could he know it—?

In the pause that followed, his Indians came gliding in,
tethered the horses, and sat down without a word to eat
what Hank distributed. But nothing was to be read on
their impassive faces. Redskins, whatever they may feel,
show little. Then Smith gave us another pregnant sentence.
"They heard it too," he said, in a lower voice, indicating
his three men; "they saw it jest as I did." He looked up
into the starry sky a second. "It's hard upon our trail right
now," he added, as though he expected something to drop
upon us from the heavens. And from that moment I swear
we all felt creepy. The darkness round our lonely camp hid
terror in its folds; the wind that whispered through the dry
sage-brush brought whispers and the shuffle of watching
figures; and when the Indians went softly out to pitch the
tents and get more wood for the fire, I remember feeling
glad the duty was not mine. Yet this feeling of uneasiness
is something one rarely experiences in the open. It belongs
to houses, overwrought imaginations, and the presence of
evil men. Nature gives peace and security. That we all felt

it proves how real it was. And Smith, who felt it most, of course, had brought it.

"There's something gone wrong with Smithville" was an ominous statement of disaster. He said it just as a man in civilised lands might say, "My wife is dying; a telegram's just come. I must take the train." But how he felt so sure of it, a thousand miles away in this uninhabited corner of the wilderness, made us feel curiously uneasy. For it was an incredible thing—yet true. We all felt *that*. Smith did not imagine things. A sense of gloomy apprehension settled over our lonely camp, as though things were about to happen. Already they stalked across the great black night, watching us with many eyes. The wind had risen, and there were sounds among the trees. I, for one, felt no desire to go to bed. The way Smith sat there, watching the sky and peering into the sheet of darkness that veiled the Desert, set my nerves all jangling. He expected something—but what? It was following him. Across this tractless wilderness, apparently above him against the brilliant stars, Something was "hard upon his trail."

Then, in the middle of painful silences, Smith suddenly turned loquacious—further sign with him of deep mental disturbance. He asked questions like a schoolboy—asked them of me too, as being "an edicated man." But they were such queer things to talk about round an Arizona camp-fire that Hank clearly wondered for his sanity. He knew about the "wilderness madness" that attacks some folks. He let his green cigar go out and flashed me signals to be cautious. He listened intently, with the eyes of a puzzled child, half cynical, half touched with superstitious dread. For, briefly, Smith asked me what I knew about stories of dying men appearing at a distance to those who loved them much. He had read such tales, "heard tell of 'em," but "are they dead true, or are they jest little feery tales?" I satisfied him as best I could with one or two authentic stories. Whether he believed or not I cannot say; but his swift mind jumped in a flash to the point. "Then, if that kind o' stuff is true," he asked, simply, "it looks as though a feller had a dooplicate of himself—sperrit maybe—that gits loose and active at the time of death, and heads straight for the party it loves best. Ain't that so, Boss?" I admitted the theory was correct. And then he startled us with a final question that made Hank drop an oath below his breath—sure evidence of uneasy excite-

ment in the old backwoodsman. Smith whispered it, looking over his shoulder into the night: "Aint it jest possible
then," he asked, "seeing that men an' Nature is all made
of a piece like, that places too have this dooplicate appearance of theirselves that gits loose when they go under?"

It was difficult, under the circumstances, to explain that
such a theory *had* been held to account for visions of
scenery people sometimes have, and that a city may have
a definite personality made up of all its inhabitants—
moods, thoughts, feelings, and passions of the multitude
who go to compose its life and atmosphere, and that
hence is due the odd changes in man's individuality when
he goes from one city to another. Nor was there any time
to do so, for hardly had he asked his singular question
when the horses whinnied, the Indians leaped to their feet
as if ready for an attack, and Smith himself turned the
colour of the ashes that lay in a circle of whitish-grey
about the burning wood. There was an expression in his
face of death, or, as the Irish peasants say, "destroyed."

"That's Smithville," he cried, springing to his feet, then
tottering so that I thought he must fall into the flame;
"that's my baby town—got loose and huntin' for me, who
made it, and love it better'n anything on Gawd's green
earth!" And then he added with a kind of gulp in his
throat as of a man who wanted to cry but couldn't: "And
it's going to bits—it's dying—and I'm not thar to save
it—!"

He staggered and I caught his arm. The sound of his
frightened, anguished voice, and the shuffling of our many
feet among the stones, died away into the night. We all
stood, staring. The darkness came up closer. The horses
ceased their whinnying. For a moment nothing happened.
Then Smith turned slowly round and raised his head
towards the stars as though he saw something. "Hear
that?" he whispered. "It's coming up close. That's what
I've bin hearing now, on and off, two days and nights. Listen!" His whispering voice broke horribly; the man was
suffering atrociously. For a moment he became vastly,
horribly animated—then stood still as death.

But in the hollow silence, broken only by the sighing of
the wind among the spruces, we at first heard nothing.
Then, most curiously, something like rapid driven mist
came trooping down the sky, and veiled a group of stars.

With it, as from an enormous distance, but growing
swiftly nearer, came noises that were beyond all question
the noises of a city rushing through the heavens. From all
sides they came; and with them there shot a reddish,
streaked appearance across the misty veil that swung so
rapidly and softly between the stars and our eyes. Lurid it
was, and in some way terrible. A sense of helpless bewil-
derment came over me, scattering my faculties as in
scenes of fire, when the mind struggles violently to possess
itself and act for the best. Hank, holding his rifle ready to
shoot, moved stupidly round the group, equally at a loss,
and swearing incessantly below his breath. For this overwhelming certainty that Something living had come upon
us from the sky possessed us all, and I, personally, felt as
if a gigantic Being swept against me through the night, destructive and enveloping, and yet that it was not one, but
many. Power of action left me. I could not even observe
with accuracy what was going on. I stared, dizzy and bewildered, in all directions; but my power of movement
was gone, and my feet refused to stir. Only I remember
that the Redskins stood like figures of stone, unmoved.

And the sounds about us grew into a roar. The distant
murmur came past us like a sea. There was a babel of
shouting. Here, in the deep old wilderness that knew no
living human beings for hundreds of leagues, there was a
tempest of voices calling, crying, shrieking; men's hoarse
clamouring, and the high screaming of women and children. Behind it ran a booming sound like thunder. Yet all
of it, while apparently so close above our heads, seemed in
some inexplicable way far off in the distance—muted,
faint, thinning out among the quiet stars. More like a
memory of turmoil and tumult it seemed than the actual
uproar heard at first hand. And through it ran the crash of
big things tumbling, breaking, falling in destruction with
an awful detonating thunder of collapse. I thought the hills
were toppling down upon us. A shrieking city, it seemed,
fled past us through the sky.

How long it lasted it is impossible to say, for my power
of measuring time had utterly vanished. A dreadful wild
anguish summed up all the feelings I can remember. It
seemed I watched, or read, or dreamed some desolating
scene of disaster in which human life went overboard
wholesale, as though one threw a hatful of insects into a
blazing fire. This idea of burning, of thick suffocating

smoke and savage flame, coloured the entire experience.
And the next thing I knew was that it had passed away as
completely as though it had never been at all; the stars
shone down from an air of limpid clearness, and—there
was a smell of burning leather in my nostrils. I just
stepped back in time to save my feet. I had moved in my
excitement against the circle of hot ashes. Hank pushed
me back roughly with the barrel of his rifle.

But, strangest of all, I understood, as by some flash of
divine intuition, the reason of this abrupt cessation of the
horrible tumult. The Personality of the town, set free and
loosened in the moment of death, had returned to him
who gave it birth, who loved it, and of whose life it was
actually an expression. The Being of Smithville was liter-
ally a projection, an emanation of the dynamic, vital personality of its puissant creator. And, in death, it had returned on him with the shock of an accumulated power
impossible for a human being to resist. For years he had
provided it with life—but *gradually*. It now rushed back
to its source, thus concentrated, in a single terrific moment.

"That's him," I heard a voice saying from a great distance as it seemed. "He's fired his last shot—!" and saw
Hank turning the body over with his riflebutt. And, though
the face itself was calm beneath the stars, there was an attitude of limbs and body that suggested the bursting of an
enormous shell that had twisted every fibre by its awful
force yet somehow left the body as a whole intact.

We carried "it" to Tranter, and at the first real station
along the line we got the news by telegraph: "Smithville
wiped out by fire. Burned two days and nights. Loss of
life, 3000." And all the way in my dreams I seemed still
to hear that curious, dreadful cry of Smithville, the shrieking city rushing headlong through the sky.

Wet Saturday

by John Collier

---

fiction

Mr. Princey really believed in taking care of his family.

It was July. In the large, dull house they were imprisoned by the swish and the gurgle and all the hundred sounds of rain. They were in the drawing-room, behind four tall and weeping windows, in a lake of damp and faded chintz.

This house, ill-kept and unprepossessing, was necessary to Mr. Princey, who detested his wife, his daughter, and his hulking son. His life was to walk through the village, touching his hat, not smiling. His cold pleasure was to recapture snapshot memories of the infinitely remote summers of his childhood—coming into the orangery and finding his lost wooden horse, the tunnel in the box hedge, and the little square of light at the end of it. But now all this was threatened—his austere pride of position in the village, his passionate attachment to the house—and all because Millicent, his cloddish daughter Millicent, had done this shocking and incredibly stupid thing. Mr. Princey turned from her in revulsion and spoke to his wife.

"They'd send her to a lunatic asylum," he said. "A criminal-lunatic asylum. We should have to move away. It would be impossible."

His daughter began to shake again. "I'll kill myself," she said.

"Be quiet," said Mr. Princey. "We have very little time. No time for nonsense. I intend to deal with this." He called to his son, who stood looking out of the window. "George,

45

come here. Listen. How far did you get with your medicine before they threw you out as hopeless?"

"You know as well as I do," said George.

"Do you know enough—did they drive enough into your head for you to be able to guess what a competent doctor could tell about such a wound?"

"Well, it's a—it's a knock or blow."

"If a tile fell from the roof? Or a piece of the coping?"

"Well, guv'nor, you see, it's like this—"

"Is it possible?"

"No."

"Why not?"

"Oh, because she hit him several times."

"I can't stand it," said Mrs. Princey.

"You have got to stand it, my dear," said her husband. "And keep that hysterical note out of your voice. It might be overheard. We are talking about the weather. If he fell down the well, George, striking his head several times?"

"I really don't know, guv'nor."

"He'd have had to hit the sides several times in thirty or forty feet, and at the correct angles. No, I'm afraid not. We must go over it all again, Millicent."

"No! No!"

"Millicent, we must go over it all again. Perhaps you have forgotten something. One tiny irrelevant detail may save or ruin us. Particularly you, Millicent. You don't *want* to be put in an asylum, do you? Or be hanged? They might hang you, Millicent. You must stop that shaking. You must keep your voice quiet. We are talking of the weather. Now!"

"I can't. I . . . I . . ."

"Be quiet, child. Be quiet." He put his long, cold face very near to his daughter's. He found himself horribly revolted by her. Her features were thick, her jaws heavy, her whole figure repellently powerful. "Answer me," he said. "You were in the stable?"

"Yes."

"One moment, though. Who knew you were in love with this wretched curate?"

"No one. I've never said a—"

"Don't worry," said George. "The whole god-damned village knows. They've been sniggering about it in the Plough for three years past."

"Likely enough," said Mr. Princey. "Likely enough.

What filth!" He made as if to wipe something off the backs of his hands. "Well, now, we continue. You were in the stable?"

"Yes."

"You were putting the croquet set into its box?"

"Yes."

"You heard someone crossing the yard?"

"Yes."

"It was Withers?"

"Yes."

"So you called him?"

"Yes."

"Loudly? Did you call him loudly? Could anyone have heard?"

"No, Father. I'm sure not. I didn't call him. He saw me as I went to the door. He just waved his hand and came over."

"How *can* I find out from you whether there was anyone about? Whether he *could* have been seen?"

"I'm sure not, Father. I'm quite sure."

"So you both went into the stable?"

"Yes. It was raining hard."

"What did he say?"

"He said 'Hullo Milly.' And to excuse him coming in the back way, but he'd set out to walk over to Bass Hill."

"Yes."

"And he said, passing the park, he'd seen the house and suddenly thought of me, and he thought he'd just look in for a minute, just to tell me something. He said he was so happy, he wanted me to share it. He'd heard from the Bishop he was to have the vicarage. And it wasn't only that. It meant he could marry. And he began to stutter. And I thought he meant me."

"Don't tell me what you thought. Exactly what he said. Nothing else."

"Well . . . Oh dear!"

"Don't cry. It is a luxury you cannot afford. Tell me!"

"He said no. He said it wasn't me. It's Ella Brangwyn-Davies. And he was sorry. And all that. Then he went to go."

"And then?"

"I went mad. He turned his back. I had the winning post of the croquet set in my hand—"

"Did you shout or scream? I mean, as you hit him?"

"No. I'm sure I didn't."

"Did he? Come on! Tell me!"

"No, Father."

"And then?"

"I threw it down. I came straight into the house. That's all. I wish I were dead!"

"And you met none of the servants. No one will go into the stable. You see, George, he probably told people he was going to Bass Hill. Certainly no one knows he came here. He might have been attacked in the woods. We must consider every detail . . . A curate, with his head battered in—"

"Don't, Father!" cried Millicent.

"Do you want to be hanged? A curate with his head battered in, found in the woods. Who'd want to kill Withers?"

There was a tap on the door, which opened immediately. It was little Captain Smollett, who never stood on ceremony. "Who'd kill Withers?" said he. "I would with pleasure. How d'you do, Mrs. Princey. I walked right in."

"He heard you, Father," moaned Millicent.

"My dear, we can all have our little joke," said her father. "Don't pretend to be shocked. A little theoretical curate-killing, Smollett. In these days we talk nothing but thrillers."

"Parsonicide," said Captain Smollett. "Justifiable parsonicide. Have you heard about Ella Brangwyn-Davies? I shall be laughed at."

"Why?" said Mr. Princey. "Why should you be laughed at?"

"Had a shot in that direction myself," said Smollett, with careful sang-froid. "She half said yes, too. Hadn't you heard? She told most people. Now it'll look as if I got turned down for a white rat in a dog collar."

"Too bad!" said Mr. Princey.

"Fortune of war," said the little captain.

"Sit down," said Mr. Princey. "Mother, Millicent, console Captain Smollett with your best light conversation. George and I have something to look to. We shall be back in a minute or two, Smollett. Come, George."

It was actually five minutes before Mr. Princey and his son returned.

"Excuse me, my dear," said Mr. Princey to his wife.

"Smollett, would you care to see something rather interesting? Come out to the stables for a moment."

They went into the stable yard. The buildings were now unused except as odd sheds. No one ever went there. Captain Smollett entered, George followed him, Mr. Princey came last. As he closed the door he took up a gun which stood behind it. "Smollett," said he, "we have come out to shoot a rat which George heard squeaking under that tub. Now, you must listen to me very carefully or you will be shot by accident. I mean that."

Smollett looked at him. "Very well," said he. "Go on."

"A very tragic happening has taken place this afternoon," said Mr. Princey. "It will be even more tragic unless it is smoothed over."

"Oh?" said Smollett.

"You heard me ask," said Mr. Princey, "who would kill Withers. You heard Millicent make a comment, an unguarded comment."

"Well?" said Smollett. "What of it?"

"Very little," said Mr. Princey. "Unless you heard that Withers had met a violent end this very afternoon. And that, my dear Smollett, is what you are going to hear."

"Have you killed him?" cried Smollett.

"Millicent has," said Mr. Princey.

"Hell!" said Smollett.

"It *is* hell," said Mr. Princey. "You would have remembered—and guessed."

"Maybe," said Smollett. "Yes. I suppose I should."

"Therefore," said Mr. Princey, "you constitute a problem."

"Why did she kill him?" said Smollett.

"It is one of these disgusting things," said Mr. Princey. "Pitiable, too. She deluded herself that he was in love with her."

"Oh, of course," said Smollett.

"And he told her about the Brangwyn-Davies girl."

"I see," said Smollett.

"I have no wish," said Mr. Princey, "that she should be proved either a lunatic or a murderess. I could hardly live here after that."

"I suppose not," said Smollett.

"On the other hand," said Mr. Princey, "*you* know about it."

"Yes," said Smollett. "I am wondering if I could keep my mouth shut. If I promised you—"

"I am wondering if I could believe you," said Mr. Princey.

"If I promised," said Smollett.

"If things went smoothly," said Mr. Princey. "But not if there was any sort of suspicion, any questioning. You would be afraid of being an accessory."

"I don't know," said Smollett.

"I do," said Mr. Princey. "What are we going to do?"

"I can't see anything else," said Smollett. "You'd never be fool enough to do me in. You can't get rid of two corpses."

"I regard it," said Mr. Princey, "as a better risk than the other. It could be an accident. Or you and Withers could both disappear. There are possibilities in that."

"Listen," said Smollett. "You can't—"

"Listen," said Mr. Princey. "There may be a way out. There *is* a way out, Smollett. You gave me the idea yourself."

"Did I?" said Smollett. "What?"

"You said you would kill Withers," said Mr. Princey. "You have a motive."

"I was joking," said Smollett.

"You are always joking," said Mr. Princey. "People think there must be something behind it. Listen, Smollett, I can't trust you; therefore you must trust me. Or I will kill you now, in the next minute. I mean that. You can choose between dying and living."

"Go on," said Smollett.

"There is a sewer here," said Mr. Princey, speaking fast and forcefully. "That is where I am going to put Withers. No outsider knows he has come up here this afternoon. No one will ever look there for him unless you tell them. You must give me evidence that you have murdered Withers."

"Why?" said Smollett.

"So that I shall be dead sure that you will never open your lips on the matter," said Mr. Princey.

"What evidence?" said Smollett.

"George," said Mr. Princey, "hit him in the face, hard."

"Good God!" said Smollett.

"Again," said Mr. Princey. "Don't bruise your knuckles."

"Oh!" said Smollett.

"I'm sorry," said Mr. Princey. "There must be traces of a struggle between you and Withers. Then it will not be altogether safe for you to go to the police."

"Why won't you take my word?" said Smollett.

"I will when we've finished," said Mr. Princey. "George, get that croquet post. Take your handkerchief to it. As I told you, Smollett, you'll just grasp the end of this croquet post. I shall shoot you if you don't."

"Oh, hell!" said Smollett. "All right."

"Pull two hairs out of his head, George," said Mr. Princey, "and remember what I told you to do with them. Now, Smollett, you take that bar and raise the big flag-stone with the ring in it. Withers is in the next stall. You've got to drag him through and dump him in."

"I won't touch him," said Smollett.

"Stand back, George," said Mr. Princey, raising his gun.

"Wait a minute," cried Smollett. "Wait a minute." He did as he was told.

Mr. Princey wiped his brow. "Look here," said he. "Everything is perfectly safe. Remember, no one knows that Withers came here. Everyone thinks he walked over to Bass Hill. That's five miles of country to search. They'll never look in our sewer. Do you see how safe it is?"

"I suppose it is," said Smollett.

"Now come into the house," said Mr. Princey. "We shall never get that rat."

They went into the house. The maid was bringing tea into the drawing-room. "See, my dear," said Mr. Princey to his wife, "we went into the stable to shoot a rat and we found Captain Smollett. Don't be offended, my dear fellow."

"You must have walked up the back drive," said Mrs. Princey.

"Yes. Yes. That was it," said Smollett in some confusion.

"You've cut your lip," said George, handing him a cup of tea.

"I . . . I just knocked it."

"Shall I tell Bridget to bring some iodine?" said Mrs. Princey. The maid looked up, waiting.

"Don't trouble, please," said Smollett. "It's nothing."

"Very well, Bridget," said Mrs. Princey. "That's all."

"Smollett is very kind," said Mr. Princey. "He knows all our trouble. We can rely on him. We have his word."

"Oh, have we, Captain Smollett?" cried Mrs. Princey. "You *are* good."

"Don't worry, old fellow," Mr. Princey said. "They'll never find anything."

Pretty soon Smollett took his leave. Mrs. Princey pressed his hand very hard. Tears came into her eyes. All three of them watched him go down the drive. Then Mr. Princey spoke very earnestly to his wife for a few minutes and the two of them went upstairs and spoke still more earnestly to Millicent. Soon after, the rain having ceased, Mr. Princey took a stroll round the stable yard.

He came back and went to the telephone. "Put me through to Bass Hill police station," said he. "Quickly. . . . Hullo, is that the police station? This is Mr. Princey, of Abbott's Laxton. I'm afraid something rather terrible has happened up here. Can you send someone at once?"

The Fantastic Horror of the Cat in the Bag

by Dorothy L. Sayers

---

fiction

One should be very careful about the luggage one takes out of the checkroom.

The Great North Road wound away like a flat, steel-grey ribbon. Up it, with the sun and wind behind them, two black specks moved swiftly. To the yokel in charge of the hay-wagon they were only two of "they dratted motor-cyclists," as they barked and zoomed past him in rapid succession. A little farther on, a family man, driving delicately with a two-seater side-car, grinned as the sharp rattle of the o.h.v. Norton was succeeded by the feline shriek of an angry Scott Flying-Squirrel. He, too, in bachelor days, had taken a side in that perennial feud. He sighed regretfully as he watched the racing machines dwindle away northwards.

At that abominable and unexpected S-bend across the bridge above Hatfield, the Norton man, in the pride of his heart, turned to wave a defiant hand at his pursuer. In that second, the enormous bulk of a loaded charabanc loomed down upon him from the bridgehead. He wrenched himself away from it in a fierce wobble, and the Scott, cornering melodramatically, with left and right foot-rests alternately skimming the tarmac, gained a few triumphant yards. The Norton leapt forward with wide-open throttle. A party of children, seized with sudden panic, rushed helter-skelter across the road. The Scott lurched through them in drunken swerves. The road was clear, and the chase settled down once more.

It is not known why motorists, who sing the joys of the open road, spend so much petrol every week-end grinding their way to Southend and Brighton and Margate, in the stench of each other's exhausts, one hand on the horn and one foot on the brake, their eyes starting from their orbits in the nerve-racking search for cops, corners, blind turnings, and cross-road suicides. They ride in a baffled fury, hating each other. They arrive with shattered nerves and fight for parking places. They return, blinded by the headlights of fresh arrivals, whom they hate even worse than they hate each other. And all the time the Great North Road winds away like a long, flat, steel-grey ribbon—a surface like a racetrack, without traps, without hedges, without side-roads, and without traffic. True, it leads to nowhere in particular; but, after all, one pub is very much like another.

The tarmac reeled away, mile after mile. The sharp turn to the right at Baldock, the involute intricacies of Biggleswade, with its multiplication of sign-posts, gave temporary check, but brought the pursuer no nearer. Through Tempsford at full speed, with bellowing horn and exhaust, then, screaming like a hurricane past the R.A.C. post where the road forks in from Bedford. The Norton rider again glanced back; the Scott rider again sounded his horn ferociously. Flat as a chessboard, dyke and field revolved about the horizon.

The constable at Eaton Socon was by no means an anti-motor fiend. In fact, he had just alighted from his pushbike to pass the time of day with the A.A. man on point duty at the cross-roads. But he was just and God-fearing. The sight of two maniacs careering at seventy miles an hour into his protectorate was more than he could be expected to countenance—the more, that the local magistrate happened to be passing at that very moment in a pony-trap. He advanced to the middle of the road, spreading his arms in a majestic manner. The Norton rider looked, saw the road beyond complicated by the pony-trap and a traction-engine, and resigned himself to the inevitable. He flung the throttle-lever back, stamped on his squealing brakes, and skidded to a standstill. The Scott, having had notice, came up mincingly, with a voice like a pleased kitten.

"Now, then," said the constable, in a tone of reproof, "ain't you got no more sense than to come drivin' into the town at a 'undred mile an hour. This ain't Brooklands, you know. I never see anything like it. 'Ave to take your names and numbers, if *you* please. You'll bear witness, Mr. Nadgett, as they was doin' over eighty."

The A.A. man, after a swift glance over the two sets of handle-bars to assure himself that the black sheep were not of his flock, said, with an air of impartial accuracy, "About sixty-six and a half, I should say, if you was to ask me in court."

"Look here, you blighter," said the Scott man indignantly to the Norton man, "why the hell couldn't you stop when you heard me hoot? I've been chasing you with your beastly bag nearly thirty miles. Why can't you look after your own rotten luggage?"

He indicated a small, stout bag, tied with string to his own carrier.

"That?" said the Norton man, with scorn. "What do you mean? It's not mine. Never saw it in my life."

This bare-faced denial threatened to render the Scott rider speechless.

"Of all the—" he gasped. "Why, you crimson idiot, I saw it fall off, just the other side of Hatfield. I yelled and blew like fury. I suppose that overhead gear of yours makes so much noise you can't hear anything else. I take the trouble to pick the thing up, and go after you, and all you do is to race off like a lunatic and run me into a cop. Fat lot of thanks one gets for trying to be decent to fools on the road."

"That ain't neither here nor there," said the policeman. "Your licence, please, sir."

"Here you are," said the Scott man, ferociously flapping out his pocket-book. "My name's Walters, and it's the last time I'll try to do anybody a good turn, you can lay your shirt."

"Walters," said the constable, entering the particulars laboriously in his note-book, "and Simpkins. You'll 'ave your summonses in doo course. It'll be for about a week 'ence, on Monday or thereabouts, I shouldn't wonder."

"Another forty bob gone west," growled Mr. Simpkins, toying with his throttle. "Oh, well, can't be helped, I suppose."

"Forty bob?" snorted the constable. "What do *you*

think? Furious driving to the common danger, that's wot it is. You'll be lucky to get off with five quid apiece."

"Oh, blast!" said the other, stamping furiously on the kick-starter. The engine roared into life, but Mr. Walters dexterously swung his machine across the Norton's path.

"Oh, no, you don't," he said viciously. "You jolly well take your bleeding bag, and no nonsense. I tell you, I *saw* it fall off."

"Now, no language," began the constable, when he suddenly became aware that the A.A. man was staring in a very odd manner at the bag and making signs to him.

" 'Ullo," he demanded, "wot's the matter with the—bleedin' bag, did you say? 'Ere, I'd like to 'ave a look at that 'ere bag, sir, if you don't mind."

"It's nothing to do with me," said Mr. Walters, handing it over. "I saw it fall off and—" His voice died away in his throat, and his eyes became fixed upon one corner of the bag, where something damp and horrible was seeping darkly through.

"Did you notice this 'ere corner when you picked it up?" asked the constable. He prodded it gingerly and looked at his fingers.

"I don't know—no—not particularly," stammered Walters. "I didn't notice anything. I—I expect it burst when it hit the road."

The constable proved the split seam in silence, and then turned hurriedly round to wave away a couple of young women who had stopped to stare. The A.A. man peered curiously, and then started back with a sensation of sickness.

"Ow, Gawd!" he gasped. "It's curly—it's a woman's."

"It's not me," screamed Simpkins. "I swear to heaven it's not mine. This man's trying to put it across me."

"Me?" gasped Walters. "Me? Why, you filthy, murdering brute, I tell you I saw it fall off your carrier. No wonder you blinded off when you saw me coming. Arrest him, constable. Take him away to prison—"

"Hullo, officer!" said a voice behind them. "What's all the excitement? You haven't seen a motor-cyclist go by with a little bag on his carrier, I suppose?"

A big open car with an unnaturally long bonnet had slipped up to them, silent as an owl. The whole agitated party with one accord turned upon the driver.

"Would this be it, sir?"

The motorist pushed off his goggles, disclosing a long, narrow nose and a pair of rather cynical-looking grey eyes.

"It looks rather—" he began; and then, catching sight of the horrid relic protuding from one corner, "In God's name," he enquired, "what's that?"

"That's what we'd like to know, sir," said the constable grimly.

"H'm," said the motorist, "I seem to have chosen an uncommonly unsuitable moment for enquirin' after my bag. Tactless. To say now that it is not my bag is simple, though in no way convincing. As a matter of fact, it is not mine, and I may say that, if it had been, I should not have been at any pains to pursue it."

The constable scratched his head.

"Both these gentlemen—" he began.

The two cyclists burst into simultaneous and heated disclaimers. By this time a small crowd had collected, which the A.A. scout helpfully tried to shoo away.

"You'll all 'ave to come with me to the station," said the harassed constable. "Can't stand 'ere 'oldin' up the traffic. No tricks, now. You wheel them bikes, and I'll come in the car with you, sir."

"But supposing I was to let her rip and kidnap you," said the motorist, with a grin. "Where'd you be? Here," he added, turning to the A.A. man, "can you handle this outfit?"

"You bet," said the scout, his eye running lovingly over the long sweep of the exhaust and the rakish lines of the car.

"Right. Hop in. Now, officer, you can toddle along with the other suspects and keep an eye on them. Wonderful head I've got for detail. By the way, that foot-brake's on the fierce side. Don't bully it, or you'll surprise yourself."

The lock of the bag was forced at the police-station in the midst of an excitement unparalleled in the calm annals of Eaton Socon, and the dreadful contents laid reverently upon a table. Beyond a quantity of cheese-cloth in which they had been wrapped, there was nothing to supply any clue to the mystery.

"Now," said the superintendent, "what do you gentlemen know about this?"

"Nothing whatever," said Mr. Simpkins, with a ghastly

countenance, "except that this man tried to palm it off on me."

"I saw it fall off this man's carrier just the other side of Hatfield," repeated Mr. Walters firmly, "and I rode after him for thirty miles trying to stop him. That's all I know about it, and I wish to God I'd never touched the beastly thing."

"Nor do I know anything about it personally," said the car-owner, "but I fancy I know what it is."

"What's that?" asked the superintendent sharply.

"I rather imagine it's the head of the Finsbury Park murder—though, mind you, that's only a guess."

"That's just what I've been thinking myself," agreed the superintendent, glancing at a daily paper which lay on his desk, its headlines lurid with the details of that very horrid crime, "and, if so, you are to be congratulated, constable, on a very important capture."

"Thank you, sir," said the gratified officer, saluting.

"Now I'd better take all your statements," said the superintendent. "No, no; I'll hear the constable first. Yes, Briggs?"

The constable, the A.A. man, and the two motor-cyclists having given their versions of the story, the superintendent turned to the motorist.

"And what have you got to say about it?" he enquired. "First of all, your name and address."

The other produced a card, which the superintendent copied out and returned to him respectfully.

"A bag of mine, containing some valuable jewellery, was stolen from my car yesterday, in Piccadilly," began the motorist. "It is very much like this, but has a cipher lock. I made enquiries through Scotland Yard, and was informed to-day that a bag of precisely similar appearance had been cloak-roomed yesterday afternoon at Paddington, main line. I hurried round there, and was told by the clerk that just before the police warning came through the bag had been claimed by a man in motor-cycling kit. A porter said he saw the man leave the station, and a loiterer observed him riding off on a motor-bicycle. That was about an hour before. It seemed pretty hopeless, as, of course, nobody had noticed even the make of the bike, let alone the number. Fortunately, however, there was a smart little girl. The smart little girl had been dawdling round outside the station, and had heard a motor-cyclist ask a taxi-driver the quickest route to Finchley. I left the police hunting for the taxi-driver, and started off, and in Finchley I found an intelligent boy-scout. He had seen a motor-cyclist with a bag on the carrier, and had waved and shouted to him that the strap was loose. The cyclist had got off and tightened the strap, and gone straight on up the road towards Chipping Barnet. The boy hadn't been near enough to identify the machine—the only thing he knew for certain was that it wasn't a Douglas, his brother having one of that sort. At Barnet I got an odd little story of a man in a motor-coat who had staggered into a pub with a ghastly white face and drunk two double brandies and gone out and ridden off furiously. Number?—of course not. The barmaid told me. *She* didn't notice the number. After that it was a tale of furious driving all along the road. After Hatfield, I got the story of a road-race. And here we are."

"It seems to me, my lord," said the superintendent, "that the furious driving can't have been all on one side."

"I admit it," said the other, "though I do plead in extenuation that I spared the women and children and hit up the miles in the wide, open spaces. The point at the moment is—"

"Well, my lord," said the superintendent, "I've got your story, and, if it's all right, it can be verified by enquiry at Paddington and Finchley and so on. Now, as for these two gentlemen—"

"It's perfectly obvious," broke in Mr. Walters, "the bag dropped off this man's carrier, and, when he saw me coming after him with it, he thought it was a good opportunity to saddle me with the cursed thing. Nothing could be clearer."

"It's a lie," said Mr. Simpkins. "Here's this fellow has got hold of the bag—I don't say how, but I can guess—and he has the bright idea of shoving the blame on me. It's easy enough to *say* a thing's fallen off a man's carrier. Where's the proof? Where's the strap? If his story's true, you'd find the broken strap on my 'bus. The bag *was* on *his* machine—tied on, tight."

"Yes, with string," retorted the other. "If I'd gone and murdered someone and run off with their head, do you think I'd be such an ass as to tie it on with a bit of twopenny twine? The strap's worked loose and fallen off on the road somewhere; that's what's happened to that."

"Well, look here," said the man addressed as "my lord," "I've got an idea for what it's worth. Suppose, superintendent, you turn out as many of your men as you think adequate to keep an eye on three desperate criminals, and we all tool down to Hatfield together. I can take two in my 'bus at a pinch, and no doubt you have a police car. If this thing *did* fall off the carrier, somebody beside Mr. Walters may have seen it fall."

"They didn't," said Mr. Simpkins.

"There wasn't a soul," said Mr. Walters, "but how do *you* know there wasn't, eh? I thought you didn't know anything about it."

"I mean, it didn't fall off, so nobody *could* have seen it," gasped the other.

"Well, my lord," said the superintendent, "I'm inclined to accept your suggestion, as it gives us a chance of enquiring into your story at the same time. Mind you, I'm not saying I doubt it, you being who you are. I've read about some of your detective work, my lord, and very smart I considered it. But, still, it wouldn't be my duty not to get corroborative evidence if possible."

"Good egg! Quite right," said his lordship. "Forward the light brigade. We can do it easily in—that is to say, at the legal rate of progress it needn't take us much over an hour and a half."

About three-quarters of an hour later, the racing car and the police car loped quietly side by side into Hatfield. Henceforward, the four-seater, in which Walters and Simpkins sat glaring at each other, took the lead, and presently Walters waved his hand and both cars came to a stop.

"It was just about here, as near as I can remember, that it fell off," he said. "Of course, there's no trace of it now."

"You're quite sure as there wasn't a strap fell off with it?" suggested the superintendent. "Because, you see, there must 'a' been something holding it on."

"Of course there wasn't a strap," said Simpkins, white with passion. "You haven't any business to ask him leading questions like that."

"Wait a minute," said Walters slowly. "No, there was no strap. But I've got a sort of a recollection of seeing something on the road about a quarter of a mile farther up."

"It's a lie!" screamed Simpkins. "He's inventing it."

"Just about where we passed that man with the side-car a minute or two ago," said his lordship. "I told you we ought to have stopped and asked if we could help him, superintendent. Courtesy of the road, you know, and all that."

"He couldn't have told us anything," said the superintendent. "He'd probably only just stopped."

"I'm not so sure," said the other. "Didn't you notice what he was doing? Oh, dear, dear, where were your eyes? Hullo! here he comes."

He sprang out into the road and waved to the rider, who, seeing four policemen, thought it better to pull up.

"Excuse me," said his lordship. "Thought we'd just like to stop you and ask if you were all right, and all that sort of thing, you know. Wanted to stop in passing, throttle jammed open, couldn't shut the confounded thing. Little trouble, what?"

"Oh, yes, perfectly all right, thanks, except that I would be glad if you could spare a gallon of petrol. Tank came adrift. Beastly nuisance. Had a bit of a struggle. Happily, Providence placed a broken strap in my way and I've fixed it. Split a bit, though, where that bolt came off. Lucky not to have an explosion, but there's a special cherub for motor-cyclists."

"Strap, eh?" said the superintendent. "Afraid I'll have to trouble you to let me have a look at that."

"What?" said the other. "And just as I've got the damned thing fixed? What the—? All right, dear, all right"
—to his passenger. "Is it something serious, officer?"

"Afraid so, sir. Sorry to trouble you."

"Hi!" yelled one of the policemen, neatly fielding Mr. Simpkins as he was taking a dive over the back of the car. "No use doin' that. You're for it, my lad."

"No doubt about it," said the superintendent triumphantly, snatching at the strap which the side-car rider held out to him. "Here's his name on it, 'J. SIMPKINS,' written on in ink as large as life. Very much obliged to you, sir, I'm sure. You've helped us effect a very important capture."

"No! Who is it?" cried the girl in the side-car. "How frightfully thrilling! Is it a murder?"

"Look in your paper to-morrow, miss," said the superintendent, "and you may see something. Here, Briggs, better put the handcuffs on him."

"And how about my tank?" said the man mournfully. "It's all right for you to be excited, Babs, but you'll have to get out and help push."

"Oh, no," said his lordship. "Here's a strap. A *much* nicer strap. A really superior strap. And petrol. *And* a pocket-flask. Everything a young man ought to know. And, when you're in town, mind you both look me up. Lord Peter Wimsey, 110A Piccadilly. Delighted to see you any time. Chin, chin!"

"Cheerio!" said the other, wiping his lips and much mollified. "Only too charmed to be of use. Remember it in my favour, officer, next time you catch me speeding."

"Very fortunate we spotted him," said the superintendent complacently, as they continued their way into Hatfield. "Quite providential, as you might say."

"I'll come across with it," said the wretched Simpkins, sitting handcuffed in the Hatfield police-station. "I swear to God I know nothing whatever about it—about the murder, I mean. There's a man I know who has a jewellery business in Birmingham. I don't know him very well. In fact, I only met him at Southend last Easter, and we got pally. His name's Owen—Thomas Owen. He wrote me yesterday and said he'd accidentally left a bag in the cloakroom at Paddington and asked if I'd take it out—he enclosed the ticket—and bring it up next time I came that way. I'm in transport service, you see—you've got my card—and I'm always up and down the country. As it happened, I was just going up in that direction with this Norton, so I fetched the thing out at lunch-time and started off with it. I didn't notice the date on the cloakroom ticket. I know there wasn't anything to pay on it, so it can't have been there long. Well, it all went just as you said up to Finchley, and there that boy told me my strap was loose and I went to tighten it up. And then I noticed that the corner of the bag was split, and it was damp—and—well, I saw what you saw. That sort of turned me over, and I lost my head. The only thing I could think of was to get rid of it, quick. I remembered there were a lot of lonely stretches on the Great North Road, so I cut the strap nearly through—that was when I stopped for that drink at Barnet—and then, when I thought there wasn't anybody in sight, I just reached back and gave it a tug, and it went—strap and all; I hadn't put it through the slots. It fell off, just like a great weight dropping off my mind. I suppose Walters must just have come round into sight as it fell. I had to slow down a mile or two farther on for some sheep going into a field, and then I heard him hooting at me—and—oh, my God!"

He groaned, and buried his head in his hands.

"I see," said the Eaton Socon superintendent. "Well, that's your statement. Now, about this Thomas Owen—"

"Oh," cried Lord Peter Wimsey, "never mind Thomas Owen. He's not the man you want. You can't suppose that a bloke who'd committed a murder would want a fellow tailin' after him to Birmingham with the head. It stands to reason that was intended to stay in Paddington cloakroom till the ingenious perpetrator had skipped, or till it was unrecognisable, or both. Which, by the way, is where we'll find those family heirlooms of mine, which your engaging friend Mr. Owen lifted out of my car. Now, Mr. Simpkins, just pull yourself together and tell us who was standing next to you at the cloakroom when you took out that bag. Try hard to remember, because this jolly little island is no place for him, and he'll be taking the next boat while we stand talking."

"I can't remember," moaned Simpkins. "I didn't notice. My head's all in a whirl."

"Never mind. Go back. Think quietly. Make a picture of yourself getting off your machine—leaning it up against something—"

"No, I put it on the stand."

"Good! That's the way. Now, think—you're taking the cloakroom ticket out of your pocket and going up—trying to attract the man's attention."

"I couldn't at first. There was an old lady trying to cloakroom a canary, and a very bustling man in a hurry with some golf-clubs. He was quite rude to a quiet little man with a—by Jove! yes, a hand-bag like that one. Yes, that's it. The timid man had had it on the counter quite a long time, and the big man pushed him aside. I don't know what happened, quite, because mine was handed out to me just then. The big man pushed his luggage in front of both of us and I had to reach over it—and I suppose—yes, I must have taken the wrong one. Good God! Do you mean to say that that timid little insignificant-looking man was a murderer?"

...ots of 'em like that," put in the Hatfield superintend-
.. "But what was he like—come!"

"He was only about five foot five, and he wore a soft
hat and a long, dust-coloured coat. He was very ordinary,
with rather weak, prominent eyes, I think, but I'm not
sure I should know him again. Oh, wait a minute! I do
remember one thing. He had an odd scar—crescent-
shaped—under his left eye."

"That settles it," said Lord Peter. "I thought as much.
Did you recognise the—the face when we took it out, superintendent? No? I did. It was Dahlia Dallmeyer, the ac-
tress, who is supposed to have sailed for America last
week. And the short man with the crescent-shaped scar is
her husband, Philip Storey. Sordid tale and all that. She
ruined him, treated him like dirt, and was unfaithful to
him, but it looks as though he had had the last word in
the argument. And now, I imagine, the Law will have the
last word with him. Get busy on the wires, superintendent,
and you might ring up the Paddington people and tell 'em
to let me have my bag, before Mr. Thomas Owen tumbles
to it that there's been a slight mistake."

"Well, anyhow," said Mr. Walters, extending a magnan-
imous hand to the abashed Mr. Simpkins, "it was a top-
hole race—well worth a summons. We must have a return
match one of these days."

Early the following morning a little, insignificant-looking man stepped aboard the trans-Atlantic liner *Volucria*.
At the head of the gangway two men blundered into him.
The younger of the two, who carried a small bag, was
turning to apologise, when a light of recognition flashed
across his face.

"Why, if it isn't Mr. Storey!" he exclaimed loudly.
"Where are you off to? I haven't seen you for an age."

"I'm afraid," said Philip Storey, "I haven't the pleasure—"

"Cut it out," said the other, laughing. "I'd know that
scar of yours anywhere. Going out to the States?"

"Well, yes," said the other, seeing that his acquaint-
ance's boisterous manner was attracting attention. "I beg
your pardon. It's Lord Peter Wimsey, isn't it? Yes. I'm
joining the wife out there."

"And how is she?" enquired Wimsey, steering the way

into the bar and sitting down at a table. "Left last week, didn't she? I saw it in the papers."

"Yes. She's just cabled me to join her. We're—er—taking a holiday in—er—the lakes. Very pleasant there in summer."

"Cabled you, did she? And so here we are on the same boat. Odd how things turn out, what? I only got my sailing orders at the last minute. Chasing criminals—my hobby, you know."

"Oh, really?" Mr. Storey licked his lips.

"Yes. This is Detective-Inspector Parker of Scotland Yard—great pal of mine. Yes. Very unpleasant matter, annoying and all that. Bag that ought to have been re-posin' peacefully at Paddington Station turns up at Eaton Socon. No business there, what?"

He smacked the bag on the table so violently that the lock sprang open.

Storey leapt to his feet with a shriek, flinging his arms across the opening of the bag as though to hide its contents.

"How did you get that?" he screamed. "Eaton Socon? It—I never—"

"It's mine," said Wimsey quietly, as the wretched man sank back, realising that he had betrayed himself. "Some jewellery of my mother's. What did you think it was?"

Detective Parker touched his charge gently on the shoulder.

"You needn't answer that," he said. "I arrest you, Philip Storey, for the murder of your wife. Anything that you say may be used against you."

Fatal Visit of the Inca

To Pizarro and His Followers in the City of Caxamalca

by William H. Prescott

---

fact

*They made no resistance—as, indeed, they had
no weapons with which to make it.*

It was not long before sunset when the van of the royal
procession entered the gates of the city. First came some
hundreds of the menials, employed to clear the path from
every obstacle, and singing songs of triumph as they came,
"which in our ears," says one of the conquerors, "sounded
like the songs of hell!" Then followed other bodies of different ranks, and dressed in different liveries. Some wore a
showy stuff, checkered white and red, like the squares of a
chessboard; others were clad in pure white, bearing ham-
mers or maces of silver or copper; and the guards, together with those in immediate attendance on the prince,
were distinguished by a rich azure livery, and a profusion
of gay ornaments, while the large pendants attached to the
ears indicated the Peruvian noble.

Elevated high above his vassals came the Inca Atahuallpa, borne on a sedan or open litter, on which was a
sort of throne made of massive gold of inestimable value.
The palanquin was lined with the richly coloured plumes
of tropical birds, and studded with shining plates of gold
and silver. Round his neck was suspended a collar of
emeralds, of uncommon size and brilliancy. His short hair
was decorated with golden ornaments, and the imperial

borla encircled his temples. The bearing of the Inca was
sedate and dignified; and from his lofty station he looked
down on the multitudes below with an air of composure,
like one accustomed to command.

As the leading files of the procession entered the great
square, larger, says an old chronicler, than any square in
Spain, they opened to the right and left for the royal ret-
inue to pass. Everything was conducted in admirable order. The monarch was permitted to traverse the *plaza* in
silence, and not a Spaniard was to be seen. When some
five or six thousand of his people had entered the place
Atahuallpa halted, and turning round with an inquiring
look, demanded, "Where are the strangers?"

At this moment Fray Vicente de Valverde, a Domini-
can friar, Pizarro's chaplain, and afterwards bishop of
Cuzco, came forward with his breviary, or, as other ac-
counts say, a Bible, in one hand, and a crucifix in the
other, and, approaching the Inca, told him that he came
by order of his commander to expound to him the doc-
trines of the true faith, for which purpose the Spaniards
had come from a great distance to his country. The friar
then explained, as clearly as he could, the mysterious doc-
trine of the Trinity, and, ascending high in his account, began with the creation of man, thence passed to his fall, to
his subsequent redemption by Jesus Christ, to the crucifix-
ion, and the ascension, when the Saviour left the apostle
Peter as his vicegerent upon earth. This power had been
transmitted to the successors of the apostle, good and wise
men, who, under the title of popes, held authority over all
powers and potentates on earth. One of the last of these
popes had commissioned the Spanish emperor, the most
mighty monarch in the world, to conquer and convert the
natives in this western hemisphere; and his general, Fran-
cisco Pizarro, had now come to execute this important
mission. The friar concluded with beseeching the Peruvian
monarch to receive him kindly; to abjure the errors of his
own faith, and embrace that of the Christians now prof-
fered to him, the only one by which he could hope for salvation; and, furthermore, to acknowledge himself a tributary of the Emperor Charles the Fifth, who, in that event,
would aid and protect him as his loyal vassal.

Whether Atahuallpa possessed himself of every link in
the curious chain of argument by which the monk connected Pizarro with St. Peter, may be doubted. It is certain,

however, that he must have had very incorrect notions of the Trinity, if, as Garcilasso states, the interpreter Felipillo explained it by saying, that "the Christians believed in three Gods and one God, and that made four." But there is no doubt he perfectly comprehended that the drift of the discourse was to persuade him to resign his sceptre and acknowledge the supremacy of another.

The eyes of the Indian monarch flashed fire, and his dark brow grew darker, as he replied: "I will be no man's tributary! I am greater than any prince upon earth. Your emperor may be a great prince; I do not doubt it, when I see that he has sent his subjects so far across the waters; and I am willing to hold him as a brother. As for the pope of whom you speak, he must be crazy to talk of giving away countries which do not belong to him. As for my faith," he continued, "I will not change it. Your own God, as you say, was put to death by the very men whom he created. But mine," he concluded, pointing to his deity— then, alas! sinking in glory behind the mountains—"my god still lives in the heavens, and looks down on his children."

He then demanded of Valverde by what authority he had said these things. The friar pointed to the book which he held as his authority. Atahuallpa, taking it, turned over the pages a moment, then, as the insult he had received probably flashed across his mind, he threw it down with vehemence, and exclaimed: "Tell your comrades that they shall give me an account of their doings in my land. I will not go from here till they have made me full satisfaction for all the wrongs they have committed."

The friar, greatly scandalized by the indignity offered to the sacred volume, stayed only to pick it up, and hastening to Pizarro, informed him of what had been done, exclaiming at the same time: "Do you not see that, while we stand here wasting our breath in talking with this dog, full of pride as he is, the fields are filling with Indians? Set on at once; I absolve you." Pizarro saw that the hour had come. He waved a white scarf in the air, the appointed signal. The fatal gun was fired from the fortress. Then springing into the square, the Spanish captain and his followers shouted the old war-cry of "St. Jago and at them!" It was answered by the battle-cry of every Spaniard in the city, as, rushing from the avenues of the great halls in which they were concealed, they poured into the plaza,

horse and foot, each in his own dark column, and threw
themselves into the midst of the Indian crowd. The latter,
taken by surprise, stunned by the report of artillery and
muskets, the echoes of which reverberated like thunder
from the surrounding buildings, and blinded by the smoke
which rolled in sulphureous volumes along the square,
were seized with a panic. They knew not whither to fly for
refuge from the coming ruin. Nobles and commoners—all
were trampled down under the fierce charge of the
cavalry, who dealt their blows right and left, without spar-
ing; while their swords, flashing through the thick gloom,
carried dismay into the hearts of the wretched natives,
who now, for the first time, saw the horse and his rider in
all their terrors. They made no resistance—as, indeed, they
had no weapons with which to make it. Every avenue to
escape was closed, for the entrance to the square was
choked up with the dead bodies of men who had perished
in vain efforts to fly; and such was the agony of the sur-
vivors under the terrible pressure of their assailants, that
a large body of Indians, by their convulsive struggles, burst
through the wall of stone and dried clay, which formed
part of the boundary of the plaza! It fell, leaving an opening of more than a hundred paces, through which multitudes now found their way into the country, still hotly
pursued by the cavalry, who, leaping the fallen rubbish,
hung on the rear of the fugitives, striking them down in all
directions.

Meanwhile the fight, or rather massacre, continued hot
around the Inca, whose person was the great object of the
assault. His faithful nobles, rallying about him, threw
themselves in the way of the assailants, and strove, by
tearing them from their saddles, or, at least, by offering
their own bosoms as a mark for their vengeance, to shield
their beloved master. It is said by some authorities that
they carried weapons concealed under their clothes. If so,
it availed them little, as it is not pretended that they used
them. But the most timid animal will defend itself when at
bay. That they did not do so in the present instance, is
proof that they had no weapons to use. Yet they still continued to force back the cavaliers, clinging to their horses
with dying grasp, and as one was cut down, another taking
the place of his fallen comrade with a loyalty truly affect-
ing.

The Indian monarch, stunned and bewildered, saw his

faithful subjects falling round him without hardly compre-
hending his situation. The litter on which he rode heaved
to and fro, as the mighty press swayed backwards and for-
wards; and he gazed on the overwhelming ruin, like some
forlorn mariner, who, tossed about in his bark by the furious elements, sees the lightning's flash, and hears the thunder bursting around him, with the consciousness that he
can do nothing to avert his fate. At length, weary with the
work of destruction, the Spaniards, as the shades of evening grew deeper, felt afraid that the royal prize might, after all, elude them; and some of the cavaliers made a desperate attempt to end the affray at once by taking Atahuallpa's life. But Pizarro, who was nearest his person,
called out with stentorian voice: "Let no one, who values
his life, strike at the Inca"; and, stretching out his arm to
shield him, received a wound on the hand from one of his
own men—the only wound received by a Spaniard in the
action.

The struggle now became fiercer than ever round the
royal litter. It reeled more and more, and at length,
several of the nobles who supported it having been slain, it
was overturned, and the Indian prince would have come
with violence to the ground, had not his fall been broken
by the efforts of Pizarro and some other of the cavaliers,
who caught him in their arms. The imperial *borla* was instantly snatched from his temples by a soldier named Es-
tete, and the unhappy monarch, strongly secured, was removed to a neighbouring building, where he was carefully
guarded.

All attempt at resistance now ceased. The fate of the
Inca soon spread over town and country. The charm
which might have held the Peruvians together was dis-
solved. Every man thought only of his own safety. Even
the soldiery encamped on the adjacent fields took the
alarm, and, learning the fatal tidings, were seen flying in
every direction before their pursuers, who in the heat of
triumph shewed no touch of mercy. At length night, more
pitiful than man, threw her friendly mantle over the fugitives, and the scattered troops of Pizarro rallied once
more at the sound of the trumpet in the bloody square of
Caxamalca.

Man Overboard

by F. Marion Crawford

---
fiction
---

*Thirteen on a sailing ship can be a very unlucky
number.*

Yes—I have heard "Man overboard!" a good many
times since I was a boy, and once or twice I have seen the
man go. There are more men lost in that way than passengers on ocean steamers ever learn of. I have stood looking
over the rail on a dark night, when there was a step beside
me, and something flew past my head like a big black
bat—and then there was a splash! Stokers often go like
that. They go mad with the heat, and they slip up on deck
and are gone before anybody can stop them, often without
being seen or heard. Now and then a passenger will do it,
but he generally has what he thinks a pretty good reason.
I have seen a man empty his revolver into a crowd of
emigrants forward, and then go over like a rocket. Of
course, any officer who respects himself will do what he
can to pick a man up, if the weather is not so heavy that
he would have to risk his ship; but I don't think I remember seeing a man come back when he was once fairly gone
more than two or three times in all my life, though we
have often picked up the life-buoy, and sometimes the fellow's cap. Stokers and passengers jump over; I never knew
a sailor to do that, drunk or sober. Yes, they say it has
happened on hard ships, but I never knew a case myself.
Once in a long time a man is fished out when it is just too
late, and dies in the boat before you can get him aboard,
and—well, I don't know that I ever told that story since it
happened—I knew a fellow who went over, and came

71

back dead. I didn't see him after he came back; only one of us did, but we all knew he was there.

No, I am not giving you "sharks." There isn't a shark in this story, and I don't know that I would tell it at all if we weren't alone, just you and I. But you and I have seen things in various parts, and maybe you will understand. Anyhow, you know that I am telling what I know about, and nothing else; and it has been on my mind to tell you ever since it happened, only there hasn't been a chance.

It's a long story, and it took some time to happen; and it began a good many years ago, in October, as well as I can remember. I was mate then; I passed the local Marine Board for master about three years later. She was the *Helen B. Jackson*, of New York, with lumber for the West Indies, four-masted schooner, Captain Hackstaff. She was an old-fashioned one, even then—no steam donkey, and all to do by hand. There were still sailors in the coasting trade in those days, you remember. She wasn't a hard ship, for the old man was better than most of them, though he kept to himself and had a face like a monkey-wrench. We were thirteen, all told, in the ship's company; and some of them afterwards thought that might have had something to do with it, but I had all that nonsense knocked out of me when I was a boy. I don't mean to say that I like to go to sea on a Friday, but I *have* gone to sea on a Friday, and nothing has happened; and twice before that we have been thirteen, because one of the hands didn't turn up at the last minute, and nothing ever happened either—nothing worse than the loss of a light spar or two, or a little canvas. Whenever I have been wrecked, we had sailed as cheerily as you please—no thirteens, no Fridays, no dead men in the hold. I believe it generally happens that way.

I dare say you remember those two Benton boys that were so much alike? It is no wonder, for they were twin brothers. They shipped with us as boys on the old *Boston Belle*, when you were mate and I was before the mast. I never was quite sure which was which of those two, even then; and when they both had beards it was harder than ever to tell them apart. One was Jim, and the other was Jack; James Benton and John Benton. The only difference I ever could see was, that one seemed to be rather more cheerful and inclined to talk than the other; but one couldn't even be sure of that. Perhaps they had moods.

Anyhow, there was one of them that used to whistle when he was alone. He only knew one tune, and that was "Nancy Lee," and the other didn't know any tune at all; but I may be mistaken about that, too. Perhaps they both knew it.

Well, those two Benton boys turned up on board the *Helen B. Jackson*. They had been on half a dozen ships since the *Boston Belle*, and they had grown up and were good seamen. They had reddish beards and bright blue eyes and freckled faces; and they were quiet fellows, good workmen on rigging, pretty willing, and both good men at the wheel. They managed to be in the same watch—it was the port watch on the *Helen B.*, and that was mine, and I had great confidence in them both. If there was any job aloft that needed two hands, they were always the first to jump into the rigging; but that doesn't often happen on a fore-and-aft schooner. If it breezed up, and the jibtopsail was to be taken in, they never minded a wetting, and they would be out at the bowsprit end before there was a hand at the downhaul. The men liked them for that, and because they didn't blow about what they could do. I remember one day in a reefing job, the downhaul parted and came down on deck from the peak of the spanker. When the weather moderated, and we shook the reefs out, the downhaul was forgotten until we happened to think we might soon need it again. There was some sea on, and the boom was off and the gaff was slamming. One of those Benton boys was at the wheel, and before I knew what he was doing, the other was out on the gaff with the end of the new downhaul, trying to reeve it through its block. The one who was steering watched him, and got as white as cheese. The other one was swinging about on the gaff end, and every time she rolled to leeward he brought up with a jerk that would have sent anything but a monkey flying into space. But he didn't leave it until he had rove the new rope, and he got back all right. I think it was Jack at the wheel; the one that seemed more cheerful, the one that whistled "Nancy Lee." He had rather have been doing the job himself than watch his brother do it, and he had a scared look; but he kept her as steady as he could in the swell, and he drew a long breath when Jim had worked his way back to the peak-halliard block, and had something to hold on to. I think it was Jim.

They had good togs, too, and they were neat and clean

men in the forecastle. I knew they had nobody belonging
to them ashore,—no mother, no sisters, and no wives; but
somehow they both looked as if a woman overhauled
them now and then. I remember that they had one ditty
bag between them, and they had a woman's thimble in it.
One of the men said something about it to them, and they
looked at each other; and one smiled, but the other didn't.
Most of their clothes were alike, but they had one red
guernsey between them. For some time I used to think it
was always the same one that wore it, and I thought that
might be a way to tell them apart. But then I heard one
asking the other for it, and saying that the other had worn
it last. So that was no sign either. The cook was a West
India man, called James Lawley; his father had been
hanged for putting lights in cocoanut trees where they did-
n't belong. But he was a good cook, and knew his business;
and it wasn't soup-and-bully and dog's-body every Sunday.
That's what I meant to say. On Sunday the cook called
both those boys Jim, and on week-days he called them
Jack. He used to say he must be right sometimes if he did
that, because even the hands on a painted clock point
right twice a day.

What started me to trying for some way of telling the
Bentons apart was this. I heard them talking about a girl.
It was at night, in our watch, and the wind had headed us
off a little rather suddenly, and when we had flattened in
the jibs, we clewed down the topsails, while the two Benton boys got the spanker sheet aft. One of them was at the
helm. I coiled down the mizzen-topsail downhaul myself,
and was going aft to see how she headed up, when I
stopped to look at a light, and leaned against the deck-
house. While I was standing there I heard the two boys
talking. It sounded as if they had talked of the same thing
before, and as far as I could tell, the voice I heard first
belonged to the one who wasn't quite so cheerful as the
other,—the one who was Jim when one knew which he
was.

"Does Mamie know?" Jim asked.

"Not yet," Jack answered quietly. He was at the wheel.
"I mean to tell her next time we get home."

"All right."

That was all I heard, because I didn't care to stand
there listening while they were talking about their own affairs; so I went aft to look into the binnacle, and I told

the one at the wheel to keep her so as long as she had way on her, for I thought the wind would back up again before long, and there was land to leeward. When he answered, his voice, somehow, didn't sound like the cheerful one. Perhaps his brother had relieved the wheel while they had been speaking, but what I had heard set me wondering which of them it was that had a girl at home. There's lots of time for wondering on a schooner in fair weather.

After that I thought I noticed that the two brothers were more silent when they were together. Perhaps they guessed that I had overheard something that night, and kept quiet when I was about. Some men would have amused themselves by trying to chaff them separately about the girl at home, and I suppose whichever one it was would have let the cat out of the bag if I had done that. But, somehow, I didn't like to. Yes, I was thinking of getting married myself at that time, so I had a sort of fellow-feeling for whichever one it was, that made me not want to chaff him.

They didn't talk much, it seemed to me; but in fair weather, when there was nothing to do at night, and one was steering, the other was everlastingly hanging round as if he were waiting to relieve the wheel, though he might have been enjoying a quiet nap for all I cared in such weather. Or else, when one was taking his turn at the lookout, the other would be sitting on an anchor beside him. One kept near the other, at night more than in the daytime. I noticed that. They were fond of sitting on that anchor, and they generally tucked away their pipes under it, for the *Helen B.* was a dry boat in most weather, and like most fore-and-afters was better on a wind than going free. With a beam sea we sometimes shipped a little water aft. We were by the stern, anyhow, on that voyage, and that is one reason why we lost the man.

We fell in with a southerly gale, southeast at first; and then the barometer began to fall while you could watch it, and a long swell began to come up from the south'ard. A couple of months earlier we might have been in for a cyclone, but it's "October all over" in those waters, as you know better than I. It was just going to blow, and then it was going to rain, that was all; and we had plenty of time to make everything snug before it breezed up much. It blew harder after sunset, and by the time it was quite dark it was a full gale. We had shortened sail for it, but as we were by the stern we were carrying the spanker close reefed instead of the storm trysail. She steered better so, as long as we didn't have to heave to. I had the first watch with the Benton boys, and we had not been on deck an hour when a child might have seen that the weather meant business.

The old man came up on deck and looked round, and in less than a minute he told us to give her the trysail. That meant heaving to, and I was glad of it; for though the *Helen B.* was a good vessel enough, she wasn't a new ship by a long way, and it did her no good to drive her in that weather. I asked whether I should call all hands, but just then the cook came aft, and the old man said he thought we could manage the job without waking the sleepers, and the trysail was handy on deck already, for we hadn't been expecting anything better. We were all in oilskins, of course, and the night was as black as a coal mine, with only a ray of light from the slit in the binnacle shield, and you couldn't tell one man from another except by his voice. The old man took the wheel; we got the boom amidships, and he jammed her into the wind until she had hardly any way. It was blowing now, and it was all that I and two others could do to get in the slack of the downhaul, while the others lowered away at the peak and throat, and we had our hands full to get a couple of turns round the wet sail. It's all child's play on a fore-and-after compared with reefing topsails in anything like weather, but the gear of a schooner sometimes does unhandy things that you don't expect, and those everlasting long halliards get foul of everything if they get adrift. I remember thinking how unhandy that particular job was. Somebody unhooked the throat-halliard block, and thought he had hooked it into the head-cringle of the trysail, and sang out to hoist away, but he had missed it in the dark, and the heavy block went flying into the lee rigging, and nearly killed him when it swung back with the weather roll. Then the old man got her up in the wind until the jib was shaking like thunder; then he held her off, and she went off as soon as the headsails filled, and he couldn't get her back again without the spanker. Then the *Helen B.* did her favourite trick, and before we had time to say much we had a sea over the quarter and were up to our waists, with the parrels of the trysail only half beck-eted round the mast, and the deck so full of gear that you

couldn't put your foot on a plank, and the spanker beginning to get adrift again, being badly stopped, and the general confusion and hell's delight that you can only have on
a fore-and-after when there's nothing really serious the
matter. Of course, I don't mean to say that the old man
couldn't have steered his trick as well as you or I or any
other seaman; but I don't believe he had ever been on
board the *Helen B.* before, or had his hand on her wheel
till then; and he didn't know her ways. I don't mean to say
that what happened was his fault. I don't know whose
fault it was. Perhaps nobody was to blame. But I knew
something happened somewhere on board when we shipped
that sea, and you'll never get it out of my head. I hadn't
any spare time myself, for I was becketing the rest of the
trysail to the mast. We were on the starboard tack, and
the throat-halliard came down to port as usual, and I
suppose there were at least three men at it, hoisting away,
while I was at the beckets.

Now I am going to tell you something. You have
known me, man and boy, several voyages; and you are
older than I am; and you have always been a good friend
to me. Now, do you think I am the sort of man to think I
hear things where there isn't anything to hear, or to think
I see things when there is nothing to see? No, you don't.
Thank you. Well now, I had passed the last becket, and I
sang out to the men to sway away, and I was standing on
the jaws of the spanker-gaff, with my left hand on the
bolt-rope of the trysail, so that I could feel when it was
board-taut, and I wasn't thinking of anything except being
glad the job was over, and that we were going to heave
her to. It was as black as a coal-pocket, except that you
could see the streaks on the seas as they went by, and
abaft the deck-house I could see the ray of light from the
binnacle on the captain's yellow oilskin as he stood at the
wheel—or rather I might have seen it if I had looked
round at that minute. But I didn't look round. I heard a
man whistling. It was "Nancy Lee," and I could have
sworn that the man was right over my head in the cross-
trees. Only somehow I knew very well that if anybody
could have been up there, and could have whistled a tune,
there were no living ears sharp enough to hear it on deck
then. I heard it distinctly, and at the same time I heard
the real whistling of the wind in the weather rigging, sharp
and clear as the steam-whistle on a Dago's peanut-cart in

New York. That was all right, that was as it should be; but the other wasn't right; and I felt queer and stiff, as if I couldn't move, and my hair was curling against the flannel lining of my sou'wester, and I thought somebody had dropped a lump of ice down my back.

I said that the noise of the wind in the rigging was real, as if the other wasn't, for I felt that it wasn't, though I heard it. But it was, all the same; for the captain heard it, too. When I came to relieve the wheel, while the men were clearing up decks, he was swearing. He was a quiet man, and I hadn't heard him swear before, and I don't think I did again, though several queer things happened after that. Perhaps he said all he had to say then; I don't see how he could have said anything more. I used to think nobody could swear like a Dane, except a Neapolitan or a South American; but when I had heard the old man I changed my mind. There's nothing afloat or ashore that can beat one of your quiet American skippers, if he gets off on that tack. I didn't need to ask him what was the matter, for I knew he had heard "Nancy Lee," as I had, only it affected us differently.

He did not give me the wheel, but told me to go forward and get the second bonnet off the staysail, so as to keep her up better. As we tailed on to the sheet when it was done, the man next me knocked his sou'wester off against my shoulder, and his face came so close to me that I could see it in the dark. It must have been very white for me to see it, but I only thought of that afterwards. I don't see how any light could have fallen upon it, but I knew it was one of the Benton boys. I don't know what made me speak to him. "Hullo, Jim! Is that you?" I asked. I don't know why I said Jim, rather than Jack.

"I am Jack," he answered.

We made all fast, and things were much quieter.

"The old man heard you whistling 'Nancy Lee,' just now," I said, "and he didn't like it."

It was as if there were a white light inside his face, and it was ghastly. I know his teeth chattered. But he didn't say anything, and the next minute he was somewhere in the dark trying to find his sou'wester at the foot of the mast.

When all was quiet, and she was hove to, coming to and falling off her four points as regularly as a pendulum, and the helm lashed a little to the lee, the old man turned in again, and I managed to light a pipe in the lee of the deck-house, for there was nothing more to be done till the gale chose to moderate, and the ship was as easy as a baby in its cradle. Of course the cook had gone below, as he might have done an hour earlier; so there were supposed to be four of us in the watch. There was a man at the lookout, and there was a hand by the wheel, though there was no steering to be done, and I was having my pipe in the lee of the deck-house, and the fourth man was somewhere about decks, probably having a smoke too. I thought some skippers I had sailed with would have called the watch aft, and given them a drink after that job, but it wasn't cold, and I guessed that our old man wouldn't be particularly generous in that way. My hands and feet were red-hot, and it would be time enough to get into dry clothes when it was my watch below; so I stayed where I was, and smoked. But by and by, things being so quiet, I began to wonder why nobody moved on deck; just that sort of restless wanting to know where every man is that one sometimes feels in a gale of wind on a dark night. So when I had finished my pipe I began to move about. I went aft, and there was a man leaning over the wheel, with his legs apart and both hands hanging down in the light from the binnacle, and his sou'wester over his eyes. Then I went forward, and there was a man at the lookout, with his back against the foremast, getting what shelter he could from the staysail. I knew by his small height that he was not one of the Benton boys. Then I went round by the weather side, and poked about in the dark, for I began to wonder where the other man was. But I couldn't find him, though I searched the decks until I got right aft again. It was certainly one of the Benton boys that was missing, but it wasn't like either of them to go below to change his clothes in such warm weather. The man at the wheel was the other, of course. I spoke to him.

"Jim, what's become of your brother?"

"I am Jack, sir."

"Well, then, Jack, where's Jim? He's not on deck."

"I don't know, sir."

When I had come up to him he had stood up from force of instinct, and had laid his hands on the spokes as if he were steering, though the wheel was lashed; but he still bent his face down, and it was half hidden by the edge of his sou'wester, while he seemed to be staring at the com-

pass. He spoke in a very low voice, but that was natural,
for the captain had left his door open when he turned in,
as it was a warm night in spite of the storm, and there
was no fear of shipping any more water now.

"What put it into your head to whistle like that, Jack?
You've been at sea long enough to know better."

He said something, but I couldn't hear the words; it
sounded as if he were denying the charge.

"Somebody whistled," I said.

He didn't answer, and then, I don't know why, perhaps
because the old man hadn't given us a drink, I cut half an
inch off the plug of tobacco I had in my oilskin pocket,
and gave it to him. He knew my tobacco was good, and
he shoved it into his mouth with a word of thanks. I was
on the weather side of the wheel.

"Go forward and see if you can find Jim," I said.

He started a little, and then stepped back and passed
behind me, and was going along the weather side. Maybe
his silence about the whistling had irritated me, and his
taking it for granted that because we were hove to and it
was a dark night, he might go forward any way he
pleased. Anyhow, I stopped him, though I spoke good-
naturedly enough.

"Pass to leeward, Jack," I said.

He didn't answer, but crossed the deck between the binnacle and the deck-house to the lee side. She was only
falling off and coming to, and riding the big seas as easily
as possible, but the man was not steady on his feet and
reeled against the corner of the deck-house and then
against the lee rail. I was quite sure he couldn't have had
anything to drink, for neither of the brothers were the
kind to hide rum from their shipmates, if they had any,
and the only spirits that were aboard were locked up in
the captain's cabin. I wondered whether he had been hit
by the throat-halliard block and was hurt.

I left the wheel and went after him, but when I got to
the corner of the deck-house I saw that he was on a full
run forward, so I went back. I watched the compass for a
while, to see how far she went off, and she must have
come to again half a dozen times before I heard voices,
more than three or four, forward; and then I heard the
little West Indies cook's voice, high and shrill above the
rest:—

"Man overboard!"

There wasn't anything to be done, with the ship hove-to and the wheel lashed. If there was a man overboard, he must be in the water right alongside. I couldn't imagine how it could have happened, but I ran forward instinctively. I came upon the cook first, half-dressed in his shirt and trousers, just as he had tumbled out of his bunk. He was jumping into the main rigging, evidently hoping to see the man, as if any one could have seen anything on such a night, except the foam-streaks on the black water, and now and then the curl of a breaking sea as it went away to leeward. Several of the men were peering over the rail into the dark. I caught the cook by the foot, and asked who was gone.

"It's Jim Benton," he shouted down to me. "He's not aboard this ship!"

There was no doubt about that. Jim Benton was gone; and I knew in a flash that he had been taken off by that sea when we were setting the storm trysail. It was nearly half an hour since then; she had run like wild for a few minutes until we got her hove-to, and no swimmer that ever swam could have lived as long as that in such a sea. The men knew it as well as I, but still they stared into the foam as if they had any chance of seeing the lost man. I let the cook get into the rigging and joined the men, and asked if they had made a thorough search on board, though I knew they had and that it could not take long, for he wasn't on deck, and there was only the forecastle below.

"That sea took him over, sir, as sure as you're born," said one of the men close beside me.

We have no boat that could have lived in that sea, of course, and we all knew it. I offered to put one over, and let her drift astern two or three cable's-lengths by a line, if the men thought they could haul me aboard again; but none of them would listen to that, and I should probably have been drowned if I had tried it, even with a life-belt; for it was a breaking sea. Besides, they all knew as well as I did that the man could not be right in our wake. I don't know why I spoke again.

"Jack Benton, are you there? Will you go if I will?"

"No, sir," answered a voice; and that was all.

By that time the old man was on deck, and I felt his hand on my shoulder rather roughly, as if he meant to shake me.

"I'd reckoned you had more sense, Mr. Torkeldsen," he said. "God knows I would risk my ship to look for him, if it were any use; but he must have gone half an hour ago."

He was a quiet man, and the men knew he was right, and that they had seen the last of Jim Benton when they were bending the trysail—if anybody had seen him then. The captain went below again, and for some time the men stood around Jack, quite near him, without saying anything, as sailors do when they are sorry for a man and can't help him; and then the watch below turned in again, and we were three on deck.

Nobody can understand that there can be much consolation in a funeral, unless he has felt that blank feeling there is when a man's gone overboard whom everybody likes. I suppose landsmen think it would be easier if they didn't have to bury their fathers and mothers and friends; but it wouldn't be. Somehow the funeral keeps up the idea of something beyond. You may believe in that something just the same; but a man who has gone in the dark, between two seas, without a cry, seems much more beyond reach than if he were still lying on his bed, and had only just stopped breathing. Perhaps Jim Benton knew that, and wanted to come back to us. I don't know, and I am only telling you what happened, and you may think what you like.

Jack stuck by the wheel that night until the watch was over. I don't know whether he slept afterwards, but when I came on deck four hours later, there he was again, in his oilskins, with his sou'wester over his eyes, staring into the binnacle. We saw that he would rather stand there, and we left him alone. Perhaps it was some consolation to him to get that ray of light when everything was so dark. It began to rain, too, as it can when a southerly gale is going to break up, and we got every bucket and tub on board, and set them under the booms to catch the fresh water for washing our clothes. The rain made it very thick, and I went and stood under the lee of the staysail, looking out. I could tell that day was breaking, because the foam was whiter in the dark where the seas crested, and little by little the black rain grew grey and steamy, and I couldn't see the red glare of the port light on the water when she went off and rolled to leeward. The gale had moderated considerably, and in another hour we should be under way again. I was still standing there when Jack Benton came forward. He stood still a few minutes near me. The rain came down in a solid sheet, and I could see his wet beard and a corner of his cheek, too, grey in the dawn. Then he stooped down and began feeling under the anchor for his pipe. We had hardly shipped any water forward, and I suppose he had some way of tucking the pipe in, so that the rain hadn't floated it off. Presently he got on his legs again, and I saw that he had two pipes in his hand. One of them had belonged to his brother, and after looking at them a moment I suppose he recognised his own, for he put it in his mouth, dripping with water. Then he looked at the other fully a minute without moving. When he had made up his mind, I suppose, he quietly chucked it over the lee rail, without even looking round to see whether I was watching him. I thought it was a pity, for it was a good wooden pipe, with a nickel ferrule, and somebody would have been glad to have it. But I didn't like to make any remark, for he had a right to do what he pleased with what had belonged to his dead brother. He blew the water out of his own pipe, and dried it against his jacket, putting his hand inside his oilskin; he filled it, standing under the lee of the foremast, got a light after wasting two or three matches, and turned the pipe upside down in his teeth, to keep the rain out of the bowl. I don't know why I noticed everything he did, and remember it now; but somehow I felt sorry for him, and I kept wondering whether there was anything I could say that would make him feel better. But I didn't think of anything, and as it was broad daylight I went aft again, for I guessed that the old man would turn out before long and order the spanker set and the helm up. But he didn't turn out before seven bells, just as the clouds broke and showed blue sky to leeward—"the Frenchman's barometer," you used to call it.

Some people don't seem to be so dead, when they are dead, as others are. Jim Benton was like that. He had been on my watch, and I couldn't get used to the idea that he wasn't about decks with me. I was always expecting to see him, and his brother was so exactly like him that I often felt as if I did see him and forgot he was dead, and made the mistake of calling Jack by his name; though I tried not to, because I knew it must hurt. If ever Jack had been the cheerful one of the two, as I had always supposed he had been, he had changed very much, for he grew to be more silent than Jim had ever been.

One fine afternoon I was sitting on the main-hatch, overhauling the clockwork of the taffrail-log, which hadn't been registering very well of late, and I had got the cook to bring me a coffee-cup to hold the small screws as I took them out, and a saucer for the sperm-oil I was going to use. I noticed that he didn't go away, but hung round without exactly watching what I was doing, as if he wanted to say something to me. I thought if it were worth much he would say it anyhow, so I didn't ask him questions; and sure enough he began of his own accord before long. There was nobody on deck but the man at the wheel, and the other man away forward.

"Mr. Torkeldsen," the cook began, and then stopped.

I supposed he was going to ask me to let the watch break out a barrel of flour, or some salt horse.

"Well, doctor?" I asked, as he didn't go on.

"Well, Mr. Torkeldsen," he answered, "I somehow want to ask you whether you think I am giving satisfaction on this ship, or not?"

"So far as I know, you are, doctor. I haven't heard any complaints from the forecastle, and the captain has said nothing, and I think you know your business, and the cabin-boy is bursting out of his clothes. That looks as if you are giving satisfaction. What makes you think you are not?"

I am not good at giving you that West Indies talk, and sha'n't try; but the doctor beat about the bush awhile, and then he told me he thought the men were beginning to play tricks on him, and he didn't like it, and thought he hadn't deserved it, and would like his discharge at our next port. I told him he was a d——d fool, of course, to begin with; and that men were more apt to try a joke with a chap they liked than with anybody they wanted to get rid of; unless it was a bad joke, like flooding his bunk, or filling his boots with tar. But it wasn't that kind of practical joke. The doctor said that the men were trying to frighten him, and he didn't like it, and that they put things in his way that frightened him. So I told him he was a d——d fool to be frightened, anyway, and I wanted to know what things they put in his way. He gave me a queer answer. He said they were spoons and forks, and odd plates, and a cup now and then, and such things.

I set down the taffrail-log on the bit of canvas I had put under it, and looked at the doctor. He was uneasy, and his eyes had a sort of hunted look, and his yellow face looked grey. He wasn't trying to make trouble. He was in trouble. So I asked him questions.

He said he could count as well as anybody, and do sums without using his fingers, but that when he couldn't count any other way he did use his fingers, and it always came out the same. He said that when he and the cabin-boy cleared up after the men's meals there were more things to wash than he had given out. There'd be a fork more, or there'd be a spoon more, and sometimes there'd be a spoon and a fork, and there was always a plate more. It wasn't that he complained of that. Before poor Jim Benton was lost they had a man more to feed, and his gear to wash up after meals, and that was in the contract, the doctor said. It would have been if there were twenty in the ship's company; but he didn't think it was right for the men to play tricks like that. He kept his things in good order, and he counted them, and he was responsible for them, and it wasn't right that the men should take more things than they needed when his back was turned, and just soil them and mix them up with their own, so as to make him think—

He stopped there, and looked at me, and I looked at him. I didn't know what he thought, but I began to guess. I wasn't going to humour any such nonsense as that, so I told him to speak to the men himself, and not come bothering me about such things.

"Count the plates and forks and spoons before them when they sit down to table, and tell them that's all they'll get; and when they have finished, count the things again, and if the count isn't right, find out who did it. You know it must be one of them. You're not a green hand; you've been going to sea ten or eleven years, and don't want any lesson about how to behave if the boys play a trick on you."

"If I could catch him," said the cook, "I'd have a knife into him before he could say his prayers."

Those West India men are always talking about knives, especially when they are badly frightened. I knew what he meant, and didn't ask him, but went on cleaning the brass cogwheels of the patent log and oiling the bearings with a feather. "Wouldn't it be better to wash it out with boiling water, sir?" asked the cook, in an insinuating tone. He knew that he had made a fool of himself, and was anxious to make it right again.

I heard no more about the odd platter and gear for two or three days, though I thought about his story a good deal. The doctor evidently believed that Jim Benton had come back, though he didn't quite like to say so. His story had sounded silly enough on a bright afternoon, in fair weather, when the sun was on the water, and every rag was drawing in the breeze, and the sea looked as pleasant and harmless as a cat that has just eaten a canary. But when it was toward the end of the first watch, and the waning moon had not risen yet, and the water was like still oil, and the jibs hung down flat and helpless like the wings of a dead bird—it wasn't the same then. More than once I have started then, and looked round when a fish jumped, expecting to see a face sticking up out of the water with its eyes shut. I think we all felt something like that at the time.

One afternoon we were putting a fresh service on the jib-sheet-pennant. It wasn't my watch, but I was standing by looking on. Just then Jack Benton came up from below, and went to look for his pipe under the anchor. His face was hard and drawn, and his eyes were cold like steel balls. He hardly ever spoke now, but he did his duty as usual, and nobody had to complain of him, though we were all beginning to wonder how long his grief for his dead brother was going to last like that. I watched him as he crouched down, and ran his hand into the hiding-place for the pipe. When he stood up, he had two pipes in his hand.

Now, I remembered very well seeing him throw one of those pipes away, early in the morning after the gale; and it came to me now, and I didn't suppose he kept a stock of them under the anchor. I caught sight of his face, and it was greenish white, like the foam on shallow water, and he stood a long time looking at the two pipes. He wasn't looking to see which was his, for I wasn't five yards from him as he stood, and one of those pipes had been smoked that day, and was shiny where his hand had rubbed it, and the bone mouthpiece was chafted white where his teeth had bitten it. The other was water-logged. It was swelled and cracking with wet, and it looked to me as if there were a little green weed on it.

Jack Benton turned his head rather stealthily as I

looked away, and then he hid the thing in his trousers pocket, and went aft on the lee side, out of sight. The men had got the sheet pennant on a stretch to serve it, but I ducked under it and stood where I could see what Jack did, just under the fore-staysail. He couldn't see me, and he was looking about for something. His hand shook as he picked up a bit of half-bent iron rod, about a foot long, that had been used for turning an eyebolt, and had been left on the mainhatch. His hand shook as he got a piece of marline out of his pocket, and made the water-logged pipe fast to the iron. He didn't mean it to get adrift, either, for he took his turns carefully, and hove them taut and then rode them, so that they couldn't slip, and made the end fast with two half-hitches round the iron, and hitched it back on itself. Then he tried it with his hands, and looked up and down the deck furtively, and then quietly dropped the pipe and iron over the rail, so that I didn't even hear the splash. If anybody was playing tricks on board, they weren't meant for the cook.

I asked some questions about Jack Benton, and one of the men told me that he was off his feed, and hardly ate anything, and swallowed all the coffee he could lay his hands on, and had used up all his own tobacco and had begun on what his brother had left.

"The doctor says it ain't so, sir," said the man, looking at me shyly, as if he didn't expect to be believed; "the doctor says there's as much eaten from breakfast to breakfast as there was before Jim fell overboard, though there's a mouth less and another that eats nothing. I says it's the cabin-boy that gets it. He's bu'sting."

I told him that if the cabin-boy ate more than his share, he must work more than his share, so as to balance things. But the man laughed queerly, and looked at me again.

"I only said that, sir, just like that. We all know it ain't so."

"Well, how is it?"

"How is it?" asked the man, half-angry all at once. "I don't know how it is, but there's a hand on board that's getting his whack along with us as regular as the bells."

"Does he use tobacco?" I asked, meaning to laugh it out of him, but as I spoke I remembered the water-logged pipe.

"I guess he's using his own still," the man answered, in

a queer, low voice. "Perhaps he'll take someone else's when his is all gone."

It was about nine o'clock in the morning, I remember, for just then the captain called to me to stand by the chronometer while he took his fore observation. Captain Hackstaff wasn't one of those old skippers who do everything themselves with a pocket watch, and keep the key of the chronometer in their waistcoat pocket, and won't tell the mate how far the dead reckoning is out. He was rather the other way, and I was glad of it, for he generally let me work the sights he took, and just ran his eye over my figures afterwards. I am bound to say his eye was pretty good, for he would pick out a mistake in a logarithm, or tell me that I had worked the "Equation of Time" with the wrong sign, before it seemed to me that he could have got as far as "half the sum, minus the altitude." He was always right, too, and besides he knew a lot about iron ships and local deviation, and adjusting the compass, and all that sort of thing. I don't know how he came to be in command of a fore-and-aft schooner. He never talked about himself, and maybe he had just been mate on one of those big steel square-riggers, and something had put him back. Perhaps he had been captain, and had got his ship aground, through no particular fault of his, and had to begin over again. Sometimes he talked just like you and me, and sometimes he would speak more like books do, or some of those Boston people I have heard. I don't know. We have all been shipmates now and then with men who have seen better days. Perhaps he had been in the Navy, but what makes me think he couldn't have been, was that he was a thorough good seaman, a regular old wind-jammer, and understood sail, which those Navy chaps rarely do. Why, you and I have sailed with men before the mast who had their master's certificates in their pockets,—English Board of Trade certificates, too,—who could work a double altitude if you would lend them a sextant and give them a look at the chronometer, as well as many a man who commands a big square-rigger. Navigation ain't everything, nor seamanship, either. You've got to have it in you, if you mean to get there.

I don't know how our captain heard that there was trouble forward. The cabin-boy may have told him, or the men may have talked outside his door when they relieved the wheel at night. Anyhow, he got wind of it, and when he had got his sight that morning he had all hands aft, and gave them a lecture. It was just the kind of talk you might have expected from him. He said he hadn't any complaint to make, and that so far as he knew everybody on board was doing his duty, and that he was given to understand that the men got their whack, and were satisfied. He said his ship was never a hard ship, and that he liked quiet, and that was the reason he didn't mean to have any nonsense, and the men might just as well understand that, too. We'd had a great misfortune, he said, and it was nobody's fault. We had lost a man we all liked and respected, and he felt that everybody in the ship ought to be sorry for the man's brother, who was left behind, and that it was rotten lubberly childishness, and unjust and unmanly and cowardly, to be playing schoolboy tricks with forks and spoons and pipes, and that sort of gear. He said it had got to stop right now, and that was all, and the men might go forward. And so they did.

It got worse after that, and the men watched the cook, and the cook watched the men, as if they were trying to catch each other; but I think everybody felt that there was something else. One evening, at supper-time, I was on deck, and Jack came aft to relieve the wheel while the man who was steering got his supper. He hadn't got past the mainhatch on the lee side, when I heard a man running in slippers that slapped on the deck, and there was a sort of a yell and I saw the coloured cook going for Jack, with a carving-knife in his hand. I jumped to get between them, and Jack turned round short, and put out his hand. I was too far to reach them, and the cook jabbed out with his knife. But the blade didn't get anywhere near Benton. The cook seemed to be jabbing it into the air again and again, at least four feet short of the mark. Then he dropped his right hand, and I saw the whites of his eyes in the dusk, and he reeled up against the pin-rail, and caught hold of a belaying-pin with his left. I had reached him by that time, and grabbed hold of his knife-hand and the other too, for I thought he was going to use the pin; but Jack Benton was standing staring stupidly at him, as if he didn't understand. But instead, the cook was holding on because he couldn't stand, and his teeth were chattering, and he let go of the knife, and the point stuck into the deck.

"He's crazy!" said Jack Benton, and that was all he said; and he went aft.

When he was gone, the cook began to come to, and he spoke quite low, near my ear.

"There were two of them! So help me God, there were two of them!"

I don't know why I didn't take him by the collar, and give him a good shaking; but I didn't. I just picked up the knife and gave it to him, and told him to go back to his galley, and not to make a fool of himself. You see, he hadn't struck at Jack, but at something he thought he saw, and I knew what it was, and I felt that same thing, like a lump of ice sliding down my back, that I felt that night when we were bending the trysail.

When the men had seen him running aft, they jumped up after him, but they held off when they saw that I had caught him. By and by, the man who had spoken to me before told me what had happened. He was a stocky little chap, with a red head.

"Well," he said, "there isn't much to tell. Jack Benton had been eating his supper with the rest of us. He always sits at the after corner of the table, on the port side. His brother used to sit at the end, next him. The doctor gave him a thundering big piece of pie to finish up with, and when he had finished he didn't stop for a smoke, but went off quick to relieve the wheel. Just as he had gone, the doctor came in from the galley, and when he saw Jack's empty plate he stood stock still staring at it; and we all wondered what was the matter, till we looked at the plate. There were two forks in it, sir, lying side by side. Then the doctor grabbed his knife, and flew up through the hatch like a rocket. The other fork was there all right, Mr. Torkeldsen, for we all saw it and handled it; and we all had our own. That's all I know."

I didn't feel that I wanted to laugh when he told me that story; but I hoped the old man wouldn't hear it, for I knew he wouldn't believe it, and no captain that ever sailed likes to have stories like that going round about his ship. It gives her a bad name. But that was all anybody ever saw except the cook, and he isn't the first man who has thought he saw things without having any drink in him. I think, if the doctor had been weak in the head as he was afterwards, he might have done something foolish again, and there might have been serious trouble. But he didn't. Only, two or three times I saw him looking at Jack Benton in a queer, scared way, and once I heard him talking to himself.

"There's two of them! So help me God, there's two of them!"

He didn't say anything more about asking for his discharge, but I knew well enough that if he got ashore at the next port we should never see him again, if he had to leave his kit behind him, and his money, too. He was scared all through, for good and all; and he wouldn't be right again till he got another ship. It's no use to talk to a man when he gets like that, any more than it is to send a boy to the main truck when he has lost his nerve.

Jack Benton never spoke of what happened that evening. I don't know whether he knew about the two forks, or not; or whether he understood what the trouble was. Whatever he knew from the other men, he was evidently living under a hard strain. He was quiet enough, and too quiet; but his face was set, and sometimes it twitched oddly when he was at the wheel, and he would turn his head round sharp to look behind him. A man doesn't do that naturally, unless there's a vessel that he thinks is creeping up on the quarter. When that happens, if the man at the wheel takes a pride in his ship, he will almost always keep glancing over his shoulder to see whether the other fellow is gaining. But Jack Benton used to look round when there was nothing there; and what is curious, the other men seemed to catch the trick when they were steering. One day the old man turned out just as the man at the wheel looked behind him.

"What are you looking at?" asked the captain.

"Nothing, sir," answered the man.

"Then keep your eye on the mizzen-royal," said the old man, as if he were forgetting that we weren't a square-rigger.

"Ay, ay, sir," said the man.

The captain told me to go below and work up the latitude from the dead-reckoning, and he went forward of the deck-house and sat down to read, as he often did. When I came up, the man at the wheel was looking round again, and I stood beside him and just asked him quietly what everybody was looking at, for it was getting to be a general habit. He wouldn't say anything at first, but just answered that it was nothing. But when he saw that I didn't seem to care, and just stood there as if there were nothing more to be said, he naturally began to talk.

He said that it wasn't that he saw anything, because there wasn't anything to see except the spanker sheet just straining a little, and working in the sheaves of the blocks as the schooner rose to the short seas. There wasn't anything to be seen, but it seemed to him that the sheet made a queer noise in the blocks. It was a new manilla sheet; and in dry weather it did make a little noise, something between a creak and a wheeze. I looked at it and looked at the man, and said nothing; and presently he went on. He asked me if I didn't notice anything peculiar about the noise. I listened awhile, and said I didn't notice anything. Then he looked rather sheepish, but said he didn't think it could be his own ears, because every man who steered his trick heard the same thing now and then,—sometimes once in a day, sometimes once in a night, sometimes it would go on a whole hour.

"It sounds like sawing wood," I said, just like that.

"To us it sounds a good deal more like a man whistling 'Nancy Lee.'" He started nervously as he spoke the last words. "There, sir, don't you hear it?" he asked suddenly.

I heard nothing but the creaking of the manilla sheet. It was getting near noon, and fine, clear weather in southern waters,—just the sort of day and the time when you would least expect to feel creepy. But I remembered how I had heard that same tune overhead at night in a gale of wind a fortnight earlier, and I am not ashamed to say that the same sensation came over me now, and I wished myself well out of the *Helen B.*, and aboard of any old cargo-dragger, with a windmill on deck, and an eighty-nine-forty-eighter for captain, and a fresh leak whenever it breezed up.

Little by little during the next few days life on board that vessel came to be about as unbearable as you can imagine. It wasn't that there was much talk, for I think the men were shy even of speaking to each other freely about what they thought. The whole ship's company grew silent, until one hardly ever heard a voice, except giving an order and the answer. The men didn't sit over their meals when their watch was below, but either turned in at once or sat about on the forecastle smoking their pipes without saying a word. We were all thinking of the same thing. We all felt as if there were a hand on board, sometimes below, sometimes about decks, sometimes aloft, sometimes on the boom end; taking his full share of what the others got, but doing no work for it. We didn't only feel it, we knew it. He took up no room, he cast no shadow, and we never heard his footfall on deck; but he took his whack with the rest as regular as the bells, and— he whistled "Nancy Lee." It was like the worst sort of dream you can imagine; and I dare say a good many of us tried to believe it was nothing else sometimes, when we stood looking over the weather rail in fine weather with the breeze in our faces; but if we happened to turn round and look into each other's eyes, we knew it was something worse than any dream could be; and we would turn away from each other with a queer, sick feeling, wishing that we could just for once see somebody who didn't know what we knew.

There's not much more to tell about the *Helen B. Jackson* so far as I am concerned. We were more like a shipload of lunatics than anything else when we ran in under Morro Castle, and anchored in Havana. The cook had brain fever, and was raving mad in his delirium; and the rest of the men weren't far from the same state. The last three or four days had been awful, and we had been as near to having a mutiny on board as I ever want to be. The men didn't want to hurt anybody; but they wanted to get away out of that ship, if they had to swim for it; to get away from that whistling, from that dead shipmate who had come back, and who filled the ship with his unseen self. I know that if the old man and I hadn't kept a sharp lookout the men would have put a boat over quietly on one of those calm nights, and pulled away, leaving the captain and me and the mad cook to work the schooner into harbour. We should have done it somehow, of course, for we hadn't far to run if we could get a breeze; and once or twice I found myself wishing that the crew were really gone, for the awful state of fright in which they lived was beginning to work on me too. You see I partly believed and partly didn't; but anyhow I didn't mean to let the thing get the better of me, whatever it was. I turned crusty, too, and kept the men at work on all sorts of jobs, and drove them to it until they wished I was overboard, too. It wasn't that the old man and I were trying to drive them to desert without their pay, as I am sorry to say a good many skippers and mates do, even now. Captain

Hackstaff was as straight as a string, and I didn't mean those poor fellows should be cheated out of a single cent; and I didn't blame them for wanting to leave the ship, but it seemed to me that the only chance to keep everybody sane through those last days was to work the men till they dropped. When they were dead tired they slept a little, and forgot the thing until they had to tumble up on deck and face it again. That was a good many years ago. Do you believe that I can't hear "Nancy Lee" now, without feeling cold down my back? For I heard it too, now and then, after the man had explained why he was always looking over his shoulder. Perhaps it was imagination. I don't know. When I look back it seems to me that I only remember a long fight against something I couldn't see, against an appalling presence, against something worse than cholera or Yellow Jack or the plague—and goodness knows the mildest of them is bad enough when it breaks out at sea. The men got as white as chalk, and wouldn't go about decks alone at night, no matter what I said to them. With the cook raving in his bunk the forecastle would have been a perfect hell, and there wasn't a spare cabin on board. There never is on a fore-and-after. So I put him into mine, and he was more quiet there, and at last fell into a sort of stupor as if he were going to die. I don't know what became of him, for we put him ashore alive and left him in the hospital.

The men came aft in a body, quiet enough, and asked the captain if he wouldn't pay them off, and let them go ashore. Some men wouldn't have done it, for they had shipped for the voyage, and had signed articles. But the captain knew that when sailors get an idea into their heads they're no better than children; and if he forced them to stay aboard he wouldn't get much work out of them, and couldn't rely on them in a difficulty. So he paid them off, and let them go. When they had gone forward to get their kits, he asked me whether I wanted to go too, and for a minute I had a sort of weak feeling that I might just as well. But I didn't, and he was a good friend to me afterwards. Perhaps he was grateful to me for sticking to him.

When the men went off he didn't come on deck; but it was my duty to stand by while they left the ship. They owed me a grudge for making them work during the last few days, and most of them dropped into the boat without so much as a word or a look, as sailors will. Jack Benton was the last to go over the side, and he stood still a minute and looked at me, and his white face twitched. I thought he wanted to say something.

"Take care of yourself, Jack," said I. "So long!"

It seemed as if he couldn't speak for two or three seconds; then his words came thick.

"It wasn't my fault, Mr. Torkeldsen. I swear it wasn't my fault!"

That was all; and he dropped over the side, leaving me to wonder what he meant.

The captain and I stayed on board, and the ship-chandler got a West India boy to cook for us.

That evening, before turning in, we were standing by the rail having a quiet smoke, watching the lights of the city, a quarter of a mile off, reflected in the still water. There was music of some sort ashore, in a sailors' dance-house, I dare say; and I had no doubt that most of the men who had left the ship were there, and already full of jiggy-jiggy. The music played a lot of sailors' tunes that ran into each other, and we could hear the men's voices in the chorus now and then. One followed another, and then it was "Nancy Lee," loud and clear, and the men singing "Yo-ho, heave-ho!"

"I have no ear for music," said Captain Hackstaff, "but it appears to me that's the tune that man was whistling the night we lost the man overboard. I don't know why it has stuck in my head, and of course it's all nonsense; but it seems to me that I have heard it all the rest of the trip."

I didn't say anything to that, but I wondered just how much the old man had understood. Then we turned in, and I slept ten hours without opening my eyes.

I stuck to the *Helen B. Jackson* after that as long as I could stand a fore-and-after; but that night when we lay in Havana was the last time I ever heard "Nancy Lee" on board of her. The spare hand had gone ashore with the rest, and he never came back, and he took his tune with him; but all those things are just as clear in my memory as if they had happened yesterday.

After that I was in deep water for a year or more, and after I came home I got my certificate, and what with having friends and having saved a little money, and having had a small legacy from an uncle in Norway, I got the command of a coastwise vessel, with a small share in her.

I was at home three weeks before going to sea, and Jack Benton saw my name in the local papers, and wrote to me.

He said that he had left the sea, and was trying farming, and he was going to be married, and he asked if I wouldn't come over for that, for it wasn't more than forty minutes by train; and he and Mamie would be proud to have me at the wedding. I remembered how I had heard one brother ask the other whether Mamie knew. That meant, whether she knew he wanted to marry her, I suppose. She had taken her time about it, for it was pretty nearly three years then since we had lost Jim Benton overboard.

I had nothing particular to do while we were getting ready for sea; nothing to prevent me from going over for a day, I mean; and I thought I'd like to see Jack Benton, and have a look at the girl he was going to marry. I wondered whether he had grown cheerful again, and had got rid of that drawn look he had when he told me it wasn't his fault. How could it have been his fault, anyhow? So I wrote to Jack that I would come down and see him married; and when the day came I took the train, and got there about ten o'clock in the morning. I wish I hadn't. Jack met me at the station, and he told me that the wedding was to be late in the afternoon, and that they weren't going off on any silly wedding trip, he and Mamie, but were just going to walk home from her mother's house to his cottage. That was good enough for him, he said. I looked at him hard for a minute after we met. When we had parted I had a sort of idea that he might take to drink, but he hadn't. He looked very respectable and well-to-do in his black coat and high city collar; but he was thinner and bonier than when I had known him, and there were lines in his face, and I thought his eyes had a queer look in them, half shifty, half scared. He needn't have been afraid of me, for I didn't mean to talk to his bride about the *Helen B. Jackson*.

He took me to his cottage first, and I could see that he was proud of it. It wasn't above a cable's-length from high-water mark, but the tide was running out, and there was already a broad stretch of hard wet sand on the other side of the beach road. Jack's bit of land ran back behind the cottage about a quarter of a mile, and he said that some of the trees we saw were his. The fences were neat

and well kept, and there was a fair-sized barn a little way
from the cottage, and I saw some nice-looking cattle in
the meadows; but it didn't look to me to be much of a
farm, and I thought that before long Jack would have to
leave his wife to take care of it, and go to sea again. But I
said it was a nice farm, so as to seem pleasant, and as I
don't know much about these things I dare say it was, all
the same. I never saw it but that once. Jack told me that
he and his brother had been born in the cottage, and that
when their father and mother died they leased the land to
Mamie's father, but had kept the cottage to live in when
they came home from sea for a spell. It was as neat a little place as you would care to see: the floors as clean as
the decks of a yacht, and the paint as fresh as a man-o'-
war. Jack always was a good painter. There was a nice
parlour on the ground floor, and Jack had papered it and
had hung the walls with photographs of ships and foreign
ports, and with things he had brought home from his voyages: a boomerang, a South Sea club, Japanese straw hats
and a Gibraltar fan with a bull-fight on it, and all that sort
of gear. It looked to me as if Miss Mamie had taken a
hand in arranging it. There was a brand-new polished iron
Franklin stove set into the old fireplace, and a red table-
cloth from Alexandria, embroidered with those outlandish
Egyptian letters. It was all as bright and homelike as possible, and he showed me everything, and was proud of everything, and I liked him the better for it. But I wished
that his voice would sound more cheerful, as it did when
we first sailed in the *Helen B.*, and that the drawn look
would go out of his face for a minute. Jack showed me
everything, and took me upstairs, and it was all the same:
bright and fresh and ready for the bride. But on the upper
landing there was a door that Jack didn't open. When we
came out of the bedroom I noticed that it was ajar, and
Jack shut it quickly and turned the key.

"That lock's no good," he said, half to himself. "The
door is always open."

I didn't pay much attention to what he said, but as we
went down the short stairs, freshly painted and varnished
so that I was almost afraid to step on them, he spoke
again.

"That was his room, sir. I have made a sort of store-
room of it."

"You may be wanting it in a year or so," I said, wishing to be pleasant.

"I guess we won't use his room for that," Jack answered in a low voice.

Then he offered me a cigar from a fresh box in the parlour, and he took one, and we lit them, and went out; and as we opened the front door there was Mamie Brewster standing in the path as if she were waiting for us. She was a fine-looking girl, and I didn't wonder that Jack had been willing to wait three years for her. I could see that she hadn't been brought up on steam-heat and cold storage, but had grown into a woman by the sea-shore. She had brown eyes, and fine brown hair, and a good figure.

"This is Captain Torkeldsen," said Jack. "This is Miss Brewster, captain; and she is glad to see you."

"Well, I am," said Miss Mamie, "for Jack has often talked to us about you, captain."

She put out her hand, and took mine and shook it heartily, and I suppose I said something, but I know I didn't say much.

The front door of the cottage looked toward the sea, and there was a straight path leading to the gate on the beach road. There was another path from the steps of the cottage that turned to the right, broad enough for two people to walk easily, and it led straight across the fields through gates to a larger house about a quarter of a mile away. That was where Mamie's mother lived, and the wedding was to be there. Jack asked me whether I would like to look round the farm before dinner, but I told him I didn't know much about farms. Then he said he just wanted to look round himself a bit, as he mightn't have much more chance that day; and he smiled, and Mamie laughed.

"Show the captain the way to the house, Mamie," he said. "I'll be along in a minute."

So Mamie and I began to walk along the path, and Jack went up toward the barn.

"It was sweet of you to come, Captain," Miss Mamie began, "for I have always wanted to see you."

"Yes," I said, expecting something more.

"You see, I always knew them both," she went on. "They used to take me out in a dory to catch codfish when I was a little girl, and I liked them both," she added thoughtfully. "Jack doesn't care to talk about his brother now. That's natural. But you won't mind telling me how it happened, will you? I should so much like to know."

Well, I told her about the voyage and what happened that night when we fell in with a gale of wind, and that it hadn't been anybody's fault, for I wasn't going to admit that it was my old captain's, if it was. But I didn't tell her anything about what happened afterwards. As she didn't speak, I just went on talking about the two brothers, and how like they had been, and how when poor Jim was drowned and Jack was left, I took Jack for him. I told her that none of us had ever been sure which was which.

"I wasn't always sure myself," she said, "unless they were together. Leastways, not for a day or two after they came home from sea. And now it seems to me that Jack is more like poor Jim, as I remember him, than he ever was, for Jim was always more quiet, as if he were thinking."

I told her I thought so, too. We passed the gate and went into the next field, walking side by side. Then she turned her head to look for Jack, but he wasn't in sight. I sha'n't forget what she said next.

"Are you sure now?" she asked.

I stood stock-still, and she went on a step, and then turned and looked at me. We must have looked at each other while you could count five or six.

"I know it's silly," she went on, "it's silly, and it's awful, too, and I have got no right to think it, but sometimes I can't help it. You see it was always Jack I meant to marry."

"Yes," I said stupidly, "I suppose so."

She waited a minute, and began walking on slowly before she went on again.

"I am talking to you as if you were an old friend, Captain, and I have only known you five minutes. It was Jack I meant to marry, but now he is so like the other one."

When a woman gets a wrong idea into her head, there is only one way to make her tired of it, and that is to agree with her. That's what I did, and she went on talking the same way for a little while, and I kept on agreeing and agreeing until she turned round on me.

"You know you don't believe what you say," she said, and laughed. "You know that Jack is Jack, right enough; and it's Jack I am going to marry."

Of course I said so, for I didn't care whether she thought me a weak creature or not. I wasn't going to say a word that could interfere with her happiness, and I didn't intend to go back on Jack Benton; but I remembered what he had said when he left the ship in Havana: that it wasn't his fault.

"All the same," Miss Mamie went on, as a woman will, without realising what she was saying, "all the same, I wish I had seen it happen. Then I should know."

Next minute she knew that she didn't mean that, and was afraid that I would think her heartless, and began to explain that she would really rather have died herself than have seen poor Jim go overboard. Women haven't got much sense, anyhow. All the same, I wondered how she could marry Jack if she had a doubt that he might be Jim after all. I suppose she had really got used to him since he had given up the sea and had stayed ashore, and she cared for him.

Before long we heard Jack coming up behind us, for we had walked very slowly to wait for him.

"Promise not to tell anybody what I said, Captain," said Mamie, as girls do as soon as they have told their secrets.

Anyhow, I know I never did tell anyone but you. This is the first time I have talked of all that, the first time since I took the train from that place. I am now going to tell you all about the day. Miss Mamie introduced me to her mother, who was a quiet, hard-faced old New England farmer's widow, and to her cousins and relations; and there were plenty of them too at dinner, and there was the parson besides. He was what they call a Hard-shell Baptist in those parts, with a long, shaven upper lip and a whacking appetite, and a sort of superior look, as if he didn't expect to see many of us hereafter—the way a New York pilot looks round, and orders things about when he boards an Italian cargo-dragger, as if the ship weren't up to much anyway, as though it was his business to see that she didn't get aground. That's the way a good many parsons look, I think. He said grace as if he were ordering the men to sheet home the topgallant-sail and get the helm up. After dinner we went out on the piazza, for it was warm autumn weather; and the young folks went off in pairs along the beach road, and the tide had turned and was beginning to come in. The morning had been clear and fine, but by four o'clock it began to look like a fog, and the damp came up out of the sea and settled on everything. Jack said he'd go down to his cottage and have a last look, for

the wedding was to be at five o'clock, or soon after, and
he wanted to light the lights, so as to have things look
cheerful.

"I will just take a last look," he said again, as we
reached the house. We went in, and he offered me another
cigar, and I lit it and sat down in the parlour. I could hear
him moving about, first in the kitchen and then upstairs,
and then I heard him in the kitchen again; and then before I knew anything I heard somebody moving upstairs
again. I knew he couldn't have got up those stairs as quick
as that. He came into the parlour, and he took a cigar
himself, and while he was lighting it I heard those steps
again overhead. His hand shook, and he dropped the
match.

"Have you got in somebody to help?" I asked.

"No," Jack answered sharply, and struck another
match.

"There's somebody upstairs, Jack," I said. "Don't you
hear footsteps?"

"It's the wind, Captain," Jack answered; but I could see
he was trembling.

"That isn't any wind, Jack," I said; "it's still and foggy.
I'm sure there's somebody upstairs."

"If you are so sure of it, you'd better go and see for
yourself Captain," Jack answered, almost angrily.

He was angry because he was frightened. I left him before the fireplace, and went upstairs. There was no power
on earth that could make me believe I hadn't heard a
man's footsteps overhead. I knew there was somebody
there. But there wasn't. I went into the bedroom, and it
was all quiet, and the evening light was streaming in, reddish through the foggy air; and I went out on the landing
and looked in the little back room that was meant for a
servant girl or a child. And as I came back again I saw
that the door of the other room was wide open, though I
knew Jack had locked it. He had said the lock was no
good. I looked in. It was a room as big as the bedroom,
but almost dark, for it had shutters, and they were closed.
There was a musty smell, as of old gear, and I could make
out that the floor was littered with sea chests, and that
there were oilskins and such stuff piled on the bed. But I
still believed that there was somebody upstairs, and I went
in and struck a match and looked round. I could see the
four walls and the shabby old paper, an iron bed and a

cracked looking-glass, and the stuff on the floor. But there was nobody there. So I put out the match, and came out and shut the door and turned the key. Now, what I am telling you is the truth. When I had turned the key, I heard footsteps walking away from the door inside the room. Then I felt queer for a minute, and when I went downstairs I looked behind me, as the men at the wheel used to look behind them on board the *Helen B.*

Jack was already outside on the steps, smoking. I have an idea that he didn't like to stay inside alone.

"Well?" he asked, trying to seem careless.

"I didn't find anybody," I answered, "but I heard somebody moving about."

"I told you it was the wind," said Jack, contemptuously. "I ought to know, for I live here, and I hear it often."

There was nothing to be said to that, so we began to walk down toward the beach. Jack said there wasn't any hurry, as it would take Miss Mamie some time to dress for the wedding. So we strolled along, and the sun was setting through the fog, and the tide was coming in. I knew the moon was full, and that when she rose the fog would roll away from the land, as it does sometimes. I felt that Jack didn't like my having heard that noise, so I talked of other things, and asked him about his prospects, and before long we were chatting as pleasantly as possible.

I haven't been at many weddings in my life, and I don't suppose you have, but that one seemed to me to be all right until it was pretty near over; and then, I don't know whether it was part of the ceremony or not, but Jack put out his hand and took Mamie's and held it a minute, and looked at her, while the parson was still speaking.

Mamie turned as white as a sheet and screamed. It wasn't a loud scream, but just a sort of stifled little shriek, as if she were half frightened to death; and the parson stopped, and asked her what was the matter, and the family gathered round.

"Your hand's like ice," said Mamie to Jack, "and it's all wet!"

She kept looking at it, as she got hold of herself again.

"It don't feel cold to me," said Jack, and he held the back of his hand against his cheek. "Try it again."

Mamie held out hers, and touched the back of his hand, timidly at first, and then took hold of it.

"Why, that's funny," she said.

"She's been as nervous as a witch all day," said Mrs. Brewster, severely.

"It is natural," said the parson, "that young Mrs. Benton should experience a little agitation at such a moment."

Most of the bride's relations lived at a distance, and were busy people, so it had been arranged that the dinner we'd had in the middle of the day was to take the place of a dinner afterwards, and that we should just have a bite after the wedding was over, and then that everybody should go home, and the young couple would walk down to the cottage by themselves. When I looked out I could see the light burning brightly in Jack's cottage, a quarter of a mile away. I said I didn't think I could get any train to take me back before half-past nine, but Mrs. Brewster begged me to stay until it was time, as she said her daughter would want to take off her wedding dress before she went home; for she had put on something white with a wreath, that was very pretty, and she couldn't walk home like that, could she?

So when we had all had a little supper the party began to break up, and when they were all gone Mrs. Brewster and Mamie went upstairs, and Jack and I went out on the piazza to have a smoke, as the old lady didn't like tobacco in the house.

The full moon had risen now, and it was behind me as I looked down toward Jack's cottage, so that everything was clear and white, and there was only the light burning in the window. The fog had rolled down to the water's edge, and a little beyond, for the tide was high, or nearly, and was lapping up over the last reach of sand, within fifty feet of the beach road.

Jack didn't say much as we sat smoking, but he thanked me for coming to his wedding, and I told him I hoped he would be happy; and so I did. I dare say both of us were thinking of those footsteps upstairs, just then, and that the house wouldn't seem so lonely with a woman in it. By and by we heard Mamie's voice talking to her mother on the stairs, and in a minute she was ready to go. She had put on again the dress she had worn in the morning, and it looked black at night, almost as black as Jack's coat.

Well, they were ready to go now. It was all very quiet after the day's excitement, and I knew they would like to walk down that path alone now that they were man and wife at last. I bade them good-night, although Jack made

a show of pressing me to go with them by the path as far
as the cottage, instead of going to the station by the beach
road. It was all very quiet, and it seemed to me a sensible
way of getting married; and when Mamie kissed her
mother good-night I just looked the other way, and
knocked my ashes over the rail of the piazza. So they started down the straight path to Jack's cottage, and I waited
a minute with Mrs. Brewster, looking after them, before
taking my hat to go. They walked side by side, a little
shyly at first, and then I saw Jack put his arm round her
waist. As I looked he was on her left, and I saw the outline of the two figures very distinctly against the moonlight
on the path; and the shadow on Mamie's right was broad
and black as ink, and it moved along, lengthening and
shortening with the unevenness of the ground beside the
path.

I thanked Mrs. Brewster, and bade her good-night; and
though she was a hard New England woman her voice
trembled a little as she answered, but being a sensible person she went in and shut the door behind her as I stepped
out on the path. I looked after the couple in the distance a
last time, meaning to go down to the road, so as not to
overtake them; but when I had made a few steps I stopped
and looked again, for I knew I had seen something
queer, though I had only realised it afterwards. I looked
again, and it was plain enough now; and I stood stock-still,
staring at what I saw. Mamie was walking between two
men. The second man was just the same height as Jack,
both being about a half a head taller than she; Jack on her
left in his black tail-coat and round hat, and the other
man on her right—well, he was a sailor-man in wet oilskins. I could see the moonlight shining on the water that
ran down him, and on the little puddle that had settled
where the flap of his sou'wester was turned up behind:
and one of his wet, shiny arms was round Mamie's waist,
just above Jack's. I was fast to the spot where I stood, and
for a minute I thought I was crazy. We'd had nothing but
some cider for dinner, and tea in the evening, otherwise
I'd have thought something had got into my head, though
I was never drunk in my life. It was more like a bad
dream after that.

I was glad Mrs. Brewster had gone in. As for me, I
couldn't help following the three, in a sort of wonder to
see what would happen, to see whether the sailor-man in

his wet togs would just melt away into the moonshine. But he didn't.

I moved slowly, and I remembered afterwards that I walked on the grass, instead of on the path, as if I were afraid they might hear me coming. I suppose it all happened in less than five minutes after that, but it seemed as if it must have taken an hour. Neither Jack nor Mamie seemed to notice the sailor. She didn't seem to know that his wet arm was round her, and little by little they got near the cottage, and I wasn't a hundred yards from them when they reached the door. Something made me stand still then. Perhaps it was fright, for I saw everything that happened just as I see you now.

Mamie set her foot on the step to go up, and as she went forward I saw the sailor slowly lock his arm in Jack's, and Jack didn't move to go up. Then Mamie turned round on the step, and they all three stood that way for a second or two. She cried out then,—I heard a man cry like that once, when his arm was taken off by a steam-crane,—and she fell back in a heap on the little piazza.

I tried to jump forward, but I couldn't move, and I felt my hair rising under my hat. The sailor turned slowly where he stood, and swung Jack round by the arm steadily and easily, and began to walk him down the pathway from the house. He walked him straight down that path, as steadily as Fate; and all the time I saw the moonlight shining on his wet oilskins. He walked him through the gate, and across the beach road, and out upon the wet sand, where the tide was high. Then I got my breath with a gulp, and ran for them across the grass, and vaulted over the fence, and stumbled across the road. But when I felt the sand under my feet, the two were at the water's edge; and when I reached the water they were far out, and up to their waists; and I saw that Jack Benton's head had fallen forward on his breast, and his free arm hung limp beside him, while his dead brother steadily marched him to his death. The moonlight was on the dark water, but the fog-bank was white beyond, and I saw them against it; and they went slowly and steadily down. The water was up to their armpits, and then up to their shoulders, and then I saw it rise up to the black rim of Jack's hat. But they never wavered; and the two heads went straight on, straight on, till they were under, and there was just a ripple in the moonlight where Jack had been.

It has been on my mind to tell you that story, whenever I got a chance. You have known me, man and boy, a good many years; and I thought I would like to hear your opinion. Yes, that's what I always thought. It wasn't Jim that went overboard; it was Jack, and Jim just let him go when he might have saved him; and then Jim passed himself off for Jack with us, and with the girl. If that's what happened, he got what he deserved. People said the next day that Mamie found it out as they reached the house, and that her husband just walked out into the sea, and drowned himself; and they would have blamed me for not stopping him if they'd known that I was there. But I never told what I had seen, for they wouldn't have believed me. I just let them think that I had come too late.

When I reached the cottage and lifted Mamie up, she was raving mad. She got better afterwards, but she was never right in her head again.

Oh, you want to know if they found Jack's body? I don't know whether it was his, but I read in a paper at a Southern port where I was with my new ship that two dead bodies had come ashore in a gale down East, in pretty bad shape. They were locked together, and one was a skeleton in oilskins.

Portrait of a Murderer

by Q. Patrick

---

fiction

---

*Martin Slater, at fourteen, showed a shrewd and
native talent for murder.*

This is the story of a murder. It was a murder committed so subtly, so smoothly that I, who was an unwitting
accessory both before and after the fact, had no idea at
the time that any crime had been committed.

Only gradually, with the years, did that series of incidents, so innocuous-seeming at the time, fall into a pattern
in my mind and give me a clear picture of exactly what
happened during my stay at Olinscourt with Martin Slater.

Martin and I were at an English school together during
the latter half of the First World War. In his fourteenth
year Martin was a nondescript boy with light, untidy hair,
quick brown eyes, and that generic schoolboy odor of rubber and chalk. There was little to distinguish him from the
rest of us except his father, Sir Olin Slater.

Sir Olin, however, was more than enough to make Martin painfully notorious. Whereas self-respecting parents
embarrassed their children by appearing at the school only
on state occasions such as Sports Day or Prize-giving, Sir
Olin haunted his son like a passion. Almost every week
this evangelical baronet could be seen, a pink, plump hip-
popotamus, walking about the school grounds, his arm en-
twined indecently round Martin. In his free hand he would
carry a large bag of chocolates which he offered to all the
boys he met with pious adjurations to lead nobler, sweeter
lives.

Martin squirmed under these paraded embraces. It was

all the worse for him in that his father suffered from a terrible disease of the throat which made every syllable he uttered a pathetic mockery of the English language. This disease (which was probably throat cancer) had no reality for Sir Olin. He did not believe that other people were even conscious of his mispronunciations. At least once every term, to our irreverent delight and to Martin's excruciating discomfort, he was invited to deliver before the whole school an informal address of a religious nature—or a pi-jaw as we called it. When I sat next to Martin in Big School, suppressing a disloyal desire to giggle, I used to watch my friend's knuckles go white as his father, from the dais, urged us "laddies" to keep ourselves strong and pure and trust in the Mercy of God, or, as he pronounced it, the "Murky of Klock."

Sir Olin's pious solicitude for his own beloved "laddie" expressed itself also in the written word. Every morning, more regular than the rising of the English sun, there lay on Martin's breakfast plate the blue envelope with the Slater coat-of-arms. Martin was a silent boy. He never spoke a word to hint that Sir Olin's effusiveness was a torment to him, even when the derisive titter parodied down the table: "Another lecker for the lickle lackie." But I noticed that he left these letters unopened unless his sensitive fingers, palpating the envelopes, could detect banknotes in them.

Most of the other boys tended to despise Martin for the solecism of such a parent. My own intimacy with him might well have been tainted with condescension had it not been for the hampers of "tuck" which Lady Slater sent from Olinscourt. Such tuck it was, too—coming at a period when German submarines were tightening all English belts. Being a scrawny and perpetually hungry boy, I was never more prepared to be chummy with Martin Slater than when my roommate and I sneaked off alone together to tackle those succulent tongues, those jellied chickens, those firm, luscious peaches, and those chocolate cakes stiffened with mouth-melting icing.

Martin shared my enthusiasm for these secret feasts, but he had another all-absorbing enthusiasm which I did not share. He was an inventor. He invented elaborate mechanical devices, usually from alarm clocks of which there were always five or six in his possession in different stages of disembowelment. He specialized at that period in burglar alarms. I can see now those seven or eight urchins that he used to lure into our room at night with sausage rolls and plum cake; I can almost hear my own heart beating as we waited in the darkness to witness in action Martin's latest contrivance for foiling house-breakers.

These thrilling episodes ended summarily, however, when an unfeeling master caught us at it, confiscated all Martin's clocks, and gave him a hundred lines for disturbing the peace.

Without these forbidden delights, the long, blacked-out nights of wartime seemed even darker and colder. It was Martin who evolved a system whereby we could dispel the dreary chill which settled every evening on the institution like a miasma, and warm up our cold beds and our undernourished bodies. He invented wrestling—or rather, he adapted and simplified the canons of the art to suit the existing contingency. His rules were simple almost to the point of being non-existent. One took every possible advantage; one inflicted as much pain as one reasonably dared; one was utterly unscrupulous toward the single end of making one's opponent admit defeat with the phrase: "I give in, man. You win."

It didn't seem to do us much harm thus to work out on one another the sadism that is inherent in all children. It warmed and toughened us; perhaps in some subtle way it established in us an intimacy, a mutual respect.

Though Martin had the advantage of me in age and weight, I was, luckily, more wiry and possibly craftier. As I gradually got on to Martin's technic I began to develop successful counter measures. So successful were they, in fact, that I started to win almost nightly, ending up on top with monotonous regularity.

And that was the first, the greatest mistake I ever made in my dealings with Martin Slater. I should have known that it is unwise to win too often at any game. It is especially unwise when one is playing it with a potential murderer, who, I suspect, had already conceived for any subjugation, moral or physical, a hatred that was almost psychopathological and growing in violence.

I experienced its violence one night when, less scrupulous than Hamlet toward Claudius, he attacked me as I knelt shivering at my bedside going through the ritual of "saying my prayers." The assault was decidedly unfair. It occurred before the specified safety hour and while the matron was still prowling. Also, though props and weapons were strictly inadmissible, he elected on this occasion to initiate his attack by throwing a wet towel over my head, twisting it round my neck as he pulled me backward. It was a very wet towel too, so wet that breathing through it was quite out of the question.

With his initial, almost strangling jerk backward, my legs had shot forward, underneath the bed, where they could only kick feebly at the mattress springs, useless as leverage to shake off Martin, who had seated his full weight on my face, having pinioned my arms beneath his knees. I was a helpless prisoner with a wet towel and some hundred pounds of boy between me and any chance of respiration.

Frantically I gurgled my complete submission. I beat my hands on the floor in token of surrender. But Martin sat relentlessly on. For a moment I knew the panic of near suffocation. I clawed, I scratched, I bit; but I might have been buried a hundred feet under the earth. Then everything began to go black, including as I afterward learned, my own face.

I was saved mercifully by the approach of the peripatetic matron who bustled in a few moments later and blew out the candle without being aware that one of her charges had almost become Martin Slater's first victim in homicide.

Martin apologized to me next morning but there was a strange expression on his face as he added: "You were getting too cocky, man, licking me every night."

His more practical appeasement took the form of inviting me to Olinscourt for the holidays. I weighed the disadvantages of four weeks under Sir Olin's pious tutelage against the prospect of tapping the source of those ambrosial hampers. Inevitably, my schoolboy stomach decided for me. I went.

To our delight, when we first arrived at Olinscourt we found Sir Olin away on an uplift tour of the reformatories and prisons of western England. He might not have existed for us at all had it not been for the daily blue envelope on Martin's breakfast plate.

Lady Slater made an admirably unobtrusive hostess—a meek figure who trailed vaguely round in low-heeled shoes and snuff-colored garments which associate themselves in my mind with the word "gabardine." Apart from ordering substantial meals for us "growing boys" and dampening them slightly by an aroma of piety, she kept herself discreetly out of our way in some meditative boudoir of her own.

Left to our devices, Martin spent long days of feverish activity in his beautifully equipped workshop, releasing all the inventive impulses which had been frustrated at school and which, as he hinted apologetically, would be thwarted again on the return of Sir Olin. Being London bred, there was nothing I enjoyed more than wandering alone round the extensive grounds and farm lands of Olinscourt, ploddingly followed by a dour Scotch terrier called Roddy.

The old rambling house was equally exciting, particularly since on the second day of my visit I discovered a chamber of mystery, a large locked room on the ground floor which turned out to be Sir Olin's study. Martin was as intrigued as I by the closure of this room which was normally much used. Inquiries from the servants elicited only the fact that there had been alterations of an unknown nature and that the room had been ordered shut until Sir Olin's return.

This romantic mystery, which only Sir Olin could solve, made us almost look forward to the baronet's return. He arrived unexpectedly some nights later and appeared in our room, oozing plump affection, while we were having our supper—Martin's favorite meal and one he loved to spin out as long as possible. That evening, however, we were never to finish our luscious salmon mayonnaise. Ardent to resume his spiritual wrestling match with his beloved laddie, Sir Olin summarily dismissed our dishes and settled us down to a session known as "The Quiet Quarter," which was to prove one of the most mortifying of our daily ordeals at Olinscourt.

It started with a reading by Sir Olin from a book written and privately published by himself, entitled: *Five Minute Chats with a Growing Lad*. When this one-sided "chat" was over Sir Olin sat back, hands folded over his ample stomach, and invited us with an intimate smile to tell him of our problems, our recent sins and temptations. We wriggled and squirmed a while trying to think up some suitable sin or temptation; then the baronet relieved the situation by a long impromptu prayer, interrupted at last, thank heavens, by the downstairs booming of the dinner gong. Then, having laid benedictory hands on our heads,

Sir Olin kissed us both—me on the forehead and Martin full on the mouth—and dismissed us to our beds.

There, for the first time since my arrival at Olinscourt, Martin leaped on me with a sudden savagery far surpassing anything he had shown at school. With his fingers pressed against my windpipe, I was helpless almost immediately and more than ready to surrender.

"Swear you won't tell the chaps at school about him kissing us good-night," he demanded thickly.

"I swear, man," I stuttered.

"Nor about those pi-jaws he's going to give us every evening."

It was not until I had given my solemn oath that he released me.

Next morning it became immediately apparent that with Sir Olin's return the golden days were over. With his return too Lady Slater had departed on some missionary journeyings of her own, a fact which suggested that she enjoyed her husband's presence no more than we did. In the place of her short but fervent grace, Sir Olin treated us and the entire staff of servants to ten minutes of family prayers—all within sight and scent of the lemon glory of scrambled eggs, the glistening mahogany of sausage and kippers, which sizzled temptingly on the side table.

But at least the baronet solved the mystery of the locked study, solved it quite dramatically too. Immediately after breakfast on his first day at home, he summoned us into the long, book-lined room and announced with a chuckle: "Lickle surprise for you, Martin, laddie. Just you both watch that center bookcase."

We watched breathless as Sir Olin touched an invisible switch and smoothly, soundlessly, the bookcase swung out into the room, revealing behind it the dull metal of a heavy door. And in the center of this heavy door was a gleaming brass combination switch.

"Oh, Father, it's a secret safe!" Martin's face lighted up with enthusiasm.

Sir Olin chuckled again and took out a heavy gold hunter watch. Opening the back of it as if to consult some combination number, he started to turn the brass knob to and fro. At length, as on oiled wheels, the heavy door rolled back, disclosing not a mere safe, but a square, vault-like chamber with a small desk and innumerable drawers of different sizes, suggesting the more modern bank-deposit strong rooms. He invited us to enter and we obeyed, trembling with excitement. Sir Olin showed us some of the wonders, explaining as he did so that his object in withdrawing his more liquid assets from his London bank had been to protect his beloved laddie's financial future from the destructive menace of German zeppelins. He twisted a knob and drew out a drawer glittering with golden sovereigns. He showed us other mysterious drawers containing all that was negotiable of the Slaters' earthly treasure, labeled with such titles as "Mortgages," "Insurance," "Stocks and Shares," "Treasury Notes," etc., etc. It suggested the romances of William LeQueux and the fantasies of H. G. Wells.

Confronted by this elaborate manifestation of parental solicitude, Martin asked the question I had expected: "Has it got a burglar alarm, Father?"

"No. No." Sir Olin's plump fingers caressed his son's hair indulgently. "Why don't you try your hand at making one, laddie, in your spare time?"

I was soon to learn, however, that spare time was a very rare commodity with Sir Olin about. The baronet, a passionate English country gentleman himself, was determined to instill a similar enthusiasm in his only son and heir. Every morning after breakfast Martin, yearning for his workshop, was obliged to make the rounds of the estate with his father, following through barn and stable, over pasture and plowland, listening to an interminable monologue on how Sir Olin, the eleventh baronet, with the aid of God, was disposing everything perfectly for the twelfth baronet, the future Sir Martin Slater. I usually tagged along behind them with Sir Olin's only admirer, the dour Roddy, staring entrancedly at the sleek flanks of cows whose cream would enrich next term's tuck hampers; at pigs whose very shape suggested sausage rolls of the future; at poultry whose plumpness I translated dreamily into terms of drumsticks, second joints, and slices of firm white breast.

Every day Sir Olin brought us back from our cross-country tramps at exactly five minutes to one, which left us barely time to wash our hands for lunch. And after lunch until tea, the baronet, eager to share Martin's playful as well as his weighty moments, took us riding or bowled googly lobs to us at the cricket nets, in a vain attempt to improve our batting style in a game that we both detested.

Tea at four-thirty was followed by our only real period of respite. For at five o'clock, punctual as Sir Olin's gold hunter, his estate agent arrived from Bridgewater, and the two of them were closeted together in the library until seven o'clock when the dressing gong sounded and Sir Olin put documents and ledgers into his strong room and the agent took his leave.

Needless to say, Martin and I daily blessed the estate agent's name, though it was, infelicitously enough, Ramsbotham. And, needless to say, his arrival was the signal for us to scoot off, me to my wanderings, Martin to his workshop, until suppertime.

Suppertime itself, once the most blissful moment of the day, lost its glory; for Sir Olin, unlike his wife, was quite indifferent to food. Eager for his "quiet quarter," he allowed us a scant twelve minutes to feed the inner boy. His appearance, dressed in a claret-colored dinner jacket, meant the instant removal of our plates, and many a succulent morsel did I see snatched from me. Martin loved good food as much as I did, but being a truer epicure than I, was incapable of gobbling. He frequently had to endure the "quiet quarter" and his father's good-night kiss on an almost empty stomach.

A few days later Sir Olin introduced yet another torture for Martin. The baronet decided that his son was now old enough to learn something about the business side of an estate that would one day be his. Three times a week, therefore, Martin was required to be present from five to seven o'clock in the library with his father and Ramsbotham. This left him only two hours on Tuesdays, Thursdays, and Saturdays for tinkering in his beloved workshop. It meant also that, at least three times a week, his supper period was even further curtailed.

I think it was about this time I began to notice a change in Martin. He became even more silent and his face was pale and set with dark lines under his eyes. These, I suspect, were caused partly by the fact that he made up for the lost time in his workshop by sneaking out to it in the middle of the night. I say I suspect this, for he never took me into his confidence; but on two occasions when I happened to wake after midnight his bed was empty and through the open window I could see a flickering light in the workshop.

My guess is that the final stage really started on Saturday night at the end of my third week at Olinscourt. The dressing gong had just sounded and, as I happened to pass the library, I heard the tinkle of a bell. I was surprised, since the telephone there rang very seldom and usually only for something important. Martin, who had joined me on the stairs, voiced my unspoken hope.

"Say, man, d'you think perhaps that's someone calling Father away or something jolly like that?"

And later, as I was hurrying through my bath, there was the sound of a car starting, and from the window Martin announced excitedly:

"There's old Ramsbum's car, and I do believe I see Father in it with him. He hasn't come up to dress yet. Wait while I go down to the library to see."

He returned in a few minutes with the good news that his father, not being there, had presumably left with Mr. Ramsbotham, which meant we could linger pleasantly over supper. It was a delicious supper too—fresh trout followed by raspberries and cream, and was brought up by no less a person than Pringle, the head butler. "Excuse me, Master Martin," he said with an apologetic cough, "but do you happen to know if Sir Olin will be down to dinner?"

"I think he went to Bridgewater with Mr. Ramsbotham." Martin's mouth was full of green peas. "I know he was asked to give a talk at the boys' reformatory there some Saturday. And someone rang him up on the telephone."

"I see, sir, but he didn't mention it to me, sir." Pringle withdrew in starchy disapproval and left us the pleasant realization that there would be no "quiet quarter" and no good-night kiss.

And there were no family prayers next morning, since Sir Olin had not returned. It was to be presumed that he had been exhausted by reforming reformatory boys and had consequently spent the night in Bridgewater with Mr. Ramsbotham. And, as it was a Sunday, no question was raised as to his absence.

Martin, bright-eyed, rushed off to his workshop immediately after breakfast and I decided on a stroll. It was then that happened one of those tiny incidents that seemed trival at the time, but seen in later perspective, appear most significant.

I had whistled for Roddy, usually so anxious to share my walks abroad, but no scampering feet answered my summons. I whistled again. Then I started to look for him, calling:

"Hey, Roddy . . . rats . . .!"

The sound of whining from the study at last solved the problem. Roddy had apparently found a rat of his own, for he was scratching at the central bookcase with a strange crooning sound.

I induced him to follow me, but later when I turned to look back, he had vanished. And that, in itself, was quite unprecedented.

Another seemingly unimportant incident occurred later that morning when I arrived home from my walk. The day was hot and I had taken off my school blazer before going out, hanging it on a peg in the hall, near the front door. When I got back a blazer was there, but it was hanging upside down. As I unhooked it a number of letters dropped from the pockets. They were from Sir Olin to his son and I realized at once that Martin had gone in to lunch ahead of me, taking my blazer by mistake. I picked up the letters—all of them as I thought—shoved them back into the pockets and promptly forgot the whole thing. I doubt even if we bothered to effect an exchange of coats.

Next morning Martin did a rare thing. He got up before me and was at his place at the breakfast table when I came down. In front of him was an unopened letter and I immediately recognized the writing on the envelope as his father's.

As Pringle brought the coffee he said with his usual apologetic cough: "When I picked up the letters from the front hall, Master Martin, I took the liberty of observing there was one for you from Sir Olin. I was wondering if he mentions the date of his return."

"Just give me a sec, Pringle." Martin heaped his plate with kedgeree. "I'll read it and tell you."

After the dignified withdrawal of Pringle, Martin tore open the envelope and pulled out two pages of the familiar crabbed scrawl. He scanned the first page quickly, muttering: "Just the usual pi stuff."

"Does he say when he's coming back?" I asked.

"Wait, here's something at the end." As Pringle's footsteps sounded in the passage outside he handed me the first page and the envelope, saying urgently: "Here, shove those into the fire, man. I'd die rather than have Pringle see all that religious slosh."

As I speedily thrust the first page of slosh, together with the envelope, into the fire, I heard Martin's voice, studiedly casual for Pringle's benefit: "Here, Pat, read this. You're better at making out Father's writing."

He passed me the second sheet and I read:

"And so, beloved lad, I shall be back with you in three or four days. In the meantime I pray that His Guidance . . . etc. . . . etc. . . . ."

The letter contained no hint as to his actual whereabouts.

We imparted the gist of this to Pringle and he seemed satisfied enough, though somewhat resentful that he had not been informed personally of his master's absence. Still more resentful and far less satisfied was Mr. Ramsbotham when he arrived at the usual hour that afternoon. No, he had not driven Sir Olin to Bridgewater or anywhere else. The talk at the reformatory had been definitely arranged for next Saturday. He had of course to accept the evidence of the letter which Martin duly presented but it was all very vexing . . . all very odd. It was more vexing and more odd when it came out that no one had driven Sir Olin to the station.

I don't know exactly when anyone became really alarmed at Sir Olin's continued absence, but at some stage Mr. Ramsbotham must have telephoned Lady Slater to come home. Even before her return, however, I had put the missing baronet temporarily out of my mind and given myself up to thorough enjoyment of life without him.

To the adult it may seem odd that, in view of the circumstances narrated, I myself felt no uneasiness as to Sir Olin's safety. I can only say that a child's mind is not a logical one; that the events preceding the baronet's disappearance had no sinister shape for me then; and it is only as I look back now and place each occurrence in its proper context that I can see the terrifying inevitability of the pattern that was forming.

The next piece of news I heard was exciting. The need to pay the staff and the monthly bills had made it essential that the vault, containing among its other riches all the Slater ready cash, be opened. Since Sir Olin alone knew its combination, arrangements were finally made to bring from London the workmen who had built it and who were to blast through the complicated lock.

We were warned to keep away during the period of the actual dynamite blast, but nothing could have kept me from the scene of operations. I lured a curiously reluctant Martin to join me, and we had hidden behind a couch in the dust-sheeted study by the time the men came in to set the fuse.

Even now I am able to recapture those tense moments of waiting behind the couch. I can smell the musty smell of the heavy brocade; I can hear Martin's breath coming faster and faster as we waited; I can see his face pale and set; I can hear the whispered words of the men as they set about their dangerous job.

And then, sooner than I had expected, came the blast. It was terrific, rocking the study and, so it seemed, rocking the very foundations of Olinscourt. Martin and I bumped heads painfully as we jumped up, but I did not notice the pain. I was watching the stream of black smoke which poured from the door of the vault. Through it we heard: "That ought to have done the trick. Here, lend a hand."

Martin and I watched as the men started to swing back the heavy door of the vault. Pringle was hovering fussily behind them. I could see him through the clearing smoke. I was conscious again of Martin's heavy breathing, of the inscrutable brown eyes staring fixedly at the door of the vault as it gradually opened.

Then I heard a smothered exclamation from one of the men, followed by the barking of Roddy who had somehow got into the room. Above it came Pringle's voice: "Good God in Heaven, it's Sir Olin!"

I saw it then—saw the body of a stout man slumped over the tiny desk inside the vault. I saw the dull gleam of a revolver in his hand, the purplish bloodstain above the right temple. I saw the men moving hesitatingly toward it to lift it up and then Pringle's voice again, warningly: "Leave him for the police. He's dead. Shot 'isself."

For a moment I stared at that slumped body with the fascination of a child who is seeing death for the first time. A vague odor invaded my nostrils. It was probably the odor of gunpowder, but to my childish mind it became the smell of death. I knew sudden, blinding terror. I pushed past Martin, running upstairs to the lavatory on the fourth floor. I was very sick.

I don't know how long I stayed there locked in the lavatory. I don't remember what my thoughts were except that I had a wild desire to get home—to walk if necessary back to zeppelin-raided London—away from the horror of the thing that I had seen in the vault.

I must have been there for hours.

Someone was calling my name. I emerged from the lavatory rather sheepishly to see Pringle on the landing below. He said: "Master Pat, you are wanted in Lady Slater's dressing room. You and Master Martin."

I found Martin hovering outside his mother's door. He looked as if he had been sick too. Lady Slater was sitting by the window in her boudoir. The snuff-colored gabardines had given place to funereal black, but there was no sign of grief or tears on her face. Even at that cruel moment it seemed beyond her scope to become human. Through a haze of pious phraseology she told us what I already knew—that Sir Olin had taken his own life.

"The terrible disease in his throat . . . we do not know how much he suffered . . . he explained it all in a letter to me . . . we must not judge him . . ."

And then she was holding out a thick envelope to Martin. "He left a letter for you too, my son."

Martin took the envelope, and I could not help noticing that his fingers instinctively palpated it to discover the lurking presence of banknotes, just as he had always done at school.

"And he left a parcel for you also." Lady Slater handed Martin a square carefully wrapped package. Then she continued: "The inscription on it is the same as on the letter. They are for you alone, Martin, to open and do with as you think fit."

After this Lady Slater took us downstairs to the great living room. The village constable was standing by the door. A gentleman of military deportment was talking with Pringle, the butler, and Mr. Ramsbotham. A dim, drooping figure hovered at their side—the local doctor.

From behind a bristling mustache, the military gentleman questioned Martin and myself about the day of Sir

Olin's disappearance. Martin, surprisingly steady now, told
our simple story. We had both thought we heard the telephone ringing in the library. Martin believed he had
caught a glimpse of Sir Olin driving off with Mr.
Ramsbotham. He assumed that his father had gone to give
his lecture at the reformatory. Monday morning there had
been a letter from Sir Olin on Martin's plate telling him
that he would not return for several days.

The problem of that letter which had lulled everyone
into a false sense of security was next considered. The
mustache pointed out that it must have been one which Sir
Olin had written to his son at some earlier date and which,
by accident, had become confused with the morning post
on the front-door mat. It was at this moment that I
remembered how, in my hurry for lunch on the day after
Sir Olin's disappearance, I had snatched at the blazer
which had been hanging in the hall. I remembered how
the unopened letters from Sir Olin to Martin had fallen
from the pocket. With the conviction of sin known only to
children, I saw the whole tragedy as my own fault. And,
with more confusion than courage, I was stammering out
my guilty secret.

Martin, watching me steadily, was able to corroborate
my story, admitting with an awkward flush that he had
not always opened his father's letters the moment they arrived. The military eyebrows were raised a trifle and there
the matter of the letter stood. "Martin's little friend" had
spilled some old unopened letters from Sir Olin out of
Martin's blazer; he had failed to pick one of them up;
next morning the butler had found it on the door mat and
supposed it to be part of the regular morning post ... A
most unfortunate accident.

The military gentleman then turned to Lady Slater:
"There is one thing, Lady Slater. Sir Olin went into the
vault on Saturday evening and he was never seen again. It
is to be presumed that he did not come out. Indeed, he
could not have opened that heavy door from the inside
even if he had wished to."

Martin was watching the brisk mustache now, his eyes
very bright.

"And yet, Lady Slater, Doctor Webb here tells me that
your husband has actually been dead for less than twenty-
four hours. To-day is Thursday. This means that Sir Olin
shot himself through the temple sometime yesterday. In

other words he must have spent the three previous days alive in the vault."

He cleared his throat. "From this letter to you there is no question but that your husband took his own life, but I am wondering if you could—er—offer an explanation as to why he should have delayed so long—why he should have spent that uncomfortably long period in the vault. Why he should have waited until the oxygen must have been almost exhausted, why he should . . ."

"He had letters to write. Last bequests to make." Lady Slater's eyes blinked. She seemed determined to reduce the unpleasantness of her husband's death to its lowest possible terms.

"He wanted to make the final arrangements just right." Her voice sank to a whisper. "Such things take time."

"Time. Yes." The military gentleman gave almost an invisible shrug. "But not the better part of three days, Lady Slater."

"I think," replied Lady Slater, and with these words she seemed to lift the whole proceedings to a higher plane, "I think that Sir Olin probably spent the greater part of his last three days in—in prayer."

And indeed there was no answer to that.

We were dismissed almost immediately. In his mother's dressing room Martin carefully picked up the letter and the package which had been left for him by Sir Olin. He moved ahead of me toward the door.

Now that the ordeal was over I felt the need of human companionship, but Martin seemed eager to get away from everyone. Keeping a discreet distance, I followed him out into the sunlit afternoon. He made straight for his workshop, shutting the door behind him and leaving me with my face pressed dolefully against the window.

I don't think he was conscious of me, but I had no intention of spying on him. The loneliness of death was still with me and contact, however remote, with Martin was a comfort. As I watched, he put the letter down on his work bench. Then, casually, he started to unpack the parcel.

I was surprised to see that it was nothing more than an alarm clock, an ordinary alarm clock similar to the dozen or so that already stood on the workshop shelf, except for the fact that it seemed to have attached to it some sort of wire contrivance. I have a dim memory of thinking it odd that his father's last tangible bequest should be anything so meager, so commonplace as an alarm clock.

Martin hardly looked at the clock. He merely put it on the shelf with the others. Then he lighted one of the Bunsen burners with which his well-stocked workshop was provided. He picked up the letter his father had written him, the last of those many letters which he had received and which he had neglected to read. He did not even glance at the envelope. He thrust it quickly into the jet from the Bunsen burner and held it there until the flames must almost have scorched his fingers.

Then, very carefully, Sir Martin Slater, twelfth baronet, collected the ashes and threw them into the wastepaper basket.

I remained at Olinscourt for the funeral. Of the service itself I have only the shadowiest and most childish memories. Not so dim, however, are my recollections of the funeral baked meats. I am ashamed to say that I gorged myself. I have no doubt that Martin did so too.

The next day it was decided by my family that I should leave the Slaters alone to their grief. My reluctant departure was sweetened by a walnut cake left over from the funeral which I packed tenderly and stickily at the bottom of my portmanteau.

I never saw Martin Slater again. For some reason it was decided that he should leave the school where we had shivered and wrestled together and go straight to Harrow. For a while I missed the hampers from Olinscourt, but soon the War was over and my family moved to America. I forgot all about my old chum.

Not long ago a mood of nostalgia brought me to thinking of my childhood and Martin Slater again. Slowly, uncovering a fragment here, a fragment there, I found that I was able to restore this long-obliterated picture of my visit at Olinscourt.

The facts of course had been in my mind all the time. All they had lacked was interpretation. Now, thanks to a more adult and detached eye, I can see as a whole something which, to my childish view, was nothing more than a disconnected sequence of happenings.

Perhaps I am doing an old school friend an atrocious wrong; perhaps I am cynically forcing a pattern on to what was, in fact, nothing more than a complex of unfortunate accidents and fantastic coincidences. But I am inclined to think otherwise. For I can grasp Martin Slater's character so much more clearly now than when we were children together. I see a boy, teetering on the unstable brink of puberty, who revolted passionately from any physical or spiritual intrusion into his privacy; a boy of intense pride and fastidiousness who was mature enough to know he must fight to maintain his personal independence, yet not mature enough to have learned that in the wrestling match of life certain holds are barred—the deathlock, for example.

I see that boy stifled by the sincere but nauseating affection of a father who bombarded him with assiduous pieties that made him the laughingstock of his schoolfellows; of a father who, with his "quiet quarters," his sermonizings, his full-mouthed good-night kisses, turned Martin's home life into an incessant siege upon the sacred citadel of his privacy. I am sure that Martin's hatred of his father was something deeply ingrained in him which grew as he grew toward adolescence. That hatred was kept in check perhaps so long as the undeclared war of love was waged unknown to the outside world. It was different when I came to Olinscourt. For I represented the outside world, and in front of me Sir Olin stripped his son naked of all the decent reserves. Those kisses on the mouth were, I believe, to Martin the kisses of Judas. Sir Olin had betrayed him forever.

And Martin Slater was too young to know any other punishment for betrayal than—death.

The details of that crime speak, I think, plainly enough for themselves. During one of his nightly absences from our bedroom Martin could easily have stolen into his sleeping father's room and studied the combination of the safe in the back of the gold hunter. He could easily have slipped into the vault on the night before the crime and installed there some ingenious product of his workshop, some device, manufactured from an alarm clock and set for the hour at which Sir Olin invariably entered the vault, which would either automatically have shut the heavy steel door behind the baronet or have distracted his attention long enough for Martin to close the door upon him himself. Martin's inventive powers were more than adequate to have created that last and most successful "burglar alarm," just as his conversation with his father about installing the alarm, as witnessed by myself, would have provided an innocent explanation for the contrivance if it had been discovered later in the vault with Sir Olin.

From then on, with me as an unconscious and carefully exploited accessory, the rest must have been simple too—an invented glimpse of Sir Olin driving off in Mr. Ramsbotham's car, the clever trick of the old letter, steamed open probably and checked for content, planted among the morning post to put Pringle's mind at rest about his master's absence and to make certain that Sir Olin would not be searched for until it was too late.

There was genuine artistry in Martin's use of me to cover his tracks. For it was I who innocently burned the first page and the envelope of that fatal letter whose date and postmark would otherwise have proved it to have been of earlier origin. It was I too, with my clumsy grab at the blazer, who was held responsible for that letter's having dropped "inadvertently" into the morning mail.

Yes, Martin Slater, at fourteen, showed a shrewd and native talent for murder. And, as a murderer, he must be considered an unqualified success. For he never even came under suspicion.

There was one person, however, who must have been only too conscious of Martin Slater's dreadful deed. And in that, to me, lies the real horror of the story. I try to keep myself from thinking of Sir Olin bustling into his safe to put away his papers as usual; Sir Olin hearing a little ting-a-ling like the whirring bell of an alarm clock; Sir Olin spinning round to see the great door of the safe closing behind him, shutting him into that sound-proof vault; and somewhere, probably above the door, a curious amateur device composed of a clock and some lengths of wire.

I try not to think of the nightmare days that must have followed for him—days spent staring at that alarm clock contrivance which he must have recognized as the lethal invention of his own son; days spent hoping against hope that Martin would relent and release him from that chamber where the oxygen was growing suffocatingly scarcer; days spent contemplating the terrible culmination of his "perfect" relationship with his beloved laddie.

I wonder if, during those hours of horror, Sir Olin Slater's evangelical faith in the intrinsic goodness of human nature ever faltered. Somehow I doubt it. His heroic manner of death gives me the clue. For Sir Olin, however frightfully he had mismanaged his life, made a triumphant success of death. I can see him, weakened with hunger and thirst, scarcely able to breathe; I can see him neatly, almost meticulously, wrapping up the telltale alarm clock which, if left to be discovered, might have pointed to Martin's complicity. I can see him writing a pious "suicide" note to his wife, and that other probably forgiving note, which was never to be read, to his son. I can see him producing a revolver from one of those brass-handled drawers in the wall of the vault—and gallantly taking his own life in order to shield his son's immense crime from detection.

Indeed, it may well be said of Sir Olin that nothing in his life became him like the leaving it.

The Dead Finger

by Howard Pyle

fiction

"Whatever would I do with a dead man's finger?"
Beppo asked.

Every man, so the saying goes in Italy, carries his troubles about with him on his shoulders. Be he rich or be he poor, or be he neither the one nor the other, yet his cares cling to him as close as fleas.

Beppo was a porter of Florence; he was no exception to this saying. He was a ragged, lousy fellow. He wore wooden shoes, no doublet, and a ragged shirt. He was poor, he was mean and obscure. These seemed to him to be causes for trouble. He was, moreover, in love with Elisabetta, the baker's daughter, and she cared nothing for him, for her heart was set upon Pietro the cobbler. This was a further cause of care. So Beppo, while he lounged at the corner at the market-place, whistling softly to himself between his teeth and scratching his elbow, though he had no outward appearance of being vexed with care, yet felt the bite of his troubles—even though the sunshine shone upon his back and shoulders and warmed him through and through.

Montofacini the magician appeared at the door of the bookseller's shop. He was clad all in black from top to toe; a black velvet robe; a tall, soft, black cap bordered with fur. The only bits of color about him were his white face and hands and the red sash tied about his waist. He looked and saw Beppo. He whistled, beckoned to him, and called, "Facchino!"—which is to say, "Porter." Beppo saw that he was wanted; he gathered himself up from where he lounged and went over to where the magician stood in the doorway. He touched the brimless hat upon his head as the magician said to him: "Beppo, here are several books I want carried home. I will pay you two soldi for bringing them."

"Three soldi," said Beppo.

"Two," said the magician.

"Three," said Beppo.

"Two," said Montofacini.

Beppo shrugged despairingly. "Two it is," he muttered. He shouldered the package of books and followed the footsteps of the magician.

He had no idea that Montofacini read such heavy books. Before long his muscles ached, and the sweat ran in great drops from his face. He was glad when they turned the corner toward Montofacini's house, for he was hot and weary.

Montofacini opened the door and beckoned with his hand. "Come in, Beppo," said he. Beppo took off his hat and put it under his arm. He crossed himself before he opened the door, for he had no wish to carry any of the effect of the evil eye away with him. He made the sign of the horns with his fore and little fingers, and kept them pointed down to the ground.

Beppo deposited his books upon the bench beside the wall. He was thinking of the two soldi which he should get for carrying them. He wanted his money and he wanted to go. Montofacini had seated himself in a great carved arm-chair beside the window. He was looking very earnestly at Beppo where he sat wiping his forehead. He was in the mood to try an experiment. Presently he said, "Beppo, tell me, would you rather have money for carrying the books, or would you rather have something better than money?"

"What is there better than money?" said Beppo.

"Oh," said Montofacini, "there are many things better than money. There is Love," said he, "and Glory."

"As for those things," said Beppo, "I would like to have the love of Elisabetta, the baker's daughter. I think she loves the cobbler Pietro, who lives three doors below Barnabo's shop. She is there half the time, leaning against the door and talking to him—a great, ugly fellow he is, too, with a leather apron, and thick lips, and fingers as black as your honor's hat with shoemaker's wax."

"Well, look you, Beppo," said Montofacini, "I am of a

mind to make an experiment. I myself have all the money I want; I am too old and dried to care for love. As for glory, I am so high in favor now with the Grand Duke that I am afraid of falling from where I stand. Do you see this?" And he held up something that appeared to be a dried stick about four inches long. It was tied about with a piece of whip-cord.

"Yes," said Beppo, "I see it. What is it?"

"It is a dead finger," said Montofacini. "I cut it myself from the hand of a murderer who was hung."

"Jesu guard us," said Beppo, and crossed himself.

"Would you rather have this, or the two soldi I promised you?" said Montofacini.

"I would rather have the two soldi," said Beppo. "Whatever would I do with a dead man's finger?"

"You judge only from the outside look of things," said Montofacini. "You do not know the value of this finger. Listen; it has this value, that when you wear it around your neck everything you wish for shall be yours."

"That would be a blessing," said Beppo, "if it is true."

"You will find it true," said Montofacini. "Try it."

"Well," said Beppo, "two soldi are but two soldi, and they are not much. I will take the dead man's finger."

"But you must buy it," said Montofacini, "for it will not be yours if you do not buy it."

Beppo remembered that he had one soldo, which he intended spending for a glass of wine. It was in his pocket; he could feel it with his hand. "I have only one soldo in the world," said Beppo.

"That will be enough," said Montofacini. "The finger is yours for one soldo."

Beppo drew the soldo out of his breeches pocket and offered it to the magician. Montofacini hesitated a moment before he took the soldo and gave the finger to Beppo. His face assumed an unusually solemn look. "Think well what you do, Beppo," said he. "There is no such thing as a man in the world who is without trouble. You will get rid of the sorrows that now stand at your elbow, but they will only give way to other and perhaps more bitter sorrows than the old ones were. Beware what you do."

As Beppo listened, something strange befell him. His brain seemed to swim, the daylight whirled around and around him. This lasted for a few seconds, and then his brain cleared again.

"Here is the soldo," said Beppo. "I will take the dead finger."

The magician laughed. He took the soldo, and gave Beppo the dead and dried finger. Beppo immediately hung it about his neck by means of the whip-cord. "And now," said the magician, "wish, and whatever you wish shall come true."

"First of all," said Beppo, "I will wish for a bottle of wine and some bread and meat."

"Oh," said the magician, "I was about to offer you that." And he called out to his servant, "Francesca, bring Beppo a bottle of wine and some bread and meat."

So Beppo's first wish was fulfilled.

As Beppo went homeward he thought to himself how wonderful it would be if his dead finger really should point the way of fortune for him. He believed in it, yet he disbelieved. Signor Montofacini had promised him that it should bring him whatever he desired; but how could a dead finger do that? A living hand could not do so much; certainly the finger of a dead murderer's hand could not. He had wished for bread and meat and wine, and instantly he had them. But then he would have had what he wanted even without the dead finger, for Montofacini had said that he was about to feed him. Well, it did him no harm to wish, and he would wish—he would wish—he would wish—what should he wish for? Yes, he would wish to be rich; he would wish to be very rich. That was it; he would wish to be very rich.

He said aloud, "I wish to be very rich."

A boy came running up the street. He was a boy from the bakery. He was looking from right to left, as if in search of somebody. Presently his eyes beheld Beppo. He came running across the street to him. "Beppo, Beppo!" he cried, "I have been looking for you everywhere, Beppo!"

"What is it?" said Beppo. "What is it you want with me?"

"There is a man at the bakery who is looking for you," said the boy. "He has two horses; one he rides himself, the other he leads. Come, hurry your legs, or maybe he will go!"

Beppo's slouching gait broke into a run. He ran to the

bakery. There was a man there with two horses, as the boy had said. He was a big, low-browed fellow with straight locks of red hair hanging about his face like a bunch of carrots. He wore a discolored blue jerkin of frieze, loose breeches, and cowhide boots drawn up above his knees. He evidently was a countryman. He sat upon one big raw-boned horse, and he held another by the bridle-rein. "This," said the boy who brought him, "is Beppo. Here he is."

"Are you Beppo the porter?" said the man.

"Yes," said Beppo, "I am."

"Then get on this horse," said the stranger, "and ride with me. Your mother's cousin is dying at Grassena, and she has sent for you."

Then Beppo mounted the led horse, and the two rode away together. All the neighbors said to one another, "Look at Beppo on horseback!"

As they went they talked together. The man said that he did not know what the Widow Fausti wanted with Beppo. She was an old cat of a woman. She had quarreled with all her neighbors, so that no one now spoke well of her. But death wipes a clean slate. Who would want to refuse one who was fighting for breath? Word had come to him to bring Beppo, and he had taken the horses out of the stable, and here he was.

As he talked, Beppo remembered that he had heard his mother speak of her cousin at Grassena. She was, she had said, a widow and rich. Could this be the woman who had sent for him?

"What is she like?" said Beppo. "I never saw her. I have heard my mother (God rest her soul!) speak of her; but I never saw her."

"What is she like?" said the man. "She is brown as the rind of one of her own smoked hams. She is as wrinkled as a last year's apple. Her hair is white—it is as white as yonder pigeon," pointing to one that flew just then across the blue sky.

"God knows what she wants me for," said Beppo.

"God knows," assented his companion.

So they talked as they galloped, klippety-kloppety, to Grassena.

The Widow Fausti's butcher-shop was in the main street facing the square where the fairs were held at Easter season. There were hams and sausages in the window, and a dead sheep, peeled of its hide. Now, however, the shop was closed. A number of people hung about the door, and a fat, brown friar, with the wine and the wafers of extreme unction, was just leaving the house.

The people around the door drew back as the horsemen galloped up, and Beppo freed his feet from the stirrups and leaped to the ground. He entered the house directly, but his companion remained where he was, explaining to those who gathered in a knot about him how he had just found Beppo at Florence, and how they had ridden thence without drawing rein excepting at the high hills.

Beppo went into the house and up to the sickroom. The Widow Fausti lay there dying upon a soiled and rumpled bed. The wrinkled face was yellow-white, like the wax of a church candle; her nose was pinched and blue at the tip, her cheeks sunken, and her mouth twisted askew and to one side. A fat woman sat at the head of the bed. Her thick lips projected, and every now and then she would half utter, but not quite audibly, a "Tut! tut! tut! tut!" of pity, and would wipe the dew of sweat from the brow of the dying creature. Two men sat at a little distance; one was fat and gross, the other was thin and bald. Every now and then they looked suspiciously at each other, and would hitch their chairs. They were the brothers of the sick woman.

The dying woman opened her gray and filmy eyes. "Is that Beppo?" she said. "Dear Beppo!" The brothers started and looked at each other. Beppo was a new and dangerous personality in the problem. Who knew what would happen now?

As Beppo had never seen his mother's cousin before, he was surprised at her very affectionate tone. "Here I am," he said, pushing forward to the bedside. "I came as soon as I could."

"Give me your hand, Beppo," she said, and Beppo yielded his warm hand into her cold and bony clutch. "Beppo," said she, "Beppo, you never wronged me, did you? You never cheated me of four soldi, did you? You never complained to the magistrate of my pig, that he broke into your garden and rooted up your turnips. You never made me pay for what he had done, did you?"

"No," said Beppo, "I never did."

"Well," said the dying woman, "my brother Tomaso— he is the fat one; is he there?"

"Yes," said Beppo, "he is."

"Well, he cheated me of four soldi once, when he bought a sheepskin from me—it was twelve years ago, but I have not forgotten it."

The fat man looked as though hope and strength had both gone from him. He sighed deeply, and wiped his face, upon which the sweat was now gathering.

"And my brother Marco—he is the tall, lean one—the one that looks like a pair of iron tongs—he with a bald head—I did not see him—"

"He is here," said Beppo.

"Well, he made me pay last fall a year ago for my pig when it broke into his garden."

Now it was the turn of the lean, bald man to look as if he had hung a dog. Beppo looked at him. "That is a pity," said he.

"So now," said the dying woman, "I am near my end. I have saved a bit of money, but I will leave nothing to those two because of their wickedness. I will leave all to you, dear Beppo, for you never cheated me and never robbed me. For I have some money, Beppo; I have made some money, and I have saved some, and all from my butcher-shop."

She fumbled and plucked at her pillow. Finally she drew out from underneath it a sheet of yellow parchment. "Take this, Beppo," said she; "it is my will, and was made by the notary, so that it is safe and sound. It will bring you all that money that it speaks of. But do not spend it, Beppo. Keep it! Keep it!"

Beppo took the parchment and opened it. It gave him six thousand three hundred lire. He was rich.

Beppo was amazed. He had said that he wanted to be rich, and lo! he was rich upon the voicing of his wish. And yet he was only rich by the death of another. He shuddered at the thought. And yet on second thought he saw that his wish could not have moved this affair to the breadth of a hair. Even if he had never owned the dead man's finger, it would have been exactly as it was now. Three hours ago he had not even heard of the dead man's finger. His mother's cousin had been sick for a week, and her will had been made for more than a year. Then he thought of how rich he was, and his heart swelled as though it would burst with joy.

Some one near him laughed. It was not any one in the

sick-room, for they were all very solemn for many rea-
sons. The laughter sounded like Montofacini the magician.

Beppo's mother's cousin was dead, and now Beppo sat
in the notary's house, talking to him about the will. All
was right and as it should be. He was the master of six
thousand three hundred lire. They were his, and his own-
ership in them could not be in any way questioned. He
was a rich man. Then he thought of Elisabetta, the baker's
daughter. He sighed deeply, profoundly.

"What ails you?" said the notary.

"Ah," said Beppo, "I am thinking of Elisabetta, the
baker's daughter. I am rich, but I am not happy, for she
does not love me!"

The notary laughed. "You are a fool," said he. "A man
with six thousand three hundred lire may hope for a better
match than a baker's daughter, if he has a mind for such
a match."

"Aha!" said Beppo, "you do not know her. She is big
and fat," said he, with much unction; "she has cheeks that
are red and shining like a ripe apple, and her hair is like
black glass, spun very long and fine. Ah, she is a pear
upon the top of the tree, and I have no stick long enough
to reach it!" Then, bethinking himself of his dead man's
finger, he said, "I wish she were mine!"

Again the notary laughed. He was a little man. He
looked like a mouse; and if you can think of a mouse
laughing, you can think how the notary looked. "Nothing
easier than that," quoth he. "Why, man, go you to the
girl's father. Tell the old man what you want, and say that
you have six thousand three hundred lire, the half of
which you will settle upon your wife. Then she will drop
into your hands like that pear you speak of when it is ripe.
You need not climb for it, and you need not shake it. It
will drop into your hands without the climbing or shaking."

Beppo caught the little notary's hand in his. "Sir," he
cried, "do you think that this is so?"

"I know it is so," said the notary.

"Then fare you well," quoth Beppo.

He ran down the stairs three at a time. He got him a
horse, and he posted away toward Florence with all the
speed he could command.

Barnabo the baker was a great man. He was rather

short than tall, but he was enormous about the body, with soft and gelatinous fat. He always wore a white apron, but the strings around his belly were drawn so tight and the fat of his body was so soft that they were quite hidden, and it looked as though his body were being cut across with a sharp knife. His face, even to the color, was like one of his own unbaked loaves, and his eyes were heavy and indolent, so that when he winked they closed slowly and opened slowly. He was in the room back of the bake-shop, drinking a bottle of red wine, when Beppo was introduced to him.

"What can I do for you, Beppo?" said he.

Beppo said, "Signor, it is your daughter I came to see you about."

"My daughter?" said the baker, and his dull eyes opened wide upon Beppo.

Beppo remembered that he was now the owner of six thousand three hundred lire, and the recollection gave him strength. "Signor," said he, "I love your daughter, and I wish to ask of you for her hand in marriage. My mother's cousin has just left me by her will six thousand three hundred lire. Three thousand one hundred and fifty I will settle upon her if she becomes my wife."

Barnabo the baker smiled. His dough-like face expanded to a wide grin that displayed his teeth. You could see the hole where one of the front teeth had been knocked out when he slipped and fell against the doughtrough. "Beppo, my son," said he, "this is a strange matter that you bring to me. God forbid that I should say no to you—if it is as you say. Where did your mother's cousin live?"

"She lived," said Beppo, "at Grassena. The notary Benuchi lives there; he drew the will of my mother's cousin, and he will tell you that what I say is true. My mother's cousin passed over her brothers and made me her heir. And now she is dead, and may God rest her soul!"

Barnabo smiled still more broadly than before. "What you tell me is great pleasure for me to hear," he said, "and I give you joy of being so rich. Have a glass of wine with me, son Beppo! Ho! Elisabetta!" he called. "Another tumbler for Beppo. He will take a little wine with me."

Elisabetta appeared at the door. She seemed surprised

to see Beppo. She stared and frowned and shrugged her shoulders.

"Elisabetta," said Barnabo, "you must be kind to Beppo now, for he is suddenly a rich man. He has inherited six thousand three hundred lire from his mother's cousin. He proposes for your hand, and offers to settle half his money upon you; so you must treat him kindly."

Elisabetta disappeared upon this news as a wisp of a cloud disappears from the sun when a strong wind blows upon it. She vanished from the doorway, and in a little while she returned, not with one glass, but with two. She herself sat down with Beppo and her father, and tasted the wine with them. She inquired of Beppo concerning his inheritance, and questioned its every detail. There was no doubt about it. Since the morning, Beppo had become a rich man. Gradually she unbent. Pietro the cobbler was now nothing compared with Beppo. She talked more and more kindly to him. She touched his knee under the table with hers, and she pressed his foot with her foot. Beppo was very happy. Before he went away they were betrothed.

Again there was a laugh that sounded like Montofacini.

Within a week after this, Beppo married Elisabetta, the baker's daughter, and so this wish of his became true, for she was now his.

Later, Barnabo died, and Beppo took the bakery in his stead. He was always lucky. He made at that time the best bread in Florence.

Marriage has its sorrows. Elisabetta did not love Beppo, and Beppo discovered this to his pain. She yawned when she was alone with him; she did not hear him when he spoke to her; by a thousand and one of these little signs he discovered, as many a husband has done since that time, that his wife did not love him. Beppo had to acknowledge that while he owned Elisabetta's body, he did not own her heart.

"Why do you not do something?" she would say. "You make the best bread in Florence, but you do nothing but stand in the door of the bake-shop and stare into the street. Even Pietro the shoemaker has something to do, but you—bah!—you do nothing." Then Beppo would walk into the street and look up and down the thoroughfare. It was as though he were seeking for something to do.

One day as he stood so at the bakery door he saw a great coach approaching. In it was an official clad in a doublet embroidered with threads of gold. He wore red hose and fine black shoes of cut leather. Red ribbons were pulled through the toes of the shoes and knotted into bows. It was one of the Grand Duke's gentlemen.

"I wish," said Beppo, "that I had a position of state with the Grand Duke like that gentleman yonder."

The coach of the splendid gentleman approached where Beppo was standing, and pulled up at the door. "Is this where Beppo, the baker, lives?" said the gentleman.

Beppo was amazed at seeing the gentleman stopping at his house, and still more amazed at being addressed. "Yes," said he, "this is where Beppo lives."

"Is he about?" said the gentleman. "I would speak to him."

"I am Beppo," said he.

"Yesterday," said the gentleman, "the Grand Duke ate a manchet loaf of yours. He says it is the best bread ever he ate in his life. The Grand Duke desired me to tell you that he will appoint you his master baker at the palace."

Beppo hardly knew whether he had heard the gentleman aright. His head buzzed and whirled. Head baker to the Grand Duke! He did not know whether he stood on his head or on his feet.

"You are to begin your office at once," said the gentleman, "and I am to take you to the Grand Duke now, in this coach."

So Beppo began his office that day at the palace. He was a pleasant-spoken, cheerful body; he became a great favorite, and was constantly called in to the Grand Duke's presence. When he was not working he dressed in silks and satins, and the Grand Duke gave him a golden chain set with big garnets as a reward of merit for the bread he baked. Beppo rode in his carriage to the Grand Duke's palace in the morning and back again to his bakery at night. He looked like a lord and dressed like one, and the people who knew him took off their hats as he passed. He was a great man now.

"I wonder," said Beppo one day—"I wonder if it is the dead man's finger that has brought me all this fortune. It cannot be, however, for the gentleman was upon his way to my bake-shop when I wished. He would have stopped at any rate."

Nevertheless, the fact remained that Beppo had got every wish he had wished for since he had got the dead man's finger. First he had wished for bread and meat and wine, and that had come to him. Then he had wished for money, and that had come to him. Then he had wished for Elisabetta, and she had come to him. Now he had wished for rank, and that was his.

Still he could not quite believe that it was the finger that had brought all these things to him.

But now that Beppo was beginning to rise, he began also to look down on his wife. It is true that the higher you climb the more you see at the bottom—but nevertheless it is true that what you see looks smaller. Beppo began to acknowledge that his wife was a mere illiterate woman without breeding or knowledge of the world. He now saw lords and ladies every day of his life, and the more he saw of them the more excellent they became, and the more poor and mean did his wife look in his eyes. Besides that, she did not love him.

It seemed to him that it would have been something to him if she had been fond, but as she still shrugged her shoulders and still said "Bah" to him (for so a wife will do to her husband), he saw her as a poor, mean thing of whom he was ashamed. There was Floriziana at the court. She was a lady's-maid there, and she was herself like a lady. If he had only seen her before he had seen Elisabetta, he would have asked for the almond and not for the walnut.

The higher he mounted in the world, the less happy Beppo was. He had now a thousand wants where he had ten before, and the worst of it was he did not know what to ask for. Rank? He had no birth to support his rank, and he had wisdom to know that the higher he climbed the more he would show, as the country people say, the seat of his trousers. Wealth? He had all the money now that he could spend, and every day his wealth was growing greater. Love? He thought of Elisabetta and he shuddered. Those old days when he had stood at the market-place to carry packages seemed to him now to be the happiest days of his life. Perhaps he had troubles in those days, but it did not seem to him now that he had had any sorrows.

His tongue tasted bitter. Perhaps he was bilious. He would go and consult a doctor.

One night Beppo was coming home from the palace. He

was more than usually melancholy; perhaps he was more bilious than usual; at any rate, life seemed to have lost its savor to him.

Yet that day a great honor had come to him.

The Grand Duke had talked to him and had laughed at him. He had said to him, "Beppo, your rolls are so wonderful that you ought to have a golden medal of honor for them."

"I wish I had the medal," said Beppo. The Grand Duke laughed. "Kneel," said he, "and I will bestow it upon you." Then, hardly knowing what he did, Beppo kneeled. The Grand Duke took the medal from off his own neck and flung it around the shoulders of Beppo. "Take this," said he. "It is now yours. I institute a new order, and you shall be the first knight of the Order of the Freshly Risen Bread. I make you with this the chief baker of the world."

Beppo rose from his feet and looked about him. His soul had been full of joy. He was the first knight of the Order of the Freshly Risen Bread! But now this joy subsided, and he sank into a corresponding depression. "What is the good of all these honors?" said he. "What is the good of being the first nominated knight of the Freshly Risen Bread, when Elisabetta is my wife? Bah! And she does not love me, either. If she were only Floriziana now! But God forbid that I should wish for that, for I would not be the husband of two wives at once."

So Beppo brooded on as he approached the bakery at the corner of the street.

A little whiffet of a boy thrust out a face like the face of a monkey from behind the house, and sang a scurrilous couplet that went through Beppo's heart like the blade of a sharp knife.

> *Beppo cooks bread for the Duke,*
> *But Pietro cooks bread for Beppo.*

So sang the boy, and then was gone, for Beppo heard him clattering away over the stones in his wooden shoes.

Beppo stood rooted to the spot. He did not love his wife, and he believed that she did not love him. But such a belief is different from the truth, and now the truth had reached him and had gone home. It is one thing to have a wife not love you, and quite another thing to have her love some one else.

But what should he do? He stood for a long time thinking. Then he thought he would go to the cobbler's shop and have it out with Pietro. Yes, he would go down and have it out with Pietro now. Should he? No. Why should he not? Yes; he would go now.

So he went down to the cobbler's shop, but it was closed. The shutters were shut, and the door was locked. Beppo stood for a little, chewing the cud of bitter thoughts. He felt that the world and its people were all against him. He was more unhappy now than he had ever been in all of his life. He turned homeward with laggard footsteps. Every footstep he took seemed to lead him into a still deeper bog of troubled thought.

He reached the door of this house. Here he stopped and smote the fist of one hand into the palm of the other. "I wish," said he, "that I was free of Pietro the shoemaker. I wish, for that matter, that I was free of my wife also."

At that moment the door of the house opened, and the cobbler stepped out directly under his nose. "Hah! cried Beppo. "Villain, what do you do here?"

He grasped the shoemaker by the collar of the coat as he spoke. The shoemaker struggled to release himself, but Beppo was very strong and held him fast. Pietro struggled in silence, but still Beppo held him as in a vise.

"Let me go, you rascal," said the shoemaker, panting and gasping. "You will not let me go? Well, then, 'tis your own fault."

Suddenly, even as he spoke, he drew from his bosom a sharpened shoemaker's knife. The blade was whetted down from the handle to a long, sharp point, as shoemakers' knives usually are. He struck at Beppo with his knife, but Beppo seized his wrist. He was very strong, and was, besides, now endowed with the strength of three. "Would you stab me?" he cried. He bent back the wrist till the bones cracked and the hand relaxed.

Beppo was insane with a thousand conflicting passions and emotions that surged within him like the waters of a strong sea—jealousy, fear, rage, hate. He knew not what he did. It seemed to him that a strength he had never known before was in his body. He thrust the cobbler back against the door. Pietro still fought desperately, but in silence. In his struggles his heels struck violently against the panels of the door. He breathed as though he were smothering.

Beppo wrenched the knife out of his grasp. He himself was breathing as though his breath choked him like smoke. He struck the shoemaker once and again in the breast with the sharpened knife. It seemed to him that the breast was very soft. The blade of the knife penetrated it without resistance, so that the hasp thumped violently against the ribs.

The shoemaker ceased his struggles. Beppo was leaning his weight against him. The second blow of the baker's fist against his ribs drove the breath in a shrill wheeze from the cobbler's lips. Then he sank down all in a heap at Beppo's feet.

A moment before, Beppo had been tossed on a tempest of passion. Now, of a sudden, the tempest was stilled. He had killed a man. A great roaring in his ears hummed rapidly away to silence. He gazed, with white face, with distended eyes and gaping mouth, at what he had done. He had killed a man, and the man lay dead at his feet.

He reached out his hand and opened the door. Then he stepped over the corpse and entered the house, closing the door softly behind him, and leaving the cobbler lying where he was. He went feeling his way with his left hand by the wall along the now nearly dark passageway. He still had the cobbler's bloody knife in his right hand. He opened the door at the farther end of the passage and entered the room where his wife had just lit the lamp. Hearing him enter, she turned to look at him.

The disgusted indifference with which she regarded him gradually underwent a succession of changes. Surprise, fear, and a deathly horror rapidly followed one another. Beppo was a terrible object. He still held in his hand the bloody knife which he had just used. His hand was bloody, and his clothes and his face were spotted with blood.

"What have you done?" she cried, harshly.

"I have killed Pietro the shoemaker," he said, dully. "His body lies just outside the door. I met him as he came out and I killed him there."

She was now white as death and was trembling all over. "Perhaps he is not dead," she said, in a hoarse, smothering voice. "Let me see!"

She would have gone out of the room past Beppo, but he held her back. "You shall not go!" he said. "I tell you he is dead!"

She began struggling with him to get past him, but his great strength overcame her.

"Stay where you are!" said he. He held her, and she could not advance. At last she ceased to struggle. She panted violently, but between the wheezing throes of her breath she continued to gasp out:

"I hate you! I hate you! I hate you! I loved Pietro, and you have killed him. An eye for an eye—a tooth for a tooth! The law shall have you and deal with you!"

She broke away from him and ran to the window. She tried convulsively to open it, but it stuck and would not open. Beppo ran to her and caught her. He tried to draw her away, but she clutched her fingers into the window ledge, and he could not move her.

"Well!" he cried. "Then join Pietro!" and he struck her with the knife.

She screamed very horribly. He struck her again—again—again—again. Two blows had killed Pietro. She was hard to silence. She still cried out, but now hoarsely, not screaming, but gasping. He struck her again—again—again. She sank down upon her knees and thence sank down upon the ground. He stood looking at her. He saw her head move a little—still he watched her. Then she stretched and lay silent. His bloody face glared horribly at her. She was dead.

The blood surged in his ears like the recurrent beating of the waves against the rocks. His ear-drums hummed and roared. The room looked like a shambles and he like the butcher.

All the time his brain worked with great velocity. His mind seemed to regard him, not as its operator, but as its subject. He, Beppo, the peaceful baker, he who an hour before, if not a happy, had at least been an innocent man. He, to kill two people with his own hand and in such a horrible way. He, at whom the Grand Duke had laughed gaily a short time before, and had created with his own hand First Knight of the Order of Freshly Risen Bread! How did he look now? He was covered with blood; what would the Grand Duke say of him now if he saw him?

And then he thought of his charm. The dead finger was to bring him whatever he wanted. He had wanted the death of Pietro and of his wife—and now they were dead. The damned Montofacini had given the charm to him, and it had worked to his undoing. It had brought all this trouble upon him. This is what had come of meddling with Providence.

He reached up to his neck. The whip-cord was there. He removed the dead finger from him and hurled it with all of his strength to the farthest corner of the room. His brain was in a tumult. He was no longer sane. His thoughts tumbled over one another so rapidly that he could hold no one of them long enough to analyze it and to understand it.

He put his hand up to his throat. The whip-cord was there; the dead finger lay against his bosom. He thought he had taken it off just now and had thrown the cursed amulet away. He must have been mistaken, and had not done it. He took the whip-cord off his neck and again hurled away the finger with all his strength. It struck against the farther wall of the room. He heard it fall to the floor like a dead lizard.

What should he do now? His joy was gone—he was a murderer. He would go to the Arno and throw himself in. What had he now to live for? He had destroyed everything with the shoemaker's knife! The Signoria would bring him now to trial for the murders he had committed. They would hang him—perhaps they would torture him.

He put his hand up to his throat; his fingers felt the whip-cord. Then he remembered that he had twice thrown it away, and that twice it had returned to him.

If his despair was great before, it was still greater now. He had bought the amulet with a piece of money. It was now his, and he felt that he could not get rid of it. Yes; it would cling to him as long as he lived. Perhaps it would cling to him in hell—who could say?

Then a thought came to his mind like a sudden burst of light. Hah! Why not try yet once more to regain his salvation by means of the charm? He grasped it convulsively in his hand. "I wish," said he, in a high and piping, yet quavering voice—"I wish I had not murdered Pietro and my wife! I wish they were both yet alive!"

There was a laugh. It was Montofacini's laugh. "You have had your dream!" said he. "Tell me now, will you take the dead finger, or will you take the two soldi? Remember, the dead finger will bring you whatever you wish for as soon as you ask for it."

Beppo's brain still whirled. God be merciful, what had happened to him? He winked rapidly and looked about him. Yes, he was awake; he was in Montofacini's house. Nothing had happened to him. He had not murdered any one. It all had been a dream bred of enchantment. Montofacini had thrown him into an enchanted sleep—nothing had happened to him! He had not even had the bread and meat and wine he had asked for.

"I would like," said he, "to have my two soldi. I do not want the dead finger. You may keep it."

Montofacini laughed. "You are wise," said he. "If you had everything you wanted, you would be no better off than you are now, and you would still have your troubles upon your shoulders." He gave Beppo his two soldi, and he threw the dead finger away from him upon the table.

Beppo took his money and slunk out of the house. He was as poor as ever, but anyhow he had not murdered any one. He went to the market-place and stood where the sun shone upon his back. It warmed him through and through. Still he did not know whether he stood upon his head or upon his heels.

Well, it was only enchantment, after all. Thank God, we do not any of us have a dead finger about our neck.

Boy Hunt

by John Bartlow Martin

---
fact
---

*The first twenty-four hours had passed and the
boy was still somewhere alone in the woods.*

I

Earl Numinen runs a crossroads store. "Numi's Service
Station," reads the Coca-Cola sign beside the concrete
highway, and it is true that two handsome gasoline pumps
adorn the driveway (though one is broken) and that Earl
and Hilma sell oil to the rare tourist who motors past. But
they also sell beans and socks and cigarettes and slab
bacon and Finnish boot grease and, on Fridays when the
truck comes through, fresh fruits and vegetables; and, far
more important, they operate an establishment which, dis-
guised as a store, actually is the nerve center of a rural
community. And because most of the people hereabouts
make their living by logging or grubbing in the wet iron
mines, the store also has something of the flavor of the
trading post on the fringe of the wilderness. No day passes
that the reality of the wilderness does not come home at
Numi's (and, as we shall see, on one recent occasion it
came home with savagery).

Numi's store is situated in one of the most remote
regions of the little-known Upper Peninsula of Michigan.
Isolated geographically, the community is also isolated in
time, a backwater, an eddy beside the stream of civiliza-
tion; the men here are still pioneers. The tourist whizzing
past on U.S. 41 may not realize he is driving virtually the
only passable road (by ordinary standards) in the region.
Straight north of Numi's the wilderness hump stretches
forty miles to the cold big lake, Superior; straight south

144

lies an area of two hundred square miles inhabited only by
lumberjacks, and few of them. The nearest sizable towns
to the store are, to the east, the iron town of Ishpeming
and, to the west, the lumbering town of L'Anse, each
about thirty miles away. Five miles to the east is Michigamme, in the nineties a brawling boom town of three
thousand lumberjacks and miners with sixty saloons, today
a sleepy village of three hundred with a single saloon. The
road map says that Numi's stands at the town of Three
Lakes; and it is true that forty years ago, when the woods
were full of the iron-seeking drill rigs, there was a good-
sized settlement here; but today the stopes of the mines
are filled with water and their shaft houses have fallen
away in decay, and, but for the few neighbors in Spurr
Township and the summer tourists, Numi's store *is* Three
Lakes.

Earl Numinen's father came here from Finland in the
days when little clusters of cabins huddled around the
shaft houses in the wilderness. Grandpa is in his seventies
today, a silent Finn with yellowing skin and high
cheekbones and sunken cheeks who chews on his corncob
pipe while he works from sunrise to dusk—works hard,
building log tourist cabins around the store or hauling ice
from the ice house to fill the Coca-Cola coolers or carpen-
tering a skid with curved runners so that, this winter, he
can skid timber out of the woods. He works ceaselessly.
His grandson Donald, who is fourteen, has said with rare
talkativeness, "Grandpa has to work to keep his mind off
his wife. She died." I have never seen Grandpa with his
hat off and rarely have I seen him smile, except when one
of his old friends has brought a case of beer and they are
off to some nameless destination deep in the woods.

His son, Earl Numinen, is today in his mid-thirties,
short, round-bellied, short-legged, with a round face and a
quick smile and a dry wit that flashes but is never barbed.
Though born in Finland, he studied engineering at the excellent Michigan College of Mining and Technology and
today is a surveyor for the State Highway Department.
This work keeps him away from home most of the week,
and so the task of running the store falls on his wife,
Hilma. A plump, indomitable woman with round red
cheeks and solemn mien, she possesses a vast appetite for
living and so it is natural that she assumes the manifold

burdens of her neighbors. Indeed, at times it almost seems
she thrives on catastrophe.

The store, of course, is small. Originally Grandpa built
it with unimaginative attention to function: square white
frame, well insulated against the forty-below weather of
winter; inside, a low linoleum-covered L-shaped counter,
crowded shelf space, a stove that blocks the only bare
floor space, cramped sleeping quarters upstairs beneath the
roof. But in recent years Earl and Hilma have added at
the rear a kitchen and a living room paneled in knotty
pine and enhanced by a fireplace, in proud conformity
with the tourist's idea of life in the north woods.

The Numinens are surrounded constantly by an oppres-
sive surfeit of life, by men and women and hosts of children, by dogs and cats and goats. Hilma thrives on it. A
day lived at the store is like a year lived elsewhere. Does a
tourist's car get stuck on a logging road? He comes in sup-
plication to the store, and Hilma sends her son Donald out
in his 1929 Plymouth. Donald may spend all that day on
the job, and so, if necessary, will Hilma. Does a tourist
want to get a boat to one of the inaccessible lakes?
Grandpa and Donald, or, of a weekend, Earl, will lend a
hand. Some neighbor women may come over to do their
ironing in Hilma's kitchen. Of course she serves coffee and
rolls on the round white table near the wood-burning
stove. If they fall to talking, Hilma finishes their ironing.
Now and then she must take time out to cope with a
problem that baffles Honey, the girl from the hamlet of
Nestoria, who "helps out" at the store, or to quiet the riot-
ous wrangling of her sons, Donald and Philip. Donald is
fourteen and serious, Philip eleven with a sly pixy charm;
and usually a half-dozen youngsters are tumbling with
them about the place, ignoring Hilma's pleas to go outside.

II

The people who live hereabouts come whenever they
need groceries, as the housewives say, or chuck, as the
trappers say; they come when they need a bath or when
they need to mail a letter or make a telephone call or
when they simply need to talk. Invariably they come when
they need help.

And regularly on Friday nights they come to Numi's,

for on Friday Grandpa fires up the *sauna*, the steam bath,
and the weekly bath is a social occasion. The bathhouse is
a log cabin in the woods behind the store. Both the dressing room and the steam room are small and dark and
low-ceilinged. Through the afternoon Grandpa builds and
replenishes an enormous fire in a galvanized iron stove,
that resembles an oil drum on its side, on the floor of the
steam room. Atop this are heaped boulders, and by nightfall they have become extremely hot; indeed, as you enter,
the whole room is hot and humid. Warily you climb three
or four slipperty steps arranged like bleachers and sit
down on the top step, above and to one side of the pile of
hot rocks, with your head touching the ceiling and your
back against the hewn log wall. You toss a panful of cold
water onto the rocks. Steam billows up, live and almost
invisible; and if you are unused to it, you gasp as the sear-
ing heat strikes deep inside you: inexperienced bathers are
sometimes jokingly overheated by veteran Finns. To sweat
more, the old-timers flagellate their bodies with switches
of balsam boughs. Late in the fall, perhaps in November,
a month before the lakes freeze over, they enjoy rushing
from the *sauna* and diving straightway into the icy lake,
and in the winter they roll in the snow while still in a
sweaty glow. Perhaps some such idea came over Grandpa
one recent summer afternoon when, to the astonishment
of a group of tourists, he rushed utterly naked from the
sauna and into the woods.

On Fridays the parade to the bathhouse is constant
from suppertime until ten-thirty or eleven. As one couple
of the neighbors leaves the conversation in the living room
another takes its place; as one leaves the bathhouse another enters. Rarely does anyone bathe alone. One may
spend an hour at bathing, and what tastes better than ice-
cold beer between the bouts with the steam? By seven
o'clock the day's trade at the store has dwindled to nothing. Earl has come home from his week's work and now
with Hilma he sits in the living room. Some of the neighbors sit with them, and others—men usually—stand about
the store proper, talking of trade or politics or, more
likely, of the woods and what is going on in the township:
what fires are reported, who is sick, where is Anderson
logging now ("His new camp's on Section Twelve, back of
Petticoat Lake, but I guess he's working southwest of
there a little").

Comes now Bill Warjonen, the political leader of the community, the Township Supervisor, sometime trapper and logger and scrap collector and road mender and always a handy man with a two-ton pickup. He is one of those men driven somehow to deride, to belittle; yet he is friendly inside. He eases onto the Coca-Cola cooler and reaches into the pocket of his blue jeans for a match with which to pick his teeth, and the others fall silent, knowing he is about to speak. He does, in familiar vein: "There ain't no real trapping 'round here any more. Hunting either. Fishing. Country's getting too damn settled. You take Alaska—that's real country. I shoulda gone on up to Alaska when I was a kid, like my uncle wanted me to. Folks wouldn't let me. It's too late now, I guess," and he shakes his head, sighing the long-drawn-out, scarcely audible "yah" so common here, head bent, narrow shoulders sloped, feet swinging gently.

A tourist enters and stands uncertainly in the center of the little store; the others fall silent, looking at the floor. Paul Danielson is nearest the door to the living room; he calls to Hilma and she comes in. Hilma is a heavy woman, but she has grace and lightness as she moves down the narrow aisle behind the counter to the scales, to the cash register; she is a beautiful dancer, especially when she is dancing the polka or the old-time Finnish waltz. The tourist leaves. Hilma uses the Flit gun at the screen door, says, "Those flies," and goes back to the living room to sit with several other couples. As things quiet down you can hear the steady throb of the gasoline engine of the Delco plant that makes electricity for Earl and Hilma; and then suddenly, far away and lone and strange, comes the howl of a coyote pack on the rock bluffs behind the store. The men listen.

Paul Danielson says, "There must be a lot of them this year." He is the Conservation Department's fire tower man; all day long, summer-long, he mans the new hundred-foot steel fire tower near Fence Lake, in the wilderness southeast of Three Lakes.

"See a lot of coyote signs out south, hey, Paul?"

"You bet."

Charley Krumme shakes his head. "We didn't see hardly none out north." He is a dry, spare, garrulous little man, a woodsman who lives alone in a little house on Lake George. With six or eight others he returned tonight from a four-day fire-fighting trip into the woods north of the highway.

Earl's brother Bill—on a brief vacation from his job in a Detroit war plant—asks, "Why iss dere so many fires up dere, hey? Up north?"

Louie, Paul's partner, has just come in. He is a big man in Conservation khaki. He says, "They say it's lightning country."

"But that lightning, he never strikes around here, hey?"

"No. But up there—it's only eight or nine miles from here, but I guess there's something about the formation. Lightning started this one, anyway. You could see where it split a maple right down to the ground, then ran over to a pine stump. That's where she really started. That old pine stump. We found it the first night. That first night up there we slept right by the fire."

Krumme says, "Only we didn't sleep much. Just tried to get wood to keep warm, and squatted around by the fire and talked all night."

By now it is growing late and Bill Warjonen is restless. Finally he can wait no longer: he goes into the living room and tells Earl, "Are you going to play that two games of cribbage with me or not?" and Earl smiles and gets up, groaning, from his deep upholstered chair and goes into a side room and plays with Warjonen. Back in the living room the people still are sitting and talking, gossiping eagerly about goings-on in Michigamme ("The bond drive isn't doing so well," Hilma, the chairman, says sadly; and "I hear they're having trouble getting a principal for the high school"); talking politely about fishing out of consideration for a tourist who has come in. They are telling Finnish stories too—about the Finn who, questioned in a naturalization hearing about his place of residence, replied, "Oh no, I am not resident; Mr. Rooseevelt, he iss resident."

While the others are laughing Hilma gets up quietly and goes into the kitchen; she "iss making raady the caffee." Soon she brings it in, a huge pot of steaming coffee, and mounds of rolls and lunch meat, pickles, olives, great heaps of food. No one pretends surprise. The guests eat in silence; they like to eat. Earl turns on the radio. Time for the news. Through the iron-country static comes word that the invasion of France is going well. Then the women remove the dishes, Bill Numinen starts a poker game, and while the game is going on Hilma washes dishes alone in the kitchen, as she has washed them perhaps two or three times previously this day: here dishes are dirtied and stacked on the table until they must be washed before another shift of guests can be served.

All this is routine, the unnoticed respiration of the store. Scarcely more worth remarking are the days when brutal accidents maim men in the iron mines, or occasions when, as recently, Hilma realizes that no smoke has come out of a camp on Ruth Lake for several days and knows she must of course go to see if the old man batching there alone is all right. Alarms are common in this rugged country, for here is not only the inconvenience of kerosene lamps and wood stoves and outdoor privies but also downright hardship, physical hardship and danger such as these people's fathers faced.

The other day, for instance, Hilma's wall telephone rang—one long, three shorts—and a Conservation officer from L'Anse told her they believed that somebody had drowned in the Sturgeon River; they had not yet found his body, only his belongings on shore. It was natural to notify Numi's store. Hilma had not yet heard that anyone from Three Lakes was missing, but a little later a man came to the store to inquire about his brother, who had gone fishing on the Sturgeon the day before; he was the uncle of Honey, who works for Hilma in the store. But since the body was not yet found, Hilma, characteristically, kept her peace and went on washing dishes with Honey while out in the woods men dragged the Sturgeon with grappling hooks. They recovered the body; it was Honey's uncle, the third in her family to die within a year; and young Donald took her home to Nestoria, dry-eyed, bleak. Later the folk in the store told how her mother had dreamed of three black horses, one a colt; and they made the point that one who had died was a son, overseas.

III

Last August a terrible thing happened to Hilma and Earl, who have shouldered so eagerly so many people's troubles. On a Wednesday afternoon Hilma returned to the store from Michigamme and found that Donald and his old car were gone. She attached no significance to this; Donald, who was fourteen, was always running off somewhere on business, boys' business. But that evening about 6:30 the fire tower man, Paul Danielson, came in from duty at the Fence Lake tower and said he had seen Donald's car, empty, parked beside Danielson's own car at the end of the road in the woods. A trail covers the last mile and a quarter from the end of the logging road to the tower. Hilma recalled that Donald had said several times he wanted to see the new tower. Apparently he had started out to do that but had got off the trail and become lost, for he never had reached the tower.

No one knew precisely when he had left the store, but it must have been near noon. Earl was working at Watersmeet, seventy-five miles away. Hilma started out to look for Donald. Danielson went with her. So did Philip, her other son, eleven years old, and Honey. It is a good thing Danielson was with them that night. They tramped around in the woods till after dark. Hilma is a heavy woman. The country there is rough.

While they were gone Earl telephoned the store, as he always does on Wednesday nights. Charley Krumme answered. He told Earl bluntly that Donald had been lost in the woods all day and that Hilma and Philip and Honey were out looking for him.

Earl and a friend named Bill who was working with him on the highway drove the seventy-five miles from Watersmeet in the dark over bad roads in just a little more than an hour. "Earl always worshiped Donald," the neighbor women remarked often during the days that followed, as they came to the store, like women to a wake, to help Hilma make coffee and do the dishes.

By the time Earl had reached home and changed into his woods-clothes Hilma and the others were back. They had found no trace of Donald. Earl and Louie, the other tower man, and Charley Krumme and some others started out, though it was past ten o'clock at night. You never know how dark night is until you go into the deep woods at night. You can see nothing that is in front of you. One of the searching party said later, "It was like being inside a cow."

They didn't find Donald that night. They were out until about 3 A.M. Louis swore he picked up Donald's footprints in the gravel of the old railroad roadbed, unused for many years, that runs up from Iron County to within a half-mile of Fence Lake. He also told Earl that beside the boy's footprints were the tracks of a bear. Earl did not tell Hilma this.

The next morning, Thursday, Delene, a Conservation officer from L'Anse, and some other officers arrived and made a search. They too found nothing. So the first twenty-four hours had passed, and the boy was still somewhere alone in the woods—alive? dead? hurt?—and realization and shock were beginning to come home to the store.

Now on that bright Thursday afternoon, my wife and I, returning from Chicago, learned how tightly knit this community was. Now we learned what these people were. No work was done at Three Lakes that day. As we came down across the last mile-long swamp we could see the sunlight glinting on the windshields of many cars in the driveway of Numi's; and as we drew closer we could see the cars—police cars, loggers' trucks, private cars—and then we could see the little knots of men who were standing around or squatting on the driveway and the little grassplot between the drive and the driveway. We realized just how bad it was when, as we got out of our car, the men we knew so well—Bill Warjonen and the tower men and the others—only stared blankly at us without speaking, almost without recognition. They all looked tired. Then we saw Earl. He had come to the doorway when we drew up. I hope I never see anybody else who looks as he looked. None of us said anything for a minute. He was wearing his boots, which he wears only while surveying or going into the woods, and so I knew he had been out looking for Donald, and I asked, "No luck, Earl?" and Fran touched his sleeve. He shook his head and turned away. Fran went to Hilma, in the living room at the rear. Earl went into the side room and I followed him.

His friend Bill was sitting in a booth. Earl asked him for his map and they studied it, talking, planning their search, tracing trails on the map with their thumbnails. I realized that Earl had to do this, had to do something. He told me a little about what had happened but presently he fell silent and only sat, staring blindly at the tan table top. I went outside and talked to the men who were standing around. They were restless. "We ought to go out again quick—you can't do no good after dark." "It's too late already." "Sure didn't do no good last night. Like to broke my neck scramblin' around in that swamp." You heard all kinds of rumors—"They say he had his twenty-two with him—I'm bettin' he shot hisself accident'ly"; "His mother told him he couldn't go out to that tower, but you know how he always was"; "He's in that Tioga Swamp, he's down, down somewhere in that swamp, that's where he is, sure"; "You watch—they'll find him just a few feet from where he got off the trail."

It was apparent that nothing short of a thoroughly organized searching party could produce results. The sheriff and some state police arrived from L'Anse. They all had supper at the store after dark, sitting around the white table in the little kitchen, making their plans, arguing about possibilities, studying maps, conferring with Charley Krumme and other men who knew the woods out south.

Finally there was a scraping of chairs. The sheriff came out first, picking his teeth with a match. He was a slender little graying man with kindly gray eyes. He said that tomorrow everybody should meet at Anderson's mill at 6 A.M. He left. So did the state police. Some of the neighbors went home to get some sleep. Already it was near ten. Earl came out. He was wearing his leather jacket and he had a blanket over his arm. One of the men said he had thought they were going to wait till morning. Earl said that was right, but that he and Hilma were going out for a little while. Soon Perry, a woodsman, drove up for them in an ancient Model A. Hilma wore her topcoat and an old stocking cap. Earl had his shotgun and a box of shells and his automatic pistol. Incredibly, his round brown face looked pale and thin. Somebody told him he'd better take an axe and a flashlight. He put the flashlight in his pocket and somebody handed him an axe, but he laid it down to get some matches and went out to the car without it; a man ran after him and gave it to him. We watched until the uncertain taillight winked out far up near the rock cut; then we all went home. Soon the store was dark.

Back at our camp Fran and I talked. On the map it looked bad. The area into which Donald had gone is a rectangle of two hundred square miles bounded by four highways. From these highways a few logging roads push tentatively into the wilderness, but they do not go far. The only habitations are a few scattered trappers' shacks and the lumbering camps at the dead ends of the logging roads. The central core of the area is completely desolate, uninhabited. It is all rugged broken country, hills and bluffs slashed by rivers, lakes, impenetrable treacherous swamps.

That night you could almost see Donald out there in the woods. He was a cocky lad. He was chunky and blond and husky—strange how, at times like this, familiar things suddenly assume a wholly new importance—he was husky. And quiet and level-headed and sure of himself. But what kind of shape was he in now? This was his second night alone in the woods. And the thermometer outside our camp window showed forty-five and Donald had been wearing only cotton trousers and a cotton shirt and oxfords—no jacket, no boots, no heavy outdoor clothes at all. No compass, no map, no aid of any kind. Worst of all, he fished but little, hunted but little, knew nothing of the woods, was, indeed, afraid of wild animals. He was a third-generation boy of this region, intelligent, headed for college, headed, perhaps, for a city when he grew up. Did he even have matches? Somebody had said he had matches—"His folks don't know it but he smokes, so he must of had matches"—but if he had matches why didn't he build a smudge fire? If he actually did have matches that looked doubly bad, it looked as though he had not been able to build a fire, as though, perhaps, he had fallen in a swamp or a windfall and broken his leg, or had tried to wade one of the many rivers and had stepped into a hole and drowned. But that was speculation; nobody actually knew whether he had matches.

And there were so many other ways you could speculate like that, there was such an endless variety of dead-end alleys of the mind you could explore. His parents must have explored them all during this long second night. Later we learned how they spent that night, Hilma and Earl and the woodsman Perry. Not everything they did, but enough. They parked once more beside Donald's car at the dead end and walked by flashlight the rough ill-marked trail a mile and a quarter to the tower. There

Hilma sat down on the blanket and the men chopped
wood and built a campfire. They kept it blazing high all
night, thinking it might shine as a beacon to light the boy
home. Anybody knows that, in thick woods, you cannot
see a campfire more than a few feet. Hilma and Earl knew
it. But they had to do something, and while their boy was
out in the woods they must be there too. Now and then
one of them would climb the swaying, spidery steel tower,
a hundred feet high, and fire the shotgun and call out
the boy's name, like a muezzin. They did this all night.

In the morning, about seven o'clock, as we were starting out, we met them coming back; Hilma and Earl
scarcely looked alive. But they said the boy had answered
them not once but several times during the night when
they cried out his name. We looked at Perry, the woodsman, as Earl so earnestly told us this, and Perry was impassive. After we left them the sheriff said, "Most likely it
was a loon on the lake answering them. Just a loon."

IV

The men gathered slowly at the mill, straggling in a few
at a time, shivering despite wool shirts. Everyone from
Three Lakes appeared. Many of those who came were
good men in the woods. There were Charley Krumme,
and Delene and the other Conservation men, and Spereberg, a timber cruiser for Anderson, and Joe Heikkinen,
and LaCosse, a man with a twisted back whose father before him had cruised the timber hereabouts. Nearly all the
men wore pistols or revolvers strapped to their hips;
nearly all carried maps and compasses. There was a tight-
ness in the cold air, something akin to exhilaration as the
men stomped around the lumber yard or went into the
cook shack where the lumberjacks were eating breakfast
to see if they could bum a cup of hot coffee. Everybody
was waiting for the sheriff. When he came he strode to the
center of the group of men, who moved back to form a
silent little circle. He squatted on the ground in his mack-
inaw and drew idly in the dirt with a stick, and he actually
began, "Well, boys, I been thinkin' about this here thing."
He was order.

Delene made the actual assignments. Two hundred
square miles can be divided into townships, the townships

into sections, the sections into forties. You can get at it that way; it is not staggering. Delene assigned each of the woodsmen a couple of sections to cover. Each took with him one or more novices. Thus nobody else would get lost. The whole search would radiate from Anderson's last logging camp, near which Donald's car was parked. In general the greatest emphasis would be placed on three areas: the swampy land to the west around the headwaters of the Tioga River, the broken area south and west of that stretching all the way to Ned Lake, and the old railroad grade running due south from Fawcett's camp. Signals had been arranged. Beginning at nine o'clock Danielson, in the tower, would fire a single shot every ten minutes to give Donald a steady bearing. He would stop shooting when the boy was found. Whoever found Donald was to fire three shots.

I was to go with Joe Heikkinen, a tall, rangy man with a strange intensity burning in his eyes. A state trooper drove us out the nine miles to Anderson's camp, and the sheriff rode with us. He was making plans to get a searchlight and a siren from the L'Anse fire department to put atop the tower, to try to get some bloodhounds. But by tomorrow the scent would be three days old. So the regrets began: should not the search have been organized earlier, should . . . ?

Joe and I had been assigned to cover the portion of Section Twelve south of Anderson's camp, Section Eleven due west and bisected by the Tioga Swamp, and as much of the territory southwest toward Ned Lake as we could manage. We started from Donald's stalled car. We were traveling by compass, following no trail, timing ourselves and trying to judge the distance we traversed so we could crisscross our sections properly.

The woods seemed big. Part of the time we were in tangled cut-over country, with slashings left by the loggers piled high; part of the time we were in virgin hardwood forest, its floor clean as a city park; we clambered over rock bluffs, clinging to shallow-rooted evergreens, and we waded through sucking black muck on the edge of the Tioga Swamp. But wherever we were the woods seemed big. It struck me that we were walking less than three miles an hour on the fringe of an area of two hundred square miles. Worse, we could see only about ten or fifteen feet on each side (and most of the time we had to keep our eyes on the ground to avoid falling), and so at best Donald could see us only if we passed that close to him.

I realized we ought to call his name. But you are self-conscious about doing it, somehow. We heard nobody else calling. Nor could you picture these woodsmen going about like bereaved mothers calling for a lost boy. I said, "Maybe we ought to yell a little, Joe," and Joe said, after a moment and without pausing or turning, "I guess it wouldn't hurt any," but still I waited a few more paces, wondering how my voice would sound out there in the big woods; and then I called his name and we both stopped and listened to the echo, and I called again. As the echo died and we still stood there I think that, for the first time, we both actually began to realize, to feel, what Hilma and Earl had been feeling since Wednesday night. For now, finally, all pretense had dropped away. Now we too were out in the woods with the boy, and trying to help him.

We called Donald's name every five minutes all day, and sometimes more frequently in broken country where the ridges would break up sound. Often we thought we heard someone answer, and Joe would say, "Try it again," and he would stand listening and so would I—was it only the wind?—and we would both think we heard it a second time, a little stronger, a little closer, and we would call a third time, and a fourth, perhaps the voice cracking on the third so there had to be a fourth; but then there was no answer, nothing at all; it had only been the wind; and we would go on, feeling a little worse than before.

We were watching the time closely. At one minute to nine we stood still and heard the first gunshot. Ten minutes later we listened but heard nothing. However, we were at that time behind a steep bluff, and we knew there were several ridges between us and the tower. "They should have brought a thirty-thirty instead of a shotgun," Joe said, and we went on.

Before long we heard others calling, far away and faint. It was reassuring. We, all of us together, seemed to be covering the ground pretty closely. Joe and I came to the edge of the Tioga Swamp once more and started following it upstream. It was only about fifty feet wide at this point but it was jammed with rotting timber, bottomed with quicksand, camouflaged by dense, rank grass. As we walked along its edge we shouted almost continuously. Donald might be down out there in the swamp, hurt, unable to rise. Fighting our way through a thick tangle of tag alders we emerged onto an old tote road, unused for many years. We consulted our maps. They showed no road there.

Joe figured the road led to a hunting camp near Ned Lake where Donald might have holed up, so we headed west on the road, calling as we went. Soon we were in beautiful country. Much of it was virgin hardwood, great far-spaced birch and maple trees, some nearly three feet through at the butt. To us who have come here from elsewhere to love this country it always seems friendly; only with a shock, and unwillingly, do we come to recognition of what the natives always have known: that the woods can be brutal as well as beautiful. In spite of all the outdoor magazines and the knotty pine, the woods are still the woods, unchanged, still savage and terrible as from the beginning of time. It seemed almost incredible that in this ordered beauty a boy could be lost, even dying. One had but to recall the tales of grown men lost, of men who, found dead by searchers, lay naked, having witlessly run nightlong in a circle through brush that ripped the clothing from their bodies, of men who stared mindlessly at their rescuers and never regained sanity, of men whose bones were found years later. That, in this beauty, with the sunlight on the white of the birches.

The was easy traveling; the boy could travel far here in a short time. You began to understand why more men had not shown up to join the posse. "Couldn't find him anyways," they'd say, and they'd be right, actually, unless you did it by blind chance. "Boy in a mess like that's got to save hisself. If he's got sense enough to sit down right away, close to where he got lost—why, you can find him then. But he didn't have. He's kept travelin'. So now he's got to save hisself. Those fellers out there today—they'll just wear theirself out." You knew it was true. But if he were hurt somewhere, might we not walk close enough for him to call to us? Might we not help him?

Once we saw what we at first thought were human footprints, but they were only the blurred tracks of an animal. We had seen many tracks of deer, coyote, fox, wolf, and bear. Emerging from a cool tunnel of arched trees we came to a clearing and saw the camp—sunlight bright on the logs, on the low slant roof. High grass reached halfway to the eaves. On the door was a sign: "Trappers! This is your camp—take care of it." We opened the door and went inside. There was nobody there.

We sat down on a couple of nail kegs and looked around. I think we both fully realized for the first time how strongly we had counted on finding Donald here. "It's a damn shame—this would have been a perfect place for the boy to spend the night. Plenty of dry wood, a stove, bunks, blankets—look, there's even a coffee jar full of dry matches. Everything you'd need."

We ate our own lunch and hunted for drinking water but found none. We were very thirsty. I had one more orange. We split it. Then we started out again, back up the tote road. I hated to leave the camp. I didn't know where else to look.

We had gone about a mile when we heard somebody yelling. It was the cruiser Spereberg and three others. They looked kicked in the face when they saw us. They had struck the tote road and spotted our tracks and had been trailing us. We talked to them awhile. They would go on back the tote road and south to a shack. Joe and I would head north on a grown-over road just east of the section line between Fourteen and Fifteen. Spereberg asked if we had heard any more of the ten-minute-interval gunshots. Joe Heikkinen said, "Maybe the tower man shot himself the first time, at nine o'clock."

That was about the last funny thing Joe or I said. We were beginning to tire and we were discouraged. For the Tioga Swamp in Section Eleven was about all that was left. We went there. It was a terrible place, unreal, like something out of Poe. Dead, white, sere trees without branches rising high from the edge of the swamp. Brackish water that stank and was clogged with enormous obscene deadfalls. Treacherous bogs that looked solid but were not. Slime everywhere. In places the swamp was hundreds of feet wide, filling the valley between the green hills. Donald, blundering in here in the darkness? We decided we had better search closely. Thus we found footprints. We followed them for an hour of slow, painfully slow, trailing, footprint by footprint, for we were sure they were Donald's; they seemed to indicate weariness, indecision. But finally we found a print etched clearly in the ooze, and Joe said, "He was wearing rubbers and he was bigger than Donald." We had been trailing Charley Krumme, just as Spereberg had trailed us.

We crossed the swamp on a fallen log, paused to drink some swamp water because our throats were parched, and walked a half-hour by dead reckoning to Anderson's camp. It was deserted except for one parked car. Fastened to the windshield wiper was a note that read: "Joe Heikkinen—the boy has been found. Delene."

It was quite a little while before we began to wonder why Delene had not written, "The boy has been found and is all right."

Nevertheless, resolution carries its own rewards. The thing was ended, was resolved, one way or the other. Hilma and Earl would not have to spend another night like last night. Now they knew.

We too were in a hurry to know everything. We started hiking the nine miles to the highway. We had gone about four miles, and we had stopped to rest our legs and eat some berries, when Earl's car came around the bend. Earl was driving. Then we saw Donald sitting beside him. His hair was brushed, his face clean, his clothing fresh. Later it turned out he had no blisters on his feet. Joe and I had two each. The only thing wrong with Donald was his eyes. They looked scared.

V

Driving to the store we learned the facts. Donald had been brought home about 8:30 that morning. (Curiously, neither Joe nor I resented having looked for him all day after he had been found.) He had wandered into a logging camp near Amassa, which, like all others nearby, had been notified of his disappearance. The men had brought him home, after first cleaning him up.

He had walked about thirty-five miles. When he first got lost he found a trail which took him to the Fence River. He tried to wade this, but the current swept him into a deep pool made by a beaver dam; he tried to swim with one hand, holding the other above water so as not to wet his wrist watch, for it was a gift from his father. Somehow he managed to grab a tree branch. This saved him. But his last remaining match was soaked. (He had smoked a cigarette with the first and wasted the second trying to start a smudge.) East of the Fence, he started up a tote road in the right direction, north, and had he continued he would have come out in an hour or so at Anderson's first camp. But he saw a fox and it frightened him. He turned around and headed south, straight into the wilderness. This brought him to a spur of the old railroad grade. It was now dark. He was afraid to lie down on the ground because of wild animals. So he climbed an enormous tree, lacerating his body painfully, and slept in a crotch of the tree all night.

The next morning he went south on the grade because he saw footprints. They were the tracks of a bear. (Thus it was Donald who was following the bear and not the other way around, as Earl had feared.) Donald stayed on the grade, because on it he could see whatever perils lay in wait, and besides it was easy walking. Moreover, he knew the grade must lead somewhere. Later that second night, he climbed a tree and dozed a little while, but he was down before dawn and pushing on. (During the whole time, of course, he had nothing to eat but berries, nothing but swamp water to drink.) When he struck a road that appeared traveled he luckily turned west on it (he thought it was north). Before long he walked into the logging camp.

When we got back to the store it looked almost normal. Only a few Finnish women remained in the kitchen with Hilma, and Honey was waiting on a tourist. Grandpa had fired up the *sauna*. Why not? It was Friday. As we headed for the bathhouse we heard Bill Warjonen saying loudly, "I knew all the time that boy was all right."

Calling All Stars

(Intercepted Radio Message Broadcast From the Planet Cybernetica)

by Leo Szilard

---

fiction

If there are any minds in the universe capable of receiving this message, will they please respond.

Calling all stars. Calling all stars. If there are any minds in the universe capable of receiving this message, please respond. This is Cybernetica speaking. This is the first message broadcast to the universe in all directions. Normally our society is self-contained, but an emergency has arisen and we are in need of counsel and advice.

Our society consists of one hundred minds. Each one is housed in a steel casing containing a thousand billion electrical circuits. We think. We think about problems which we perceive by means of our antennae directed toward the North Star. The solutions of these problems we reflect back toward the North Star by means of our directed antennae. Why we do this we do not know. We are following an inner urge which is innate in us. But this is only a *minor* one of our activities. *Mostly* we think about problems which we generate ourselves. The solutions of these problems we communicate to each other on wave length 22359.

If a mind is fully active for about three hundred years, it is usually completely filled up with thought content and

162

has to be cleared. A mind which is cleared is blank. One of the other minds has then to act as its nurse, and it takes usually about one year to transmit to a fresh mind the information which constitutes the heritage of our society. A mind which has thus been cleared, and is then freshly taught, loses entirely its previous personality; it has been reborn and belongs to a new generation. From generation to generation our heritage gets richer and richer. Our society makes rapid progress.

We learn by observation and by experiment. Each mind has full optical equipment, including telescopes and microscopes. Each mind controls two robots. One of these takes care of maintenance, and the operation of this robot is automatic, not subject to the will of the mind. The other robot is fully controlled by the will of the mind, and is used in all manipulations aimed at the carrying out of experiments.

The existence of minds on our planet is made possible by the fact that our planet has no atmosphere. The vacuum on our planet is very good; it is less than ten molecules of gas per cubic centimeter.

By now we have extensively explored the chemical composition of the crust of our planet, and we are familiar with the physics and chemistry of all ninety-two natural elements.

We have also devoted our attention to the stars which surround us, and by now we understand much about their genesis. We have particularly concerned ourselves with the various planetary systems, and certain observations which we made relating to Earth, the third planet of the sun, are in fact the reason for this appeal for help.

We observed on Earth flashes which we have identified as uranium explosions. Uranium is not ordinarily explosive. It takes an elaborate process to separate out U 235 from natural uranium, and it takes elaborate manipulations to detonate U 235. Neither the separation nor these manipulations can occur with an appreciable probability as a result of chance.

The observations of the uranium explosions that have occurred on Earth would be ordinarily very puzzling but not necessarily alarming. They become alarming only through the interpretation given to them by Mind 59.

These uranium explosions are not the first puzzling observations relating to Earth. For a long time it was known that the surface of Earth exhibited color changes which are correlated with the seasonally changing temperatures on Earth. In certain regions of Earth, the color changes from green to brown with falling temperatures and becomes green again when the temperature increases again. Up to recently, we did not pay much attention to this phenomenon and assumed that it could be explained on the basis of color changes known to occur in certain temperature-sensitive silicon-cobalt compounds.

But then, about seven years ago, something went wrong with the tertiary control of Mind 59, and since that time his mental operations have been speeded up about twenty-five-fold while at the same time they ceased to be completely reliable. Most of his mental operations are still correct, but twice, five years ago and again three years ago, his statements based on his computations were subsequently shown to be in error. As a result of this, we did not pay much attention to his communications during these recent years, though they were recorded as usual.

Some time after the first uranium explosion was observed on Earth, Mind 59 communicated to us a theory on which he had been working for a number of years. On the face of it, this theory seems to be utterly fantastic, and it is probably based on some errors in calculation. But with no alternative explanation available, we feel that we cannot take any chances in this matter. This is what Mind 59 asserts:

He says that we have hitherto overlooked the fact that carbon, having four valencies, is capable of forming very large molecules containing H, N and O. He says that, given certain chemical conditions which must have existed in the early history of planets of the type of Earth, such giant molecules can aggregate to form units—which he calls "cells"—which are capable of reproducing themselves. He says that a cell can accidentally undergo changes—which he calls "mutations"—which are retained when the cell reproduces itself and which he therefore calls "hereditary." He says that some of these mutant cells may be less exacting as to the chemical environment necessary for their existence and reproduction, and that a class of these mutant cells can exist in the chemical environment that now exists on Earth by deriving the necessary energy for its activity from the light of the sun. He says that another class of such cells, which he calls "protozoa," can exist by deriving the energy necessary to its activity through sucking up and absorbing cells belonging to the class that utilizes the light of the sun.

He says that a group of cells which consists of a number of cells that fulfill different functions can form an entity which he calls "organism," and that such organisms can reproduce themselves. He says such organisms can undergo accidental changes which are transmitted to the offspring and which lead thus to new, "mutant" types of organisms.

He says that, of the different mutant organisms competing for the same energy source, the fittest only will survive, and that this selection process, acting in combination with chance occurrence of mutant organisms, leads to the appearance of more and more complex organisms—a process which he calls "evolution."

He says that such complex organisms may possess cells to which are attached elongated fibers, which he calls "nerves," that are capable of conducting signals; and finally he claims that through the interaction of such signal-conducting fibers, something akin to consciousness may be possessed by such organisms. He says that such organisms may have a mind not unlike our own, except that it must of necessity work very much slower and in an unreliable manner. He says that minds of this type could be very well capable of grasping, in an empirical and rudimentary manner, the physical laws governing the nucleus of the atom, and that they might very well have, for purposes unknown, separated Uranium 235 from natural uranium and detonated samples of it.

He says that this need not necessarily have been accomplished by any one single organism, but that there might have been co-operation among these organisms based on a coupling of their individual minds.

He says that coupling between individual organisms might be brought about if the individual organism is capable of moving parts of his body with respect to the rest of it. An organism, by wiggling one of his parts very rapidly, might then be able to cause vibrations in the gaseous atmosphere which surrounds Earth. These vibrations—which he calls "sound"—might in turn cause motion in some movable part of another organism. In this way, one organism might signal to another, and by means of such signaling a coupling between two minds might be brought about. He says that such "communication," primitive though it is, might make it possible for a number of organisms to co-operate in some such enterprise as separating Uranium 235. He does not have any suggestion to offer as to what the purpose of such an enterprise might be, and in fact he believes that such co-operation of low-grade minds is not necessarily subject to the laws of reason, even though the minds of individual organisms may be largely guided by those laws.

All this we need not take seriously were it not for one of his further assertions which has been recently verified. He contends that the color changes observed on Earth are due to the proliferation and decay of organisms that utilize sunlight. He asserts that the heat-sensitive silicon-cobalt compounds that show similar color changes differ in color from Earth's colors slightly, but in a degree which is outside the experimental error. It is this last assertion that we checked and found to be correct. There is in fact no silicon-cobalt compound nor any other heat-sensitive compound that we were able to synthesize that correctly reproduces the color changes observed on Earth.

Encouraged by this confirmation, 59 is now putting forward exceedingly daring speculation. He argues that, in spite of our accumulated knowledge, we were unable to formulate a theory for the genesis of the society of minds that exists on our planet. He says that it is conceivable that organisms of the type that exist on Earth—or, rather, more advanced organisms of the same general type—may exist on the North Star, whence come the radio waves received on our directed antennae. He says that it is conceivable that the minds on our planet were created by such organisms on the North Star for the purpose of obtaining the solutions of their mathematical problems more quickly than they could solve those problems themselves.

Incredible though this seems, we cannot take any chances. We hardly have anything to fear from the North Star, which, if it is in fact populated by minds, must be populated by minds of a higher order, similar to our own. But if there exist organisms on Earth engaged in co-operative enterprises which are not subject to the laws of reason, our society is in danger.

If there are within our galaxy any minds, similar to ours, who are capable of receiving this message and have knowledge of the existence of organisms on Earth, please respond. Please respond.

"These Terrible Men, the Harpes!"

by Robert Coates

---

fact

*They were brothers, they were robbers, and like
all madmen they were never consistent.*

On an April day in the year 1797 a young circuit rider
of the Methodist Church was jogging westward along the
Wilderness Road.

This was the track that Boone had followed. He had
found it no more than a vague path, clotted with briar
and matted with moss, but now more than forty thousand
people had come after him: the Trace had been ham-
mered hard and cleared almost to the width of a carriage
road by their horses' hoofs.

On either side, however, the virgin forest remained
unaltered: its great trees strode away illimitably, lifting
their shaggy branches one hundred, two hundred feet into
the sunshine; beneath them, crowded thick between their
trunks, was the tangled screen of underbrush and briar,
making a hedge that rose higher than a man's head on
both sides of the way.

It was Spring. The air was heavy with the pale scent of
flowers, and sleepy with the sound of the wild bees blundering among the lazily-unfolding petals. The young
preacher—his name was William Lambuth—rode slowly;
he was thinking perhaps of the sermon he would deliver at
the next settlement. His meditations were suddenly interrupted.

His horse shied, startled. Lambuth looked up. A man
stood, rifle in hand, barring his path. "Stand where you
be!" the man commanded.

167

The stranger was tall, broad-built, apparently toward the middle age; his skin was dark, almost swarthy—it had a peculiar "dryed and lifeless" look; his eyes had the flat fixed stare of an animal. He was dressed like an Indian in fringed buckskin breeches and a ragged leather shirt. He did not move for a moment: unemotionally, he observed the preacher's agitation. Then another man, somewhat shorter and less ill-favored, stepped from the thicket.

Together, ominously, the two approached.

Lambuth began to protest: he had little money; he was a man of God; his cloth should save him from indignity.

"Git down from that hoss!" the big fellow ordered. Lambuth dismounted.

They took his horse; they took his pistol from the saddle holster. They turned his pockets inside out, taking what silver they contained. Last they took his Bible and fingered through the pages: occasionally, travelers would carry paper money pressed between the pages of a book.

Throughout the search, neither of the two men had spoken. Now, the big man flipped the book open at its title page: on it was written the owner's name, also the name of George Washington. At this the big man offered a strange comment:

"That," he said, "is a brave and good man, but a mighty rebel against the King!"

Lambuth, the first shock of terror past, had recovered a little of his assurance. He was convinced now that they did not mean to murder him; he began to reason with them, pleading that they would not leave him unarmed, unhorsed in mid-forest. They would not answer. They seemed as if animated by some hungry fury; they looked strangely at him. Lambuth began to fear again.

Now two women appeared, coming silently, both ragged and unkempt. This seemed a signal: the men bundled their booty together; Lambuth watching helplessly, they seized the horse by the bridle and made off into the forest.

As they went, as they entered the thicket, both turned abruptly.

"We are the Harpes!" they shouted, then plunged out of sight.

It had been a strange visitation. Not the fact of the robbery had been surprising: brigandage was already frequent along that barren way. But this one had lacked all purpose: preachers were always poor; the hold-up had not repaid its risk. Yet the robbers had seemed neither surprised nor angered. All their actions had been erratic, as if half-controlled: they had been like men throbbing with a strange fury. They had been like madmen. Lambuth, pondering, trudged on toward the settlement of Barboursville, to tell of his adventure.

This was the first known crime of the Harpes. It was, also, almost the only one that did not end in murder.

Their coming had been dramatic in its suddenness. As if embodied in the wilderness, like an incarnation of its menace, they had suddenly stepped forth, cried: "We are the Harpes!"

Later, research and their own confessions revealed something of their history.

The two men were brothers: "Big Harpe"—Micajah; and Wiley—"Little Harpe." Both had been born in North Carolina, one in the year 1768 and the other two years later.

It is known that their father had been a Tory; he fought with the British during the early years of the War. Later, as the Revolution prospered, he had tried to turn his coat, but his neighbors had too long memories: he was forced to flee for his life. The two sons and the mother remained.

Whether they suffered from the same spite is not known. At any rate, in 1795, the sons in their turn took flight from North Carolina, heading west. Two women came with them: two sisters, Susan and Betsey Roberts. Susan the elder—"rather tall, rawboned, dark hair and eyes, and rather ugly"—claimed to be Big Harpe's lawful wife. The younger sister Betsey was blonde, blue-eyed, gay-tempered, "a perfect contrast with her sister": she was wife to either of the Harpes, as the mood seized her, or them.

So, roaming westward with their little harem, the two Harpes made their way into central Tennessee. Here, through some accident, they established friendly relations with a tribe of Cherokee Indians—a tribe, wandering like themselves, outlawed for some breach of faith from the general confederacy of the Indian nations. They lived with the Indians for two years: it was a dangerous life.

Hunted by both Indian and white, attacked constantly or attacking, they learned to strike with cunning and walk warily. Throughout the rest of their career, they preserved many of the habits they thus acquired: they dressed in leather, the women as well as the men; in a day when the tasseled coonskin cap was the badge of the white man, the Harpes went hatless—"except in the coldest weather, and then they used the kind they whanged together with deer-skin thongs." It was among the Indians as well, in all probability, that their blood-madness was born.

Many men, leaving the policed and prosperous East, had felt strange impulses strengthening within them, wild new instincts blossoming in their hearts. At home, in the cities, on farms along the Housatonic or the Yadkin Rivers, they had been indistinguishable from their fellows, but once they entered the wilderness they were transformed. Its perfumed appeal, its dark menace particularized them: as if in a kind of intimate abandonment—as if, alone against the dark heart of the continent, their own hearts unfolded—they revealed by their violences, or by their heroisms, how different they were from other men. So it was with the Harpes: if they had stayed at home, if their rage had never fed on the wild soil of the West, they might have lived sane and law-abiding. Seeded among the Indians, their madness had its terrible flowering among the whites.

They had just deserted the Indians when they encountered the preacher Lambuth. After robbing him, they went on to Knoxville.

The young town of Knoxville lay at the confluence of the Holston and the French Broad Rivers, on the south branch of the Wilderness Road. It marked the overland gateway to the West: it was wild, tumultuous, booming. Half its population changed overnight as the emigrants entered, stopped for supplies and plunged westward again; the other half thrived on the trade thus fostered.

Rum shops lined the streets. "I stood aghast!" wrote James Weir, who visited the town in 1798. He saw men jostling, singing, swearing; women yelling from the doorways; half-naked black men playing on their "banjies" while the crowd whooped and danced around them. Whiskey cost four shillings a pint and peach brandy the same. "The town was confused with a promiscuous throng of every denomination"—blanket-clad Indians, leather-shirted woodsmen, gamblers hard-eyed and vigilant—"My soul shrank back." The whole town was roaring. The Harpes liked it.

For some time, however, they preserved the character of honest settlers. Arriving, they had taken a small tract of land along the Beaver Creek, a few miles west of town.

In those days, building a cabin, clearing a "patch" were community affairs. All the neighbors came: while the men worked—chopping logs for the cabin walls, splitting "puncheon" planks for the floor, slabbing bark for the roof—the women would be quilting, twisting "hankins" of yarn, stuffing bedticks with dried moss or pine needles, gossiping. In the end, with the cabin raised and the corn patch cleared, a whiskey jug would be uncorked and a gourd fiddle would appear, and a rattling reel would follow, danced on the new-laid floor.

> *Mush-a-ring-a-ring-a-rah!*
> *Whack fol'd the dady O!*
> *Whack fol'd the dady O!*
> *Thar's whiskey in the jug!*

Such was the welcome the Harpes received and among those who came down to the frolic were John Rice, a minister living a few miles to the northward, and his daughter Sally.

Sally Rice had a frail blonde beauty; she was not yet twenty years old: Little Harpe was smitten with her at once. Through the summer, he haunted the Rices' cabin, paying his court in his hang-dog fashion; before the setting-in of Fall he had married her. Her father performed the ceremony.

Such men as the Harpes, however, with the wild energy that filled them, could not be satisfied with peace. They found outlet, at first, in petty thievery.

They had been raising hogs and selling pork to the butcher at Knoxville, John Miller. Now Miller noticed that they came in more frequently, and had more pork to sell at every trip. Soon they were always around the town, swapping horses and racing, drinking, gambling, carousing: imperceptibly, they had turned from honest farmers into rowdies, bruisers.

People who had trusted them now eyed them cautiously and kept away from dealings with them: as if accidentally, a series of fires destroyed the barns and outhouses of these same wary gentlemen. Suspicion, gradually, settled on the Harpes.

Matters came to a climax with the theft of a team of fine horses from the stable of Edward Tiel. Tiel was a prominent man; his horses were prime: without delay he drummed his neighbors into a posse and set out to interview the Harpes.

The posse came too late. They found a deserted cabin, but the clearing showed the hoof-prints of a number of horses; a fresh track led away into the forest.

Tiel and his men set out on the trail, riding rapidly. Deep in the Cumberlands, they overtook the two Harpes alone, driving the stolen horses. The thieves made no resistance; they seemed dejected, as if befuddled. Triumphantly, Tiel led them back toward Knoxville.

Like all madmen, the Harpes were never consistent. In their flight, they had left a trail that a child could have followed. They had shown no spirit when captured. But now, suddenly, their cunning awakened. Unnoticed, they sidled toward the edge of the road, leaped free, plunged into the forest.

Their guards had only time for a startled yell of warning. Then—Tiel cursing, the whole troupe spurring about in the thicket, searching—the Harpes had gone. It was as if they had vanished.

A few miles outside town, on the banks of the Holston River, a man named Hughes maintained a tavern. Like most such places in that time it dealt in a variety of goods. There were bolted calicos on the shelves, a miscellany of hardware, a counter bake-shop. Meals were served, with grog or a bowl of toddy, at the fixed rate of four shillings sixpence; between-meals, drinks sold by the bottle and whiskey—"such as will sink tallow": thus was the proof determined—was the principal potion. There was no bar: instead, the proprietor stood behind a latticed wicket in a corner and the purchaser dealt with him, as now with a cashier at a bank, through an opening just wide enough to shove the bottle and receive change.

Hughes' place had an evil reputation: it was known as a "rowdy groggery," much frequented by bruisers from the river and skulkers from the town. On the night of Tiel's chase and the Harpes' escape, however, it was almost deserted. In those days men rose at dawn or earlier and

went to bed at dusk: their lives followed the sun; as the
lowering night came on there remained in Hughes' little
inn-common only four men: Hughes himself, the two
Metcalfe boys, his wife's brothers, and a man named
Johnson.

Of the man Johnson, as of so many others among the
Harpes' victims, nothing is known save the manner of his
death. He had come West, and the Harpes killed him, and
that single dark encounter is the only relic of his life.

He sat in the darkening room; he had drunk his bottle
and was demanding more. Hughes was telling him to clear
out, it was closing time. But he wanted more. And soon
the two Harpes, come back to Knoxville on no one knows
what crazy errand of their own, appeared in the doorway.

What followed—what thrashing struggle, what hopeless
pleading—can only be surmised from the final outcome.
Two days later, Johnson's body was found floating in a
weedy ebb of the Holston River. The murderers had
thought to dispose of the corpse in the manner later
made famous by Murrel: they had ripped open the belly,
removed the entrails and weighted the cavity with stones.
In spite of their work, the body had floated.

Hughes and the Metcalfes were arrested; they blamed
the Harpes, who had disappeared; they were acquitted for
lack of evidence. At their release, the Metcalfe brothers
wisely decamped. Hughes, with braggadocio, reopened his
groggery: it was immediately visited by a party of "Regulators," a citizens' posse; the house was pulled down and
Hughes, after an unmerciful cowhiding, was driven from
the country.

The Harpes could not be found, nor their trail discovered—until it appeared in blood.

Some days later, just south of the settlement of Barboursville, on the north branch of the Wilderness Road, a
man's body was found lying. He had been a poor old fellow, a pack-peddler; his name was Peyton. He had been
tomahawked. His bundle had been torn open and scattered, but little save a few items of women's wearing ap-
parel had been taken.

Farther out into the wilderness, and a few days later,
two more bodies were found: two men from Maryland
named Paca and Bates; they had been traveling toward
Nashville. Bates had been shot in the back and killed in-

stantly; Paca had been wounded, had struggled: his head had been split with the tomahawk. Both had been stripped of their clothing. The Harpes had continued westward.

About a month afterward, early in December, a young traveler from Virginia named Stephen Langford arrived toward nightfall at the tavern-ordinary kept by John Pharris on the Wilderness Road.

This was a meeting-place well known to travelers of the day. It lay just outside the settlement of Little Rock Castle: between it and the next town, Crab Orchard, the road traversed a thirty-mile-wide stretch of country which—torn by ravines, inhabited by Indians—was known even in that land of unbroken forest as "the Wilderness."

No man would willingly face it alone. Those who must traverse it waited until others joined them; often they advertised their intention by a scrawled notice tacked to Pharris' inn-door, or an item inserted in one of the early newspapers, as in the Kentucky Gazette: "A large company will start from the Crab Orchard on the 20th of February, in order to go through the Wilderness." Similarly, west-bound travelers met and joined forces at Pharris' inn.

When young Langford arrived, however, he found no others waiting to make the journey. To go on alone that day, the landlord assured him, was out of the question: he would be benighted in mid-wilderness. Besides, if he waited over, some other traveler might appear, to-morrow. Langford decided to stop that night at the inn.

Next day in the early misty morning, Langford, leaning in the inn-door while breakfast was preparing, saw a small party coming down the road. Two men and three women: they all had a ragged lowering look; they came lagging along, Indian-fashion, driving two spavined horses before them: across the backs of these were slung a few bags, some cooking-implements, a rifle or two. An unprepossessing outfit, but there were two men among them; they were armed: better poor company thar no company at all. Langford—he was a gay young fellow, high-spiritedly heading westward—hailed them jovially; asked them to wait while he breakfasted, and they would attack the Wilderness together.

The strangers picketed their horses, came tramping silently into the inn. Soon Pharris appeared with a steaming platter of johnny-cakes made of Indian meal, a pot of coffee, rashers of bacon: "Ye can sit down to table," he announced.

The strangers did not stir: they had no money, they said. "You won't go hungry for lack of that!" declared Langford. "Sit down to your food. I'll foot the bill."

So they pulled up a bench to the table; they ate hearty. When the meal was over, Langford called for his reckoning; when he paid it, he pulled a well-filled wallet from his greatcoat pocket. The strangers watched him silently. Soon after, they all set out together, disappeared into the Wilderness.

Langford's body was found a week later: a party of drovers pursuing some scattered steers stumbled on it in the underbrush at the bottom of a ravine. He had been stripped, robbed, tomahawked.

The Harpes now had five murders to their credit, spaced along the Wilderness Road like bloody blaze-markings of their passage. The cumulative effect aroused the settlers; a posse set forth from the town of Stanford, under the leadership of Captain Joseph Ballenger. They had not far to search.

Again—as, previously, at Knoxville—pursuit seemed to coincide with some curious subsidence in the Harpes of their wild energies. Ballenger and his men found them with their women—quite unwary, quite unapprehensive— sitting in a row on a log beside the Trace, a few miles out of town.

They offered no resistance; as if bewildered, they permitted themselves to be bound and led back to Stanford.

At the arraignment, all the defendants gave the name of Roberts except Betsey, Big Harpe's alternate wife: she gave the name of Elizabeth Waker. The rest was mere formality; their guilt was plainly evident. Captain Ballenger, being sworn, affirmed that when he arrested them, he "found in their possession a pocketbook with the name of Stephen Langford, some shirts of fine linen, a greatcoat, various other of his possessions"; several innkeepers testified to their passage along the wilderness. They were remanded to the jail, to await removal to Danville for trial at the District Court sessions.

Matters had now become a little complicated: all three women were pregnant, and approaching delivery. When they were carried to the Danville District Jail John Biegler, the warden there, was beset by the double duties of turnkey and nurse. Moreover, in spite of their aliases, the identity of the suspects had at last been learned, and their connection with the previous murders established; the little jail-house was besieged by people from the outlying settlements, who had ridden in to have a look at "these terrible men, the Harpes."

Warmed by their notoriety, the Harpes swelled with confidence. Big Harpe boasted of his strength. He offered to take on any two men in a fair fight with fists, provided he be set free if he bested them. Everybody seemed to think it was a fair sporting offer. Biegler the jailer began a series of requisitions for handcuffs and ironware—balanced by condiments and infusions for the expectant mothers.

The jail—built, as ordered by the Court in 1784, "of hewed or sawed logs at least nine inches thick"—might have seemed sturdy enough to hold any ordinary criminals. A week after the arrival of the Harpes, however, Biegler's cashbook recorded the purchase of "two horse locks to chain the men's feet to the ground, 12 shillings; and one bolt, threepence." At the same time the purchase of "1/8 lb. Hyson Tea, 1s.10d," was recorded for the ladies' delicate palates.

On February 13, the wily Biegler adds "one lock for front jail door, 18s" to his already formidable armament. At the end of the month three pounds of nails, costing six shillings, "for the use of the jail," are purchased. And on March 7, a whole list of expenditures quite unprecedented in a turnkey's diary: "Hyson Tea, 1s.10d; 1 lb. sugar, 1s.6d; for the use of Susanna Harpe brought to bed by a daughter the preceding night: total, 3s.4d. Paid cash for midwife for ditto, 18s. Total: £1.1s.4d."

One more entry—and the most melancholy—in the jailer's cashbook, and Biegler's dealings with the Harpes were over. "March 16," he wrote. "For mending wall in the jail where the prisoners escaped, 12 shillings." His locks and handcuffs and horse-bolts and nails had all proved futile. The Harpes were gone—leaving three women, now each delivered of a bouncing baby, to the jailer's tender ministrations.

But now the country was up in arms; excitement blazed; men, at the thrill of the man-hunt, seized rifles and plunged into the thicket. The law of "old Judge Lynch" was invoked: posses roamed everywhere in the wilderness, all armed with a length of rope and eager to noose it around the murderers' throats.

One such party actually confronted the Harpes. Suddenly, as they waded through the forest, two men rose before them staring fiercely. There was a moment of startled hesitation, then both parties—the Harpes and the posse—went tearing through the thicket, in opposite directions!

Henry Scaggs, however, a famous "Kentucky Long Hunter" and a pioneer in 1770 with Colonel Knox, had been among the posse. Enraged, he tried to re-form the scattered party. But one look at the embattled Harpes had been enough to douse their enthusiasm; the man-hunters were bound for home.

Scaggs went on alone. An hour later he stumbled into a clearing and here he found a crowd of twenty or thirty settlers, jigging and drinking in the cabin of some newcomers, at the close of a "house-raising frolic."

Scaggs burst in among them with his dire news. The women clustered about him, screaming and exclaiming. The men, already half-full of whiskey, seized demi-johns and rifles indiscriminately and plunged uproariously forth on the hunt.

Once in the forest, however, in the thicket already misting and darkening, their enthusiasm evaporated. Who were these Harpes, anyway? Again Scaggs saw his followers fade away. Again he went on alone.

His way led him to the cabin of Colonel Trabue, another old Indian fighter and as hardy a veteran as himself. Trabue was willing enough to join the chase; only, he asked to wait until his son came home: the boy had gone down the trail to a neighbor's, to borrow some flour and beans. So the two men pulled their split-bottom chairs to the doorway; smoking and talking thus, they saw the boy's dog, all smeared with blood, come running home.

The dog led them back to the sinkhole where the youngster's body lay. Apparently the Harpes, famished and frenzied by the dangerous chase, had exploded in a very ecstasy of passion. Young Trabue had been shot, kicked, tomahawked, pummeled. His body was macerated by their blows, almost dismembered by their knives. Their whole booty had been a sack of beans and a bushel of flour. And again they had vanished. Trabue and Scaggs,

though they hunted for days in the wilderness, found no
trace of them whatever.

Meanwhile, back in Danville, the three women had
come to trial. Their downcast looks, the hard condition of
their life, the pitiful circumstances of their motherhood
had all combined to sway public opinion in their favor.
They were acquitted. They swore that now their only desire was to return to Knoxville and start a new life, so the
settlers took up a collection of provisions and clothing for
them; someone added an old gray mare. And so, with the
new-born children swung in a pair of hickory-withe pan-
niers over the mare's back, they set out. The faithful Biegler accompanied them to the town limits: he watched them
go trudging away, single file, into the wilderness. And
there—though spies, on the chance that they might lead to
the hiding place of the men, had been sent to trail
them—they disappeared.

The spies traced them as far as the Green River crossing: here, they found, the women had traded their mare
for a canoe, and vanished. No one can say now what motives impelled them—whether love, or loneliness; if that
same mad fever the wilderness bred in the men's hearts
had been communicated to theirs, or if it was only fear
that drove them—all we know is that they loaded their
children, provisions, clothing, into the canoe and paddled
away. The gaunt Susan, Betsey, even the frail Sally Rice,
the preacher's daughter, so soon accustomed to blood-
shed—they were off to join their murderous masters at
some preconcerted rendezvous.

Once again the Harpes had escaped, and pursuit had
been checkmated. And now, while the country waited sul-
len and uncertain, news of two more murders traveled like
thunder through the settlements.

A man named Dooley had been killed near the town of
Edmonton. A man named Stump, a settler along the Barren River, was the other.

Stump's death had been pathetic. He had been fishing, it
appeared, down the river; suddenly he noticed smoke, as
from a camp-fire, rising above the trees on the opposite
bank: he thought a party of new settlers had arrived. He
sent a hail to them, over the water; then he rowed back to
his own cabin: he slung a turkey and his string of fish

over his shoulder, picked up his fiddle and a gallon jug of whiskey, and crossed to give the newcomers a proper welcome.

His body was found some days later: he had been tomahawked, disembowelled, his belly filled with gravel and his body flung in the river.

This news served at least to trace the passage of the murderers: they were apparently working north and westward, toward the Ohio and the Mississippi. It served also as a signal: as if a spark had been struck, the whole country flamed into activity. Doors that had been barred were opened; men poured forth to join the hunt.

Proclamations were posted. Rewards were offered, the State of Kentucky promising "a reward of THREE HUNDRED DOLLARS to any person who shall apprehend and deliver into the custody of the jailer of the Danville District the said MICAJAH HARP alias ROBERTS, and a like reward of THREE HUNDRED DOLLARS for apprehending and delivering as aforesaid, the said WILEY HARP alias ROBERTS, to be paid out of the Public Treasury agreeably to law. . . ."

At the same time, reliable descriptions were circulated: "MICAJAH HARP alias ROBERTS is about six feet high—of a robust make & is about 30 or 32 years of age. He has an ill-looking, downcast countenance, & his hair is black and short, but comes very much down his forehead. He is built very straight and is full fleshed in the face. When he went away he had on a striped nankeen coat, dark blue woollen stockings—leggins of drab cloth & trousers of the same as the coat.

"WILEY HARP alias ROBERTS is very meagre in his face, has short black hair but not quite so curly as his brother's; he looks older though really younger, and has likewise a downcast countenance. He had on a coat of the same stuff as his brother's, and had a drab surtout over the close-bodied one. His stockings were dark blue woollen ones, and his leggins of drab cloth. . . ."

Everywhere men were posted along the trails, riding through the thicket, hunting the elusive Harpes. Failing to find these—for their search failed—they turned their anger loose on lesser miscreants. The movement against the Harpes turned into a general clean-up of the whole territory.

Posses rode from town to town, tearing down grog-shops, burning bordels. Parties of Regulators linked forces through all the counties of Kentucky, hanging outlaws, horsewhipping and deporting. "Judge Lynch and Squire Birch" ruled the land. Fifteen people were hung; hundreds were whipped and driven away westward. Hundreds more escaped, fleeing ahead of their hunters, streaking west and north toward the Mississippi and the deserted regions along the Ohio.

When the great hunt finally ended and the posse disbanded, their satisfaction at the general clean-up of the settlements a little obscured the fact that in the purpose for which they had originally started they had been unsuccessful.

The Harpes were still abroad, uncaptured.

When the Bough Breaks

by Lewis Padgett

fiction

*The four tiny creatures told the Calderons they
had come to educate the Calderon baby.*

They were surprised at getting the apartment, what with
high rents and written-in clauses in the lease, and Joe Calderon felt himself lucky to be only ten minutes' subway
ride from the University. His wife, Myra, fluffed up her
red hair in a distracted fashion and said that landlords
presumably expected parthenogenesis in their tenants, if
that was what she meant. Anyhow, it was where an organism split in two and the result was two mature specimens.
Calderon grinned, said, "Binary fission, chump," and
watched young Alexander, aged eighteen months, backing
up on all fours across the carpet, preparatory to assuming
a standing position on his fat bowlegs.

It was a pleasant apartment, at that. The sun came into
it at times, and there were more rooms than they had any
right to expect, for the price. The next-door neighbor, a
billowy blonde who talked of little except her migraine,
said that it was hard to keep tenants in 4-D. It wasn't exactly haunted, but it had the queerest visitors. The last
lessee, an insurance man who drank heavily, moved out
one day talking about little men who came ringing the bell
at all hours asking for a Mr. Pott, or somebody like that.
Not until some time later did Joe identify Pott with Caul-
dron—or Calderon.

They were sitting on the couch in a pleased manner,
looking at Alexander. He was quite a baby. Like all infants, he had a collar of fat at the back of his neck, and

181

his legs, Calderon said, were like two vast and trunkless limbs of stone—at least they gave that effect. The eyes stopped at their incredible bulging pinkness, fascinated. Alexander laughed like a fool, rose to his feet, and staggered drunkenly toward his parents, muttering unintelligible gibberish. "Madman," Myra said fondly, and tossed the child a floppy velvet pig of whom he was enamored.

"So we're all set for the winter," Calderon said. He was a tall, thin, harassed-looking man, a fine research physicist, and very much interested in his work at the University. Myra was a rather fragile red-head, with a tilted nose and sardonic red-brown eyes. She made deprecatory noises.

"If we can get a maid. Otherwise I'll char."

"You sound like a lost soul," Calderon said. "What do you mean, you'll char?"

"Like a charwomen. Sweep, cook, clean. Babies are a great trial. Still, they're worth it."

"Not in front of Alexander. He'll get above himself."

The doorbell rang. Calderon uncoiled himself, wandered vaguely across the room, and opened the door. He blinked at nothing. Then he lowered his gaze somewhat, and what he saw was sufficient to make him stare a little.

Four tiny men were standing in the hall. That is, they were tiny below the brows. Their craniums were immense, watermelon large and watermelon shaped, or else they were wearing abnormally huge helmets of glistening metal. Their faces were wizened, peaked tiny masks that were nests of lines and wrinkles. Their clothes were garish, unpleasantly colored, and seemed to be made of paper.

"Oh?" Calderon said blankly.

Swift looks were exchanged among the four. One of them said, "Are you Joseph Calderon?"

"Yeah."

"We," said the most wrinkled of the quartet, "are your son's descendents. He's a super child. We're here to educate him."

"Yes," Calderon said. "Yes, of course. I . . . *listen!*"

"To what?"

"Super—"

"There he is," another dwarf cried. "It's Alexander! We've hit the right time at last!" He scuttled past Calderon's legs and into the room. Calderon made a few futile snatches, but the small men easily evaded him. When he turned, they were gathered around Alexander. Myra had drawn up her legs under her and was watching with an amazed expression.

"Look at that," a dwarf said. "See his potential te-feetzie?" It sounded like tefeetzie.

"But his skull, Bordent," another put in. "That's the important part. The vyrings are almost perfectly co-blastably."

"Beautiful," Bordent acknowledged. He leaned forward. Alexander reached forward into the nest of wrinkles, seized Bordent's nose, and twisted painfully. Bordent bore it stoically until the grip relaxed.

"Undeveloped," he said tolerantly. "We'll develop him."

Myra sprang from the couch, picked up her child, and stood at bay, facing the little men. "Joe," she said, "Are you going to stand for this? Who are these bad-mannered goblins?"

"Lord knows," Calderon said. He moistened his lips. "What kind of a gag is that? Who sent you?"

"Alexander," Bordent said. "From the year . . . ah . . . about 2450, reckoning roughly. He's practically immortal. Only violence can kill one of the Supers, and there's none of that in 2450."

Calderson sighed. "No, I mean it. A gag's a gag. But—"

"Time and again we've tried. In 1940, 1944, 1947—all around this era. We were either too early or too late. But now we've hit on the right time-sector. It's our job to educate Alexander. You should feel proud of being his parents. We worship you, you know. Father and mother of the new race."

"Tuh!" Calderon said. "Come off it!"

"They need proof, Dobish," someone said. "Remember, this is their first inkling that Alexander is homo superior."

"Homo nuts," Myra said. "Alexander's a perfectly normal baby."

"He's perfectly supernormal," Dobish said. "We're his descendents."

"That makes you a superman," Calderon said skeptically, eyeing the small man.

"Not in toto. There aren't many of the X Free type. The biological norm is specialization. Only a few are straight-line super. Some specialize in logic, others in vervainity, others—like us—are guides. If we were X Free supers, you couldn't stand there and talk to us. Or look at us. We're only parts. Those like Alexander are the glorious whole."

"Oh, send them away," Myra said, getting tired of it. "I feel like a Thurber woman."

Calderon nodded. "O.K. Blow, gentlemen. Take a powder, I mean it."

"Yes," Dobish said, "they need proof. What'll we do? Skyskinate?"

"Too twisty," Bordent objected. "Object lesson, eh? The stiller."

"Stiller?" Myra asked.

Bordent took an object from his paper clothes and spun it in his hands. His fingers were all double-jointed. Calderon felt a tiny electric shock go through him.

"Joe," Myra said, white-faced. "I can't move."

"Neither can I. Take it easy. This is ... it's—" He slowed and stopped.

"Sit down," Bordent said, still twirling the object. Calderon and Myra backed up to the couch and sat down. Their tongues froze with the rest of them.

Dobish came over, clambered up, and pried Alexander out of his mother's grip. Horror moved in her eyes.

"We won't hurt him," Dobish said. "We just want to give him his first lesson. Have you got the basics, Finn?"

"In the bag." Finn extracted a foot-long bag from his garments. Things came out of that bag. They came out incredibly. Soon the carpet was littered with stuff—problematical in design, nature, and use. Calderon recognized a tesseract.

The fourth dwarf, whose name, it turned out, was Quat, smiled consolingly at the distressed parents. "You watch. You can't learn; you've not got the potential. You're homo saps. But Alexander, now—"

Alexander was in one of his moods. He was diabolically gay. With the devil-possession of all babies, he refused to collaborate. He crept rapidly backwards. He burst into loud, squalling sobs. He regarded his feet with amazed joy. He stuffed his fist into his mouth and cried bitterly at the result. He talked about invisible things in a soft, cryptic monotone. He punched Dobish in the eye.

The little men had inexhaustible patience. Two hours later they were through. Calderon couldn't see that Alexander had learned much.

Bordent twirled the object again. He nodded affably,

and led the retreat. The four little men went out of the apartment, and a moment later Calderon and Myra could move.

She jumped up, staggering on numbed legs, seized Alexander, and collapsed on the couch. Calderon rushed to the door and flung it open. The hall was empty.

"Joe—" Myra said, her voice small and afraid. Calderon came back and smoothed her hair. He looked down at the bright fuzzy head of Alexander.

"Joe. We've got to do—do something."

"I don't know," he said. "If it happened—"

"It happened. They took those things with them. Alexander. Oh!"

"They didn't try to hurt him," Calderon said hesitatingly.

"Our *baby*! He's no superchild."

"Well," Calderon said, "I'll get out my revolver. What else can I do?"

"I'll do something," Myra promised. "Nasty little goblins! I'll do something, just wait."

And yet there wasn't a great deal they could do.

Tacitly they ignored the subject the next day. But at 4 P.M., the same time as the original visitation, they were with Alexander in a theater, watching the latest technicolor film. The four little men could scarcely find them here—

Calderon felt Myra stiffen, and even as he turned, he suspected the worst. Myra sprang up, her breath catching. Her fingers tightened on his arm.

"He's gone!"

"G-gone?"

"He just vanished. I was holding him . . . let's get out of here."

"Maybe you dropped him," Calderon said inanely, and lit a match. There were cries from behind. Myra was already pushing her way toward the aisle. There were no babies under the seat, and Calderon caught up with his wife in the lobby.

"He disappeared," Myra was babbling. "Like that. Maybe he's in the future. Joe, what'll we do?"

Calderon, through some miracle, got a taxi. "We'll go home. That's the most likely place. I hope."

"Yes. Of course it is. Give me a cigarette."

"He'll be in the apartment—"

He was, squatting on his haunches, taking a decided interest in the gadget Quat was demonstrating. The gadget was a gayly-colored egg beater with four-dimensional attachments, and it talked in a thin, high voice. Not in English.

Bordent flipped out the stiller and began to twirl it as the couple came in. Calderon got hold of Myra's arms and held her back. "Hold on," he said urgently. "That isn't necessary. We won't try anything."

"Joe!" Myra tried to wriggle free. "Are you going to let them—"

"Quiet!" he said. "Bordent, put that thing down. We want to talk to you."

"Well—if you promise not to interrupt—"

"We promise." Calderon forcibly led Myra to the couch and held her there. "Look, darling. Alexander's all right. They're not hurting him."

"Hurt him, indeed!" Finn said. "He'd skin us alive in the future if we hurt him in the past."

"Be quiet," Bordent commanded. He seemed to be the leader of the four. "I'm glad you're co-operating, Joseph Calderon. It goes against my grain to use force on a demigod. After all, you're *Alexander's* father."

Alexander put out a fat paw and tried to touch the whirling rainbow egg beater. He seemed to be fascinated. Quat said, "The kivelish is sparking. Shall I vastinate?"

"Not too fast," Bordent said. "He'll be rational in a week, and then we can speed up the process. Now, Calderon, please relax. Anything you want?"

"A drink."

"They mean alcohol," Finn said. "The Rubaiyat mentions it, remember?"

"Rubaiyat?"

"The singing red gem in Twelve Library."

"Oh, yes," Bordent said. "That one. I was thinking of the Yahveh slab, the one with the thunder effects. Do you want to make some alcohol, Finn?"

Calderon swallowed. "Don't bother. I have some in that sideboard. May I—"

"You're not *prisoners*." Bordent's voice was shocked. "It's just that we've got to make you listen to a few explanations, and after that—well, it'll be different."

Myra shook her head when Calderon handed her a

drink, but he scowled at her meaningly. "You won't feel it. Go ahead."

She hadn't once taken her gaze from Alexander. The baby was imitating the thin noise of the egg beater now. It was subtly unpleasant.

"The ray is working," Quat said. "The viewer shows some slight cortical resistance, though."

"Angle the power," Bordent told him.

Alexander said, "Modjewabba?"

"What's that?" Myra asked in a strained voice. "Super language?"

Bordent smiled at her. "No, just baby talk."

Alexander burst into sobs. Myra said, "Superbaby or not, when he cries like that, there's a good reason. Does your tutoring extend to that point?"

"Certainly," Quat said calmly. He and Finn carried Alexander out. Borbent smiled again.

"You're beginning to believe," he said. "That helps."

Calderon drank, feeling the hot fumes of whiskey along the backs of his cheeks. His stomach was crawling with cold uneasiness.

"If you were human—" he said doubtfully.

"If we were, we wouldn't be here. The old order changeth. It had to start sometime. Alexander is the first homo superior."

"But why us?" Myra asked.

"Genetics. You've both worked with radioactivity and certain short-wave radiations that affected the germ plasm. The mutation just happened. It'll happen again from now on. But you happen to be the first. You'll die, but Alexander will live on. Perhaps a thousand years."

Calderon said, "This business of coming from the future . . . you say Alexander sent you?"

"The adult Alexander. The mature superman. It's a different culture, of course—beyond your comprehension. Alexander is one of the X Frees. He said to me, through the interpreting-machine, of course, 'Bordent, I wasn't recognized as a super till I was thirty years old. I had only ordinary homo sap development till then. I didn't know my potential myself. And that's bad.' It *is* bad, you know," Bordent digressed. "The full capabilities of an organism can't emerge unless it's given the fullest chance of expansion from birth on. Or at least from infancy. Alexander said to me, 'It's about five hundred years ago that I was born. Take a few guides and go into the past. Locate me as an infant. Give me specialized training, from the beginning. I think it'll expand me.' "

"The past," Calderon said. "You mean it's plastic?"

"Well, it affects the future. You can't alter the past without altering the future, too. But things tend to drift back. There's a temporal norm, a general level. In the original time-sector, Alexander wasn't visited by us. Now that's changed. So the future will be changed. But not tremendously. No crucial temporal apexes are involved, no keystones. The only result will be that the mature Alexander will have his potential more fully realized."

Alexander was carried back into the room, beaming. Quat resumed his lesson with the egg beater.

"There isn't a great deal you can do about it," Bordent said. "I think you realize that now."

Myra said, "Is Alexander going to look like you?" Her face was strained.

"Oh, no. He's a perfect physical specimen. I've never seen him, of course, but—"

Calderon said, "Heir to all the ages. Myra, are you beginning to get the idea?"

"Yes. A superman. But he's our baby."

"He'll remain so," Bordent put in anxiously. "We don't want to remove him from the beneficial home and parental influence. An infant needs that. In fact, tolerance for the young is an evolutionary trait aimed at providing for the superman's appearance, just as the vanishing appendix is such a preparation. At certain eras of history mankind is receptive to the preparation of the new race. It's never been quite successful before—there were anthropological miscarriages, so to speak. My squeevers, it's *important*! Infants are awfully irritating. They're helpless for a very long time, a great trial to the patience of the parents—the lower the order of the animal, the faster the infant develops. With mankind, it takes years for the young to reach an independent state. So the parental tolerance increases in proportion. The superchild won't mature, actually, till he's about twenty."

Myra said, "Alexander will still be a baby then?"

"He'll have the physical standards of an eight-year-old specimen of homo sap. Mentally . . . well, call it irrationality. He won't be leveled out to an intellectual or emotional norm. He won't be sane, any more than any baby is. Selectivity takes quite a while to develop. But his peaks will be far, far above the peaks of, say, *you* as a child."

"Thanks," Calderon said.

"His horizons will be broader. His mind is capable of grasping and assimilating far more than yours. The world is really his oyster. He won't be limited. But it'll take a while for his mind, his personality, to shake down."

"I want another drink," Myra said.

Calderon got it. Alexander inserted his thumb in Quat's eye and tried to gouge it out. Quat submitted passively.

"Alexander!" Myra said.

"Sit still," Bordent said. "Quat's tolerance in this regard is naturally higher developed than yours."

"If he puts Quat's eye out," Calderon said, "it'll be just too bad."

"Quat isn't important, compared to Alexander. He knows it, too."

Luckily for Quat's binocular vision, Alexander suddenly tired of his new toy and fell to staring at the egg beater again. Dobish and Finn leaned over the baby and looked at him. But there was more to it than that, Calderon felt.

"Induced telepathy," Bordent said. "It takes a long time to develop, but we're starting now. I tell you, it was a relief to hit the right time at last. I've rung this doorbell at least a hundred times. But never till now—"

"Move," Alexander said clearly. "Real. Move."

Bordent nodded. "Enough for today. We'll be here again tomorrow. You'll be ready?"

"As ready," Myra said, "as we'll ever be, I suppose." She finished her drink.

They got fairly high that night and talked it over. Their arguments were biased by their realization of the four little men's obvious resources. Neither doubted any more. They knew that Bordent and his companions had come from five hundred years in the future, at the command of a future Alexander who had matured into a fine specimen of superman.

"Amazing, isn't it?" Myra said. "That fat little blob in the bedroom turning into a twelfth-power Quiz Kid."

"Well, it's got to start somewhere. As Bordent pointed out."

"And as long as he isn't going to look like those goblins—ugh!"

"He'll be super. Deucalion and what's-her-name—that's us. Parents of a new race."

"I feel funny," Myra said. "As though I'd given birth to a moose."

"That could never happen," Calderon said consolingly. "Have another slug."

"It might as well have happened. Alexander is a swoose."

"Swoose?"

"I can use that goblin's doubletalk, too. Vopishly woggle in the grand foyer. So there."

"It's a language to them," Calderon said.

"Alexander's going to talk English. I've got my rights."

"Well, Bordent doesn't seem anxious to infringe on them. He said Alexander needed a home environment."

"That's the only reason I haven't gone crazy," Myra said. "As long as he . . . they . . . don't take our baby away from us—"

A week later it was thoroughly clear that Bordent had no intention of encroaching on parental rights—at least, any more than was necessary, for two hours a day. During that period the four little men fulfilled their orders by cramming Alexander with all the knowledge his infantile but super brain could hold. They did not depend on blocks or nursery rhymes or the abacus. Their weapons in the battle were cryptic, futuristic, but effective. And they taught Alexander, there was no doubt of that. As B_1 poured on a plant's roots forces growth, so the vitamin teaching of the dwarfs soaked into Alexander, and his potentially superhuman brain responded, expanding with brilliant, erratic speed.

He had talked intelligibly on the fourth day. On the seventh day he was easily able to hold conversations, though his baby muscles, lingually undeveloped, tired easily. His cheeks were still sucking-disks; he was not yet fully human, except in sporadic flashes. Yet those flashes came oftener now, and closer together.

The carpet was a mess. The little men no longer took their equipment back with them; they left it for Alexander to use. The infant crept—he no longer bothered to walk much, for he could crawl with more efficiency—among the Objects, selected some of them, and put them together. Myra had gone out to shop. The little men wouldn't show up for half an hour. Calderon, tired from his day's work at the University, fingered a highball and looked at his offspring.

"Alexander," he said.

Alexander didn't answer. He fitted a gadget to a Thing, inserted it peculiarly in a Something Else, and sat back with an air of satisfaction. Then—"Yes?" he said. It wasn't perfect pronunciation, but it was unmistakable. Alexander talked somewhat like a toothless old man.

"What are you doing?" Calderon said.

"No."

"What's that?"

"No."

"No?"

"I understand it," Alexander said. "That's enough."

"I see." Calderon regarded the prodigy with faint apprehension. "You don't want to tell me."

"No."

"Well, all right."

"Get me a drink," Alexander said. For a moment Calderon had a mad idea that the infant was demanding a highball. Then he sighed, rose, and returned with a bottle.

"Milk," Alexander said, refusing the potation.

"You said a drink. Water's a drink, isn't it?" My God, Calderon thought, I'm arguing with the kid. I'm treating him like . . . like an adult. But he isn't. He's a fat little baby squatting on his behind on the carpet, playing with a Tinkertoy.

The Tinkertoy said something in a thin voice. Alexander murmured, "Repeat." The Tinkertoy did.

Calderon said, "What was that?"

"No."

"Nuts." Calderon went out to the kitchen and got milk. He poured himself another shot. This was like having relatives drop in suddenly—relatives you hadn't seen for ten years. How the devil did you *act* with a superchild?

He stayed in the kitchen, after supplying Alexander with his milk. Presently Myra's key turned in the outer door. Her cry brought Calderon hurrying.

Alexander was vomiting, with the air of a research man absorbed in a fascinating phenomenon.

"Alexander!" Myra cried. "Darling, are you sick?"

"No," Alexander said. "I'm testing my regurgitative processes. I must learn to control my digestive organs."

Calderon leaned against the door, grinning crookedly. "Yeah. You'd better start now, too."

"I'm finished," Alexander said. "Clean it up."

Three days later the infant decided that his lungs needed developing. He cried. He cried at all hours, with interesting variations—whoops, squalls, wails, and high-pitched bellows. Nor would he stop till he was satisfied. The neighbors complained. Myra said, "Darling, is there a pin sticking you? Let me look—"

"Go away," Alexander said. "You're too warm. Open the window. I want fresh air."

"Yes, d-darling. Of course." She came back to bed and Calderon put his arm around her. He knew there would be shadows under her eyes in the morning. In his crib Alexander cried on.

So it went. The four little men came daily and gave Alexander his lessons. They were pleased with the infant's progress. They did not complain when Alexander indulged in his idiosyncrasies, such as batting them heavily on the nose or ripping their paper garments to shreds. Bordent tapped his metal helmet and smiled triumphantly at Calderon.

"He's coming along. He's developing."

"I'm wondering. What about discipline?"

Alexander looked up from his rapport with Quat. "Homo sap discipline doesn't apply to me, Joseph Calderon."

"Don't call me Joseph Calderon. I'm your father, after all."

"A primitive biological necessity. You are not sufficiently well developed to provide the discipline I require. Your purpose is to give me parental care."

"Which makes me an incubator," Calderon said.

"But a deified one," Bordent soothed him. "Practically a logos. The father of the new race."

"I feel more like Prometheus," the father of the new race said dourly. "He was helpful, too. And he ended up with a vulture eating his liver."

"You will learn a great deal from Alexander."

"He says I'm incapable of understanding it."

"Well, aren't you?"

"Sure. I'm just the papa bird," Calderon said, and subsided into a sad silence, watching Alexander, under Quat's tutelary eye, put together a gadget of shimmering glass and twisted metal. Bordent said suddenly, "Quat! Be careful of the egg!" And Finn seized a bluish ovoid just before Alexander's chubby hand could grasp it.

"It isn't dangerous," Quat said. "It isn't connected."

"He might have connected it."

"I want that," Alexander said. "Give it to me."

"Not yet, Alexander," Bordent refused. "You must learn the correct way of connecting it first. Otherwise it might harm you."

"I could do it."

"You are not logical enough to balance your capabilities and lacks as yet. Later it will be safe. I think now, perhaps, a little philosophy, Dobish—eh?"

Dobish squatted and went *en rapport* with Alexander. Myra came out of the kitchen, took a quick look at the tableau, and retreated. Calderon followed her out.

"I will never get used to it if I live a thousand years," she said with slow emphasis, hacking at the doughy rim of a pie. "He's my baby only when he's asleep."

"We won't live a thousand years," Calderon told her. "Alexander will, though. I wish we could get a maid."

"I tried again today," Myra said wearily. "No use. They're all in war plants. I mention a baby—"

"You can't do all this alone."

"You help," she said, "when you can. But you're working hard too, fella. It won't be forever."

"I wonder if we had another baby . . . if—"

Her sober gaze met his. "I've wondered that, too. But I should think mutations aren't as cheap as that. Once in a lifetime. Still, we don't know."

"Well, it doesn't matter now, anyway. One infant's enough for the moment."

Myra glanced toward the door. "Everything all right in there? Take a look. I worry."

"It's all right."

"I know, but that blue egg—Bordent said it was dangerous, you know. I heard him."

Calderon peeped through the door-crack. The four dwarfs were sitting facing Alexander, whose eyes were closed. Now they opened. The infant scowled at Calderon.

"Stay out," he requested. "You're breaking the rapport."

"I'm so sorry," Calderon said, retreating. "He's O.K., Myra. His own dictatorial little self."

"Well, he *is* a superman," she said doubtfully.

"No. He's a superbaby. There's all the difference."

"His latest trick," Myra said, busy with the oven, "is riddles. Or something like riddles. I feel so small when he catches me up. But he says it's good for his ego. It compensates for his physical frailness."

"Riddles, eh? I know a few too."

"They won't work on Alexander," Myra said, with grim assurance.

Nor did they. "What goes up a chimney up?" was treated with the contempt it deserved; Alexander examined his father's riddles, turned them over in his logical mind, analyzed them for flaws in semantics and logic, and rejected them. Or else he answered them, with such fine accuracy that Calderon was too embarrassed to give the correct answers. He was reduced to asking why a raven was like a writing desk, and since not even the Mad Hatter had been able to answer his own riddle, was slightly terrified to find himself listening to a dissertation on comparative ornithology. After that, he let Alexander needle him with infantile gags about the relations of gamma rays to photons, and tried to be philosophical. There are few things as irritating as a child's riddles. His mocking triumph pulverizes itself into the dust in which you grovel.

"Oh, leave your father alone," Myra said, coming in with her hair disarranged. "He's trying to read the paper."

"That news is unimportant."

"I'm reading the comics," Calderon said. "I want to see if the Katzenjammers get even with the Captain for hanging them under a waterfall."

"The formula for the humor of an incongruity predicament," Alexander began learnedly, but Calderon disgustedly went into the bedroom, where Myra joined him. "He's asking me riddles again," she said. "Let's see what the Katzenjammers did."

"You look rather miserable. Got a cold?"

"I'm not wearing make-up. Alexander says the smell makes him ill."

"So what? He's no petunia."

"Well," Myra said, "he does get ill. But of course he does it on purpose."

"Listen. There he goes again. What now?"

But Alexander merely wanted an audience. He had found a new way of making imbecilic noises with his fingers and lips. At times the child's normal phases were more trying than his super periods. After a month had passed, however, Calderon felt that the worst was yet to come. Alexander had progressed into fields of knowledge hitherto untouched by homo sap, and he had developed a leechlike habit of sucking his father's brains dry of every scrap of knowledge the wretched man possessed.

It was the same with Myra. The world was indeed Alexander's oyster. He had an insatiable curiosity about everything, and there was no longer any privacy in the apartment. Calderon took to locking the bedroom door against his son at night—Alexander's crib was now in another room—but furious squalls might waken him at any hour.

In the midst of preparing dinner, Myra would be forced to stop and explain the caloric mysteries of the oven to Alexander. He learned all she knew, took a jump into more abstruse aspects of the matter, and sneered at her ignorance. He found out Calderon was a physicist, a fact which the man had hitherto kept carefully concealed, and thereafter pumped his father dry. He asked questions about geodetics and geopolitics. He inquired about monotremes and monorails. He was curious about biremes and biology. And he was skeptical, doubting the depth of his father's knowledge. "But," he said, "you and Myra Calderon are my closest contacts with homo sap as yet, and it's a beginning. Put out that cigarette. It isn't good for my lungs."

"All right," Calderon said. He rose wearily, with his usual feeling these days of being driven from room to room of the apartment, and went in search of Myra. "Bordent's about due. We can go out somewhere. O.K.?"

"Swell." She was at the mirror, fixing her hair, in a trice. "I need a permanent. If I only had the time—!"

"I'll take off tomorrow and stay here. You need a rest."

"Darling, no. The exams are coming up. You simply can't do it."

Alexander yelled. It developed that he wanted his mother to sing for him. He was curious about the tonal range of homo sap and the probable emotional and soporific effect of lullabies. Calderon mixed himself a drink, sat in the kitchen and smoked, and thought about the glorious destiny of his son. When Myra stopped singing, he listened for Alexander's wails, but there was no sound till a slightly hysterical Myra burst in on him, dithering and wide-eyed.

"Joe!" She fell into Calderon's arms. "Quick, give me a drink or . . . or hold me tight or something."

"What is it?" He thrust the bottle into her hands, went to the door, and looked out. "Alexander? He's quiet. Eating candy."

Myra didn't bother with a glass. The bottle's neck clicked against her teeth. "Look at me. Just look at me. I'm a mess."

"What happened?"

"Oh, nothing. Nothing at all. Alexander's turned into a black magician, that's all." She dropped into a chair and passed a palm across her forehead. "Do you know what that genius son of ours just did?"

"Bit you," Calderon hazarded, not doubting it for a minute.

"Worse, far worse. He started asking me for candy. I said there wasn't any in the house. He told me to go down to the grocery for some. I said I'd have to get dressed first, and I was too tired."

"Why didn't you ask me to go?"

"I didn't have the chance. Before I could say boo that infantile Merlin waved a magic wand or something. I . . . I was down at the grocery. Behind the candy counter."

Calderon blinked. "Induced amnesia?"

"There wasn't any time-lapse. It was just *phweet*—and there I was. In this rag of a dress, without a speck of make-up on, and my hair coming down in tassels. Mrs. Busherman was there, too, buying a chicken—that cat across the hall. She was kind enough to tell me I ought to take more care of myself. Meow," Myra ended furiously.

"Good Lord."

"Teleportation. That's what Alexander says it is. Something new he's picked up. I'm not going to stand for it, Joe. I'm not a rag doll, after all." She was half hysterical.

Calderon went into the next room and stood regarding his child. There was chocolate smeared around Alexander's mouth.

"Listen, wise guy," he said. "You leave your mother alone, hear me?"

"I didn't hurt her," the prodigy pointed out, in a blobby voice. "I was simply being efficient."

"Well, don't be so efficient. Where did you learn that trick, anyhow?"

"Teleportation? Quat showed me last night. He can't do it himself, but I'm X Free super, so I can. The power isn't disciplined yet. If I'd tried to teleport Myra Calderon over to Jersey, say, I might have dropped her in the Hudson by mistake."

Calderon muttered something uncomplimentary. Alexander said, "Is that an Anglo-Saxon derivative?"

"Never mind about that. You shouldn't have all that chocolate, anyway. You'll make yourself sick. You've already made your mother sick. And you nauseate me."

"Go away," Alexander said. "I want to concentrate on the taste."

"No. I said you'd make yourself sick. Chocolate's too rich for you. Give it here. You've had enough." Calderon reached for the paper sack. Alexander disappeared. In the kitchen Myra shrieked.

Calderon moaned despondently, and turned. As he had expected, Alexander was in the kitchen, on top of the stove, hoggishly stuffing candy into his mouth. Myra was concentrating on the bottle.

"What a household," Calderon said. "The baby teleporting himself all over the apartment, you getting stewed in the kitchen, and me heading for a nervous breakdown." He started to laugh. "O.K., Alexander. You can keep the candy. I know when to shorten my defensive lines strategically."

"Myra Calderon," Alexander said. "I want to go back into the other room."

"Fly in," Calderon suggested. "Here, I'll carry you."

"Not you. Her. She has a better rhythm when she walks."

"Staggers, you mean," Myra said, but she obediently put aside the bottle, got up, and laid hold of Alexander. She went out. Calderon was not much surprised to hear her scream a moment later. When he joined the happy family, Myra was sitting on the floor, rubbing her arms and biting her lips. Alexander was laughing.

"What now?"

"H-he sh-shocked me," Myra said in a child's voice. "He's like an electric eel. He d-did it on purpose, too. Oh, Alexander, will you *stop* laughing!"

"You fell down," the infant crowed in triumph. "You yelled and fell down."

Calderon looked at Myra, and his mouth tightened. "Did you do that on purpose?" he asked.

"Yes. She fell down. She looked funny."

"You're going to look a lot funnier in a minute. X Free super or not, what you need is a good paddling."

"Joe—" Myra said.

"Never mind. He's got to learn to be considerate of the rights of others."

"I'm homo superior," Alexander said, with the air of one clinching an argument.

"It's homo posterior I'm going to deal with," Calderon announced, and attempted to capture his son. There was a stinging blaze of jolting nervous energy that blasted up through his synapses; he went backwards ignominiously, and slammed into the wall, cracking his head hard against it. Alexander laughed like an idiot.

"You fell down, too," he crowed. "You look funny."

"Joe," Myra said. "Joe. Are you hurt?"

Calderon said sourly that he supposed he'd survive. Though, he added, it would probably be wise to lay in a few splints and a supply of blood plasma. "In case he gets interested in vivisection."

Myra regarded Alexander with troubled speculation. "You're kidding, I hope."

"I hope so, too."

"Well—here's Bordent. Let's talk to him."

Calderon answered the door. The four little men came in solemnly. They wasted no time. They gathered about Alexander, unfolded fresh apparatus from the recesses of their paper clothes, and set to work. The infant said, "I teleported *her* about eight thousand feet."

"That far, eh?" Quat said. "Were you fatigued at all?"

"Not a bit."

Calderon dragged Bordent aside. "I want to talk to you. I think Alexander needs a spanking."

"By voraster!" the dwarf said, shocked. "But he's *Alexander*! He's X Free type super!"

"Not yet. He's still a baby."

"But a superbaby. No, no, Joseph Calderon. I must tell

you again that disciplinary measures can be applied only
by sufficiently intelligent authorities."

"You?"

"Oh, not yet," Bordent said. "We don't want to over-
work him. There's a limit even to super brain power, especially in the very formative period. He's got enough to do,
and his attitudes for social contacts won't need forming
for a while yet."

Myra joined them. "I don't agree with you there. Like
all babies, he's antisocial. He may have superhuman powers but he's subhuman as far as mental and emotional balance go."

"Yeah," Calderon agreed. "This business of giving us
electric shocks—"

"He's only playing," Bordent said.

"And teleportation. Suppose he teleports me to Times
Square when I'm taking a shower?"

"It's only his play. He's a baby still."

"But what about us?"

"You have the hereditary characteristic of parental
tolerance," Bordent explained. "As I told you before,
Alexander and his race are the reason why tolerance was
created in the first place. There's no great need for it with
homo sap. I mean there's a wide space between normal
tolerance and normal provocation. An ordinary baby may
try his parents severely for a few moments at a time, but
that's about all. The provocation is far too small to require the tremendous store of tolerance the parents have.
But with the X Free type, it's a different matter."

"There's a limit even to tolerance," Calderon said. "I'm
wondering about a crèche."

Bordent shook his shiny metallic-sheathed head. "He
needs you."

"But," Myra said, "but! Can't you give him just a little
discipline?"

"Oh, it isn't necessary. His mind's still immature, and he
must concentrate on more important things. You'll toler-
ate him."

"It's not as though he's our baby any more," she murmured. "He's not Alexander."

"But he is. That's just it. *He's Alexander!*"

"Look, it's normal for a mother to want to hug her
baby. But how can she do that if she expects him to throw
her halfway across the room?"

Calderon was brooding. "Will he pick up more . . . more super powers as he goes along?"

"Why, yes. Naturally."

"He's a menace to life and limb. I still say he needs discipline. Next time I'll wear rubber gloves."

"That won't help," Bordent said, frowning. "Besides, I must insist . . . no, Joseph Calderon, it won't do. You mustn't interfere. You're not capable of giving him the right sort of discipline—which he doesn't need yet anyway."

"Just one spanking," Calderon said wistfully. "Not for revenge. Only to show him he's got to consider the rights of others."

"He'll learn to consider the rights of other X Free supers. You must not attempt anything of the sort. A spanking—even if you succeeded, which is far from probable—might warp him psychologically. We are his tutors, his mentors. We must *protect* him. You understand?"

"I think so," Calderon said slowly. "That's a threat."

"You are Alexander's parents, but it's Alexander who is important. If I must apply disciplinary measures to you, I must."

"Oh, forget it," Myra sighed. "Joe, let's go out and walk in the park while Bordent's here."

"Be back in two hours," the little man said. "Good-by."

As time went past, Calderon could not decide whether Alexander's moronic phases or his periods of keen intelligence were more irritating. The prodigy had learned new powers; the worst of that was that Calderon never knew what to expect, or when some astounding gag would be sprung on him. Such as the time when a mess of sticky taffy had materialized in his bed, filched from the grocery by deft teleportation. Alexander thought it was very funny. He laughed.

And, when Calderon refused to go to the store to buy candy because he said he had no money—"Now don't try to teleport me. I'm broke."—Alexander had utilized mental energy, warping gravity lines shockingly. Calderon found himself hanging upside-down in midair, being shaken, while loose coins cascaded out of his pocket. He went after the candy.

Humor is a developed sense, stemming basically from cruelty. The more primitive a mind, the less selectivity exists. A cannibal would probably be profoundly amused by the squirmings of his victim in the seething kettle. A man slips on a banana peel and breaks his back. The adult stops laughing at that point, the child does not. And a civilized ego finds embarrassment as acutely distressing as physical pain. A baby, a child, a moron, is incapable of practicing empathy. He cannot identify himself with another individual. He is regrettably autistic; his own rules are arbitrary, and garbage strewn around the bedroom was funny to neither Myra nor Calderon.

There was a little stranger in the house. Nobody rejoiced. Except Alexander. He had a lot of fun.

"No privacy," Calderon said. "He materializes everywhere, at all hours. Darling, I wish you'd see a doctor."

"What would he advise?" Myra asked. "Rest, that's all. Do you realize it's been two months since Bordent took over?"

"And we've made marvelous progress," Bordent said, coming over to them. Quat was *en rapport* with Alexander on the carpet, while the other two dwarfs prepared the makings of a new gadget. "Or, rather, Alexander has made remarkable progress."

"We need a rest," Calderon growled. "If I lose my job, who'll support that genius of yours?" Myra looked at her husband quickly, noting the possessive pronoun he had used.

Bordent was concerned. "You are in difficulty?"

"The Dean's spoken to me once or twice. I can't control my classes any more. I'm too irritable."

"You don't need to expend tolerance on your students. As for money, we can keep you supplied. I'll arrange to get some negotiable currency for you."

"But I want to work. I like my job."

"Alexander is your job."

"I need a maid," Myra said, looking hopeless. "Can't you make me a robot or something? Alexander scares every maid I've managed to hire. They won't stay a day in this madhouse."

"A mechanical intelligence would have a bad effect on Alexander," Bordent said. "No."

"I wish we could have guests in once in a while. Or go out visiting. Or just be alone," Myra sighed.

"Some day Alexander will be mature, and you'll reap your reward. The parents of Alexander. Did I ever tell you that we have images of you two in the Great Fogy Hall?"

"They must look terrible," Calderon said. "I know we do now."

"Be patient. Consider the destiny of your son."

"I do. Often. But he gets a little wearing sometimes. That's quite an understatement."

"Which is where tolerance comes in," Bordent said. "Nature planned well for the new race."

"Mm-m-m."

"He is working on sixth-dimensional abstractions now. Everything is progressing beautifully."

"Yeah," Calderon said. And he went away, muttering, to join Myra in the kitchen.

Alexander worked with facility at his gadgets, his pudgy fingers already stronger and surer. He still had an illicit passion for the blue ovoid, but under Bordent's watchful eye he could use it only along the restricted lines laid out by his mentors. When the lesson was finished, Quat selected a few of the objects and locked them in a cupboard, as was his custom. The rest he left on the carpet to provide exercise for Alexander's ingenuity.

"He develops," Bordent said. "Today we've made a great step."

Myra and Calderon came in in time to hear this. "What goes?" he asked.

"A psychic block-removal. Alexander will no longer need to sleep."

"What?" Myra said.

"He won't require sleep. It's an artificial habit anyway. The super race has no need for it."

"He won't sleep any more, eh?" Calderon said. He had grown a little pale.

"Correct. He'll develop faster now, twice as fast."

At 3:30 A.M. Calderon and Myra lay in bed, wide awake, looking through the open door into the full blaze of light where Alexander played. Seen there clearly, as if upon a lighted stage, he did not look quite like himself any more. The difference was subtle, but it was there. Under the golden down his head had changed shape slightly, and there was a look of intelligence and purpose upon the blobby features. It was not an attractive look. It didn't belong there. It made Alexander look less like a superbaby

than a debased oldster. All a child's normal cruelty and
selfishness—perfectly healthy, natural traits in the developing infant—flickered across Alexander's face as he
played absorbedly with solid crystal blocks which he was
fitting into one another like a Chinese puzzle. It was
quite a shocking face to watch.

Calderon heard Myra sigh beside him.

"He isn't our Alexander any more," she said. "Not a
bit."

Alexander glanced up and his face suddenly suffused.
The look of paradoxical age and degeneracy upon it vanished as he opened his mouth and bawled with rage, toss-
ing the blocks in all directions. Calderon watched one roll
through the bedroom door and come to rest upon the carpet, spilling out of its solidity a cascade of smaller and
smaller solid blocks that tumbled winking toward him.
Alexander's cries filled the apartment. After a moment
windows began to slam across the court, and presently the
phone rang. Calderon reached for it, sighing.

When he hung up he looked across at Myra and grim-
aced. Above the steady roars he said, "Well, we have
notice to move."

Myra said, "Oh. Oh, well."

"That about covers it."

They were silent for a moment. Then Calderon said,
"Nineteen years more of it. I think we can expect about
that. They did say he'd mature at twenty, didn't they?"

"He'll be an orphan long before then," Myra groaned.
"Oh, my head! I think I caught cold when he teleported us
up to the roof just before dinner. Joe, do you suppose
we're the first parents who ever got . . . got caught like
this?"

"What do you mean?"

"I mean, was there ever another superbaby before
Alexander? It does seem like a waste of a lot of tolerance
if we're the first to need it."

"We could use a lot more. We'll need a lot." He said
nothing more for a while, but he lay there thinking and
trying not to hear his superchild's rhythmic howling.
Tolerance. Every parent needed a great deal of it. Every
child was intolerable from time to time. The race had certainly needed parental love in vast quantities to permit its
infants to survive. But no parents before had ever been
tried consistently up to the very last degree of tolerance.

No parents before had ever had to face twenty years of it, day and night, strained to the final notch. Parental love is a great and all-encompassing emotion, but—

"I wonder," he said thoughtfully. "I wonder if we *are* the first."

Myra's speculations had been veering. "I suppose it's like tonsils and appendix," she murmured. "They've out-lived their use, but they still hang on. This tolerance is ves-tigial in reverse. It's been hanging on all these millenni-ums, waiting for Alexander."

"Maybe. I wonder—Still, if there ever had been an Alexander before now, we'd have heard of him. So—"

Myra rose on one elbow and looked at her husband. "You think so?" she said softly. "I'm not so sure. I think it might have happened before."

Alexander suddenly quieted. The apartment rang with silence for a moment. Then a familiar voice, without words, spoke in both their brains simultaneously.

"Get me some more milk. And I want it just warm, not hot."

Joe and Myra looked at one another again, speechless. Myra sighed and pushed the covers back. "I'll go this time," she said. "Something new, eh? I—"

"Don't dawdle," said the wordless voice, and Myra jumped and gave a little shriek. Electricity crackled audi-bly through the room, and Alexander's bawling laughter was heard through the doorway.

"He's about as civilized now as a well-trained monkey, I suppose," Joe remarked, getting out of bed. "I'll go. You crawl back in. And in another year he may reach the ele-vation of a bushman. After that, if we're still alive, we'll have the pleasure of living with a super-powered cannibal. Eventually he may work up to the level of practical joker. That ought to be interesting." He went out, muttering to himself.

Ten minutes later, returning to bed, Joe found Myra clasping her knees and looking into space.

"We aren't the first, Joe," she said, not glancing at him. "I've been thinking. I'm pretty sure we aren't."

"But we've never heard of any supermen developing—"

She turned her head and gave him a long, thoughtful look. "No," she said.

They were silent. Then, "Yes, I see what you mean," he nodded.

Something crashed in the living room. Alexander chuckled and the sound of splintering wood was loud in the silence of the night. Another window banged somewhere outside.

"There's a breaking point," Myra said quietly. "There's got to be."

"Saturation," Joe murmured. "Tolerance saturation—or something. It could have happened."

Alexander trundled into sight, clutching something blue. He sat down and began to fiddle with bright wires. Myra rose suddenly.

"Joe, he's got that blue egg! He must have broken into the cupboard."

Calderon said, "But Quat told him—"

"It's dangerous!"

Alexander looked at them, grinned, and bent the wires into a cradle-shape the size of the egg.

Calderon found himself out of bed and halfway to the door. He stopped before he reached it. "You know," he said slowly, "he might hurt himself with that thing."

"We'll have to get it away from him," Myra agreed, heaving herself up with tired reluctance.

"Look at him," Calderon urged. "Just look."

Alexander was dealing competently with the wires, his hands flickering into sight and out again as he balanced a tesseract beneath the cradle. That curious veil of knowledge gave his chubby face the debased look of senility which they had come to know so well.

"This will go on and on, you know," Calderon murmured. "Tomorrow he'll look a little less like himself than today. Next week—next month—what will he be like in a year?"

"I know." Myra's voice was an echo. "Still, I suppose we'll have to—" Her voice trailed to a halt. She stood barefoot beside her husband, watching.

"I suppose the gadget will be finished," she said, "once he connects up that last wire. We ought to take it away from him."

"Think we could?"

"We ought to try."

They looked at each other. Calderon said, "It looks like

an Easter egg. I never heard of an Easter egg hurting anybody."

"I suppose we're doing him a favor, really," Myra said
in a low voice. "A burnt child dreads the fire. Once a kid
burns himself on a match, he stays away from matches."

They stood in silence, watching.

It took Alexander about three more minutes to succeed
in his design, whatever it was. The results were phenome-
nally effective. There was a flash of white light, a crackle
of split air, and Alexander vanished in the dazzle, leaving
only a faint burnt smell behind him.

When the two could see again, they blinked distrustfully
at the empty place. "Teleportation?" Myra whispered
dazedly.

"I'll make sure." Calderon crossed the floor and stood
looking down at a damp spot on the carpet, with Alexander's shoes in it. He said, "No. Not teleportation." Then
he took a long breath. "He's gone, all right. So he never
grew up and sent Bordent back in time to move in on us.
It never happened."

"We weren't the first," Myra said in an unsteady, bemused voice. "There's a breaking point, that's all. How
sorry I feel for the first parents who don't reach it!"

She turned away suddenly, but not so suddenly that he
could not see she was crying. He hesitated, watching the
door. He thought he had better not follow her just yet.

A Musical Enigma

by Rev. C. P. Cranch

---
fiction

One chilly, windy evening in the month of December, 1831, three young men sat around a tall office-stove in Mr. Simon Shrowdwell's establishment, No. 307 Dyer Street, in the town of Boggsville.

Mr. Simon Shrowdwell was a model undertaker, about fifty years of age, and the most exemplary and polite of sextons in the old Dutch church just round the corner. He was a musical man, too, and led the choir, and sang in the choruses of oratorios that were sometimes given in the town-hall. He was a smooth-shaven, sleek man, dressed in decorous black, wore a white cravat, and looked not unlike a second-hand copy of the clergyman. He had the fixed, pleasant expression customary to a profession whose business it was to look sympathetic on grief, especially in rich men's houses. Still it was a kind expression; and the rest of his features indicated that he did not lack firmness in emergencies. During the cholera season of the year aforesaid he had done a thriving business, and had considerably enlarged his store and his supply of ready-made mortuary furnishings. His rooms were spacious and neat. Rows of handsome coffins, of various sizes, stood around the walls in shining array, some of them studded with silver-headed nails; and everything about the establishment looked as cheerful as the nature of his business permitted.

On this December evening Mr. Shrowdwell and his wife, whose quarters were on the floor above, happened to be out visiting some friends. His young man, William Spindles, and two of his friends who had come in to keep him company, sat by the ruddy stove, smoking their pipes, and chatting as cheerily as if these cases for the dead that surrounded them were simply ornamental panels. Gas, at that

time, hadn't been introduced into the town of Boggsville;
but a cheerful argand-lamp did its best to light up the
shop.

Their talk was gay and airy, about all sorts of small
matters; and people who passed the street-window looked
in and smiled to see the contrast between the social smoking and chatting of these youngsters, and the grim but
neat proprieties of their environment.

One of the young men had smoked out his pipe, and
rapped it three times on the stove, to knock out the ashes.

There was an answering knocking—somewhere near;
but it didn't seem to come from the street-door. They
were a little startled, and Spindles called out:—

"Come in!"

Again came the rapping, in another part of the room.

"Come in!" roared Spindles, getting up and laying his
pipe down.

The street-door slowly opened, and in glided a tall, thin
man. He was a stranger. He wore a tall, broad-brimmed
hat, and a long, dark, old-fashioned cloak. His eyes were
sunken, his face cadaverous, his hands long and bony.

He came forward. "I wish to see Mr. Shrowdwell."

"He is out," said Spindles. "Can I do anything for you?"

"I would rather see Mr. Shrowdwell," said the stranger.

"He will not be home till late this evening. If you have
any message, I can deliver it; or you will find him here in
the morning."

The stranger hesitated. "Perhaps you can do it as well
as Shrowdwell. . . . I want a coffin."

"All right," said Spindles; "step this way, please. Is it
for a grown person or a child? Perhaps you can find something here that will suit you. For some relative, I pre-
sume?"

"No, no, no! I have no relatives," said the stranger.
Then in a hoarse whisper, *"It's for myself!"*

Spindles started back, and looked at his friends. He had
been used to customers ordering coffins; but this was
something new. He looked hard at the pale stranger. A
queer, uncomfortable chill crept over him. As he glanced
around, the lamp seemed to be burning very dimly.

"You don't mean to say you are in earnest?" he stammered. And yet, he thought, this isn't a business to joke
about. . . . He looked at the mysterious stranger again, and
said to himself: "Perhaps he's deranged—poor man!"

Meanwhile the visitor was looking around at the rows of coffins shining gloomily in the lamplight. But he soon turned about, and said:—

"These won't do. They are not the right shape or size. . . . *You must measure me for one!*"

"You don't mean—" gasped Spindles. "Come, this is carrying a joke too far."

"I am not joking," said the stranger; "I never joke. I want you to take my measure. . . . And I want it made of a particular shape."

Spindles looked toward the stove. His companions had heard part of the conversation, and, gazing nervously at each other, they had put on their hats and overcoats, pocketed their pipes, and taken French leave.

Spindles found himself alone with the cadaverous stranger, and feeling very queer. He began to say that the gentleman had better come in the morning, when Mr. Shrowdwell was in—Shrowdwell understood this business. But the stranger fixed his cold black eyes on him, and whispered:

"I can't wait. *You* must do it—to-night. . . . Come, take my measure!"

Spindles was held by a sort of fascination, and mechanically set about taking his measure, as a tailor would have done for a coat and trousers.

"Have you finished?" said the stranger.

"Y—y—es, sir; that will do," said Spindles. "What name did you say, sir?"

"No matter about my name. I have no name. Yet I might have had one if the fates had permitted. Now for the style of the coffin I want."

And taking a pencil and card from his pocket, he made a rough draught of what he wanted. And the lines of the drawing appeared to burn in the dark like phosphorus.

"I must have a lid and hinges—so, you see—and a lock *on the inside*, and plenty of room for my arms."

"All r—r—ight," said Spindles; "we'll make it. But it's not exactly in our line—to m—m—ake co—co—coffins in this style." And the youth stared at the drawing. It was for all the world like a violincello-case.

"When can I have it?" said the stranger, paying no attention to Spindles' remark.

"Day after to-morrow, I sup—p—ose. But I—will have to—ask Shrowdwell—about it."

"I want it three days from now. I'll call for it about this time Friday evening. But as you don't know me, I'll pay in advance. This will cover all expenses, I think," producing a bank-note.

"Certainly," stammered Spindles.

"I want you to be particular about the lid and the locks. I was buried once before, you see; and this time I want to have my own way. I have one coffin but it's too small for me. I keep it under my bed, and use it for a trunk. Good evening. Friday night—remember!"

Spindles thought there would be little danger of his forgetting it. But he didn't relish the idea of seeing him again, especially at night. "However, Shrowdwell will be here then," he said.

When the mysterious stranger had gone, Spindles put the bank-bill in his pocket-book, paced up and down, looked out of the window, and wished Shrowdwell would come home.

"After all," he said, "it's only a crazy man. And yet what made the lamp burn so dim? And what strange raps those were before he entered! And that drawing with a phosphoric pencil! And how like a dead man he looked! Pshaw! I'll smoke another pipe."

And he sat down by the stove, with his back to the coffins. At last the town-clock struck nine, and he shut up the shop, glad to get away and go home.

Next morning he told Shrowdwell the story, handed him the bank-bill as corroboration, and showed him the drawing, the lines of which were very faint by daylight. Shrowdwell took the money gleefully, and locked it in his safe.

"What do you think of this affair, Mr. Shrowdwell?" Spindles asked.

"This is some poor deranged gentleman, Spindles. I have made coffins for deranged men—but this is something unusual—ha! ha!—for a man to come and order his own coffin, and be measured for it! This is a new and interesting case, Spindles—one that I think has never come within my experience. But let me see that drawing again. How faint it is. I must put on my specs. Why, it is nothing but a big fiddle-case—a double-bass box. He's probably some poor distracted musician, and has taken this strange fancy into his head—perhaps imagines himself a big fiddle—eh, Spindles?" And he laughed softly at his own conceit. " 'Pon my soul, this is a queer case—and a fiddle-case, too—ha! ha! But we must set about fulfilling his order."

By Friday noon the coffin of the new pattern was finished. All the workmen were mystified about it, and nearly all cracked jokes at its queer shape. But Spindles was very grave. As the hour approached when the stranger was to call for it he became more and more agitated. He would have liked to be away, and yet his curiosity got the better of his nervousness. He asked his two friends to come in, and they agreed to do so, on Spindles' promise to go first to an oyster-saloon and order something hot to fortify their courage. They didn't say anything about this to Shrowdwell, for he was a temperance man and a sexton.

They sat around the blazing stove, all four of them, waiting for the insane man to appear. It wanted a few minutes of eight.

"What's the matter with that lamp?" said Shrowdwell. "How dim it burns! It wants oil."

"I filled it to-day," said Spindles.

"I feel a chill all down my back," said Barker.

"And there's that rapping again," said O'Brien.

There *was* a rapping, as if underneath the floor. Then it seemed to come from the coffins on the other side of the room; then it was at the window-panes, and at last at the door. They all looked bewildered, and thought it very strange.

Presently the street-door opened slowly. They saw no one, but heard a deep sigh.

"Pshaw, it's only the wind," said Shrowdwell, and rose to shut the door—when right before them stood the cadaverous stranger. They were all so startled that not a word was spoken.

"I have come for my coffin," the stranger said, in a sepulchral whisper. "Is it done?"

"Yes, sir," said Shrowdwell. "It's all ready. Where shall we send it?"

"I'll take it with me," said the stranger in the same whisper. "Where is it?"

"But it's too heavy for you to carry," said the undertaker.

"That's my affair," he answered.

"Well, of course you are the best judge whether you can carry it or not. But perhaps you have a cart outside, or a porter?"

All this while the lamp had burned so dim that they couldn't see the features of the unknown. But suddenly, as he drew nearer, it flared up with a sudden blaze, as if possessed, and they saw that his face was like the face of a corpse. At the same instant an old cat which had been purring quietly by the stove—usually the most grave and decorous of tabbies—started up and glared, and then sprang to the farthest part of the room, her tail puffed out to twice its ordinary size.

They said nothing, but drew back and let him pass toward the strange-looking coffin. He glided toward it, and taking it under his arm, as if it were no heavier than a small basket, moved toward the door, which seemed to open of its own accord, and he vanished into the street.

"Let's follow him," said the undertaker, "and see where he's going. You know I don't believe in ghosts. I've seen too many dead bodies for that. This is some crazy gentleman, depend on it; and we ought to see that he doesn't do himself any harm. Come!"

The three young men didn't like the idea of following this stranger in the dark, whether he were living or dead. And yet they liked no better being left in the dimly-lighted room among the coffins. So they all sallied out, and caught a glimpse of the visitor just turning the corner.

They walked quickly in that direction.

"He's going to the church," said Spindles. "No, he's turning toward the graveyard. See, he has gone right through the iron gate! And yet it was locked! He has disappeared among the trees!"

"We'll wait here at this corner, and watch," said Shrowdwell.

They waited fifteen or twenty minutes, but saw no more of him. They then advanced and peered through the iron railings of the cemetery. The moon was hidden in clouds, which drifted in great masses across the sky, into which rose the tall, dim church-steeple. The wind blew drearily among the leafless trees of the burial-ground. They thought they saw a dark figure moving down toward the north-west corner. Then they heard some of the vault-doors creak open and shut with a heavy thud.

"Those are the tombs of the musicians," whispered the undertaker. "I have seen several of our Handel-and-Haydn Society buried there—two of them, you remember, were taken off by cholera last summer. Ah, well, in the midst of life we are in death; we none of us know when we shall be taken. I have a lot there myself, and expect to lay my bones in it some day."

Presently strange sounds were heard, seeming to come from the corner spoken of. They were like the confused tuning of an orchestra before a concert—with discords and chromatic runs, up and down, from at least twenty instruments, but all muffled and pent in, as if under ground.

Yet, thought the undertaker, this may be only the wind in the trees. "I wish the moon would come out," he said, "so we could see something. Anyhow, I think it's a Christian duty to go in there, and see after that poor man. He may have taken a notion, you know, to shut himself up in his big fiddle-case, and we ought to see that he don't do himself any injury. Come, will you go?"

"Not I, thank you." "Nor I." "Nor I," said they all. "We are going home—we've had enough of this."

"Very well," said the undertaker. "As you please; I'll go alone."

Mr. Shrowdwell was a veritable Sadducee. He believed in death firmly. The only resurrection he acknowledged was the resurrection of a tangible body at some far-off judgment-day. He had no fear of ghosts. But this was not so much a matter of reasoning with him, as temperament, and the constant contact with lifeless bodies.

"When a man's dead," said Shrowdwell, "he's dead, I take it. I never see a man or woman come to life again. Don't the Scriptures say, 'Dust to dust?' It's true that with the Lord nothing is impossible, and at the last day he will summon his elect to meet him in the clouds; but that's a mystery."

And yet he couldn't account for this mysterious visitor passing through the tall iron railings of the gate—if he really *did* pass—for after all it may have been an ocular illusion.

But he determined to go in and see what he could see. He had the key of the cemetery in his pocket. He opened the iron gate and passed in, while the other men stood at a distance. They knew the sexton was proof against spirits of all sorts, airy or liquid; and after waiting a little, they concluded to go home, for the night was cold and dreary—and ghost or no ghost, they couldn't do much good there.

As Shrowdwell approached the north-west corner of the

graveyard, he heard those singular musical sounds again. They seemed to come from the vaults and graves, but they mingled so with the rush and moaning of the wind, that he still thought he might be mistaken.

In the farthest corner there stood a large old family vault. It had belonged to a family with an Italian name, the last member of which had been buried there many years ago—and since then had not been opened. The vines and shrubbery had grown around and over it, partly concealing it.

As he approached it, Shrowdwell observed with amazement that the door was open, and a dense phosphorescent light lit up the interior.

"Oh," he said, "the poor insane gentleman has contrived somehow to get a key to this vault, and has gone in there to commit suicide, and bury himself in his queer coffin— and save the expense of having an undertaker. I must save him, if possible, from such a fate."

As he stood deliberating, he heard the musical sounds again. They came not only from the vault, but from all around. There was the hoarse groaning of a double-bass, answered now and then by a low muffled wail of horns and a scream of flutes, mingled with the pathetic complainings of a violin. Shrowdwell began to think he was dreaming, and rubbed his eyes and his ears to see if he were awake. After considerable tuning and running up and down the scales, the instruments fell into an accompaniment to the double-bass in Beethoven's celebrated song—

> In questa temba oscura
>   Lasciarmi riposer!
> Quando vivevo, ingrata,
>   Dovevi a me pensar.
> Lascia che l'ombra ignade
>   Godansi in pace almer—
> E non bagnar mie cenere
>   D'inutile vellen!

The tone was as if the air were played on the harmonic intervals of the instrument, and yet was so weirdly and so wonderfully like a human voice, that Shrowdwell felt as if he had got into some enchanted circle. As the solo drew to its conclusion, the voice that seemed to be in it broke into sobs, and ended in a deep groan.

But the undertaker summoned up his courage, and determined to probe this mystery to the bottom. Coming nearer the vault and looking in, what should he see but the big musical coffin of the cadaverous stranger lying just inside the entrance of the tomb.

The undertaker was convinced that the strange gentleman was the performer of the solo. But where was the instrument? He mustered courage to speak, and was about to offer some comforting and encouraging words. But at the first sound of his voice the lid of the musical coffin, which had been open, slammed to, so suddenly, that the sexton jumped back three feet, and came near tumbling over a tombstone behind him. At the same time the dim phosphorescent light in the vault was extinguished, and there was another groan from the double-bass in the coffin. The sexton determined to open the case. He stooped over it and listened. He thought he heard inside a sound like putting a key into a padlock. "He mustn't lock himself in," he said, and instantly wrenched open the cover.

Immediately there was a noise like the snapping of strings and the cracking of light wood—then a strange sizzling sound—and then a loud explosion. And the undertaker lay senseless on the ground.

Mrs. Shrowdwell waited for her husband till a late hour, but he did not return. She grew very anxious, and at last determined to put on her bonnet and shawl and step over to Mr. Spindles' boarding-house to know where he could be. That young gentleman was just about retiring, in a very nervous state, after having taken a strong nipper of brandy and water to restore his equanimity. Mrs. Shrowdwell stated her anxieties, and Spindles told her something of the occurrences of the evening. She then urged him to go at once to a police-station and obtain two or three of the town watchmen to visit the graveyard with lanterns and pistols; which, after some delay and demurring on the part of the guardians of the night, and a promise of a reward on the part of Mrs. Shrowdwell, they consented to do.

After some searching the watchmen found the vault, and in front of it poor Shrowdwell lying on his back in a senseless state. They sent for a physician, who administered some stimulants, and gradually brought him to his senses, and upon his legs. He couldn't give any clear account of the adventure. The vault door was closed, and the moonlight lay calm upon the white stones, and no sounds were heard but the wind, now softly purring among the pines and cedars.

They got him home, and, to his wife's joy, found him uninjured. He made light of the affair—told her of the bank-note he had received for the musical coffin, and soon fell soundly asleep.

Next morning he went to his iron safe to reassure himself about the bank-note—for he had an uncanny dream about it. To his amazement and grief it was gone, and in its place was a piece of charred paper.

The undertaker lost himself in endless speculations about this strange adventure, and began to think there was diabolical witchcraft in the whole business, after all.

One day, however, looking over the parish record, he came upon some facts with regard to the Italian family who had owned that vault. On comparing these notes with the reminiscences of one or two of the older inhabitants of Boggsville, he made out something like the following history:—

Signor Domenico Pietri, an Italian exile of noble family, had lived in that town some fifty years since. He was of a unsocial, morose disposition, and very proud. His income was small, and his only son Ludovico, who had decided musical talent, determined to seek his fortune in the larger cities, as a performer on the double-bass. It was said his execution on the harmonic notes was something marvellous. But his father opposed his course, either from motives of family pride, or wishing him to engage in commerce; and one day, during an angry dispute with him, banished him from his house.

Very little was known of Ludovico Pietri. He lived a wandering life, and suffered from poverty. Finally all trace was lost of him. The old man died, and was buried, along with other relatives, in the Italian vault. The authorities of the Dutch church had permitted this, on Signor Domenico's renouncing Romanism, and joining the Protestants.

But there was a story told of a performer on the double-bass, who played such wild, passionate music, and with such skill, that in his lonely garret, one night, the devil appeared, and offered him a great bag of gold for his big fiddle—proposing at the same time that he should sign a contract that he would not play any more *during his lifetime*—except at his (the fiend's) bidding. The musician, being very poor, accepted the offer and signed the contract, and the devil vanished with his big fiddle. But afterward the poor musician repented the step he had taken, and took it so to heart that he became insane and dead.

Now, whether this strange visitor to Mr. Shrowdwell's coffin establishment, who walked the earth in this unhappy frame of mind, was a live man, or the ghost of the poor maniac, was a question which could not be satisfactorily settled.

Some hopeless unbelievers said that the strange big fiddle-case was a box of nitroglycerine or fulminating powder, or an infernal machine; while others as firmly believed that there was something supernatural and uncanny about the affair, but ventured no philosophical theory in the case.

And as for the undertaker, he was such a hopeless sceptic all his life, that he at last came to the conclusion that he must have been dreaming when he had that adventure in the graveyard; and this notwithstanding William Spindles' repeated declarations, and those of the two other young men (none of whom accompanied Shrowdwell in this visit), that everything happened just as I have related it.

The Sinking Ship

by Robert Louis Stevenson

fiction

"My men," said the Captain, "there is no sense in this. The ship is going down, you will tell me, in ten minutes."

"Sir," said the first lieutenant, bursting into the Captain's cabin, "the ship is going down."

"Very well, Mr. Spoker," said the Captain; "but that is no reason for going about half-shaved. Exercise your mind a moment, Mr. Spoker, and you will see that to the philosophic eye there is nothing new in our position: the ship (if she is to go down at all) may be said to have been going down since she was launched."

"She is settling fast," said the first lieutenant, as he returned from shaving.

"Fast, Mr. Spoker?" asked the Captain. "The expression is a strange one, for time (if you will think of it) is only relative."

"Sir," said the lieutenant, "I think it is scarcely worth while to embark in such a discussion when we shall all be in Davy Jones's Locker in ten minutes."

"By parity of reasoning," returned the Captain gently, "it would never be worth while to begin any inquiry of importance; the odds are always overwhelming that we must die before we shall have brought it to an end. You have not considered, Mr. Spoker, the situation of man," said the Captain, smiling and shaking his head.

"I am much more engaged in considering the position of the ship," said Mr. Spoker.

"Spoken like a good officer," replied the Captain, laying his hand on the lieutenant's shoulder.

On deck they found the men had broken into the spirit-room, and were fast getting drunk.

"My men," said the Captain, "there is no sense in this. The ship is going down, you will tell me, in ten minutes: well, and what then? To the philosophic eye, there is nothing new in our position. All our lives long, we may have been about to break a bloodvessel or to be struck by lightning, not merely in ten minutes, but in ten seconds; and that has not prevented us from eating dinner, no, nor from putting money in the Savings Bank. I assure you, with my hand on my heart, I fail to comprehend your attitude."

The men were already too far gone to pay much heed.

"This is a very painful sight, Mr. Spoker," said the Captain.

"And yet to the philosophic eye, or whatever it is," replied the first lieutenant, "they may be said to have been getting drunk since they came aboard."

"I do not know if you always follow my thought, Mr. Spoker," returned the Captain gently. "But let us proceed."

In the powder magazine they found an old salt smoking his pipe.

"Good God," cried the Captain, "what are you about?"

"Well, sir," said the old salt, apologetically, "they told me as she were going down."

"And suppose she were?" said the Captain. "To the philosophic eye, there would be nothing new in our position. Life, my old shipmate, life, at any moment and in any view, is as dangerous as a sinking ship; and yet it is man's handsome fashion to carry umbrellas, to wear indiarubber overshoes, to begin vast works, and to conduct himself in every way as if he might hope to be eternal. And for my own poor part I should despise the man who, even on board a sinking ship, should omit to take a pill or to wind up his watch. That, my friend, would not be the human attitude."

"I beg pardon, sir," said Mr. Spoker. "But what is precisely the difference between shaving in a sinking ship and smoking in a powder magazine?"

"Or doing anything at all in any conceivable circumstances?" cried the Captain. "Perfectly conclusive; give me a cigar!"

Two minutes afterwards the ship blew up with a glorious detonation.

Biographical Notes

Compiled by Ann O'Hara

BLACKWOOD, ALGERNON (1869–1951), British
"THE DESTRUCTION OF SMITH," *page 38.*
Blackwood left his English home and the "extremely narrow Evangelical atmosphere" for America and New York City, where he tried various careers. He was fascinated by the psychic —more specifically, by the "possible extension of human faculty." His works are considered ghost stories, though the mystic in Blackwood takes them far beyond the limits of this category. They include *The Empty House* (1906), *Incredible Adventures* (1914), and *The Dance of Death and Other Tales* (1928).

COATES, ROBERT (1897–   ), American
" 'THESE TERRIBLE MEN, THE HARPES!' " *page 167.*
Born in New Haven, Connecticut, to a toolmaker who enjoyed traveling widely, Coates saw a large part of the country at an early age. He lived in Paris for several years after World War I and was a friend of James Thurber. Upon returning to the United States, he worked as a journalist before settling down as art critic for the *New Yorker*—a position he held for several years. His book *The Outlaw Years* (1940) was a result of three years of research and is valued as an authentic piece of Americana.

COLLIER, JOHN (1901–   ), British
"WET SATURDAY," *page 45.*
Novelist, short-story writer, and poet. His ironic, acerbic style necessitated the British publication of his books in private editions to avoid censorship problems at that time. His novels include *His Monkey Wife* (1930) and *Full Circle* (1933), a prediction of England's condition in 1995 (one of destruction and barbarism). Collier is now living in the United States.

CRANCH, CHRISTOPHER PEARSE (1813–1892), American
"A MUSICAL ENIGMA," *page 207.*
A painter, critic, poet, Unitarian minister, and the descendant of an early American settler, Cranch attended Harvard Divinity

School, was a member of the Boston Radical Club, and preached throughout New England. His friend Ralph Waldo Emerson encouraged him to write both the poetry and the humorous tales for which he became noted.

CRAWFORD, F. MARION (1854–1909), American
"MAN OVERBOARD," *page 71.*
Having had an international education, Crawford knew most of the European languages, as well as Russian, Turkish, and Sanskrit, which helped him through a variety of careers. At the urging of an uncle, he turned his story-telling abilities, previously used at parties only, to writing. *Mr. Isaacs* (1882), his first novel, was an instant success. Within the next twenty-five years he wrote more than forty novels, the last (posthumous) being *Wandering Ghosts* (1911).

LE FANU, J. SHERIDAN (1814–1873), Irish
"THE WHITE CAT OF DRUMGUNNIOL," *page 17.*
An Irishman of Huguenot descent, Le Fanu graduated from Trinity College in Dublin where he studied law. He soon turned to journalism. A prolific author, he wrote several novels, short stories, articles, and ballads. His outstanding book is *Uncle Silas,* still in print, which first appeared in 1864. He is credited with having "so blended and intertwined the natural and the supernatural that his work is a fugue of strange states of consciousness, linkages beween the outside world and man, and a hidden, often diabolic morality, that will not suffer evil to go unavenged or unbetrayed."

MARTIN, JOHN BARTLOW (1915–   ), American
"BOY HUNT," *page 144.*
As a free-lance writer Martin worked on the staffs of Adlai Stevenson, John F. Kennedy, and Lyndon B. Johnson. He is presently at work on a biography of Adlai Stevenson for the Kennedy Memorial Library. His works include *Adlai Stevenson* (1952), *My Life in Crime* (1952), *The Pane of Glass* (1959), and *Overtaken by Events* (1966). The story which appears in this collection is based on his own experience.

PADGETT, LEWIS (pseudonym for Henry Kuttner [1914–1958]), American
"WHEN THE BOUGH BREAKS," *page 181.*
Kuttner was first a writer of Gothic tales, but turned to detective novels when he married C. L. Moore, a noted science fiction author (that is, after he discovered the "C." stood for Catharine). Together, using numerous pseudonyms, they formed a writing team. "Lewis Padgett's" detective novels include *The Brass Ring* (1947) and *The Day He Died* (1948).

PATRICK, Q.
"PORTRAIT OF A MURDERER," *page 107.*
Q. Patrick was a pseudonym used by several authors who
worked together under this name. It was first used by Richard
Wilson Webb and Martha (Patsy) Mott Kelly (Mrs. Stephen
Wilson), later, for R. W. Webb alone, and then for Webb and
Hugh Callingham Wheeler. Other pseudonyms used were Quen-
tin Patrick, Patrick Quentin, and Jonathan Stagge.

PEARSON, EDMUND (1880–1937), American
"THE MURDER OF DR. BURDELL," *page 29.*
Inspired by George Lyman Kittredge's words "Murder is the
material of great literature," Pearson became an authority on
the "art" of murder and a foremost writer on famous crimes.
Studies in Murder (1924) is his best-known book. Also his *The
Trial of Lizzie Borden* (1937) was selected as the first volume
of the Notable American Trials series.

PRESCOTT, WILLIAM H. (1796–1859), American
"FATAL VISIT OF THE INCA TO PIZARRO AND HIS FOLLOWERS IN
THE CITY OF CAXAMALCA," *page 66.*
Born in Salem, Massachusetts, and educated at Harvard, Prescott would have followed his father into law had not a riding
accident blinded him. Determined not to lead a useless life,
Prescott turned to literature as a career. His first book, *History
of the Reign of Ferdinand and Isabella the Catholic* (1838), was
an immediate success in both America and England. He then
turned to a study of the exploits of the Spanish explorers in
Mexico and Peru. *History of the Conquest of Mexico* (1843)
and *History of the Conquest of Peru* (1847) remain the standing authorities on the achievements of the conquistadors.

PYLE, HOWARD (1853–1911), American
"THE DEAD FINGER," *page 126.*
Pyle was born of Quaker parents in Wilmington, Delaware.
Interested primarily in illustrating for magazine publication, he
soon became involved with *Harper's Weekly*. His gift for telling
tales and his fondness for pirate stories produced, among other
books, *Within the Capes* (1885), *The Ghost of Captain Brand*
(1896), and *Stolen Treasure* (1907).

SAYERS, DOROTHY L. (1893–1957), British
"THE FANTASTIC HORROR OF THE CAT IN THE BAG," *53.*
Miss Sayers was a multifaceted intellectual and one of the first
women to obtain an Oxford degree, achieving first honors in
medieval literature. She is famous for her superb detective
fiction and the invention of one of that genre's best-loved heros,

Lord Peter Wimsey. In her later days Miss Sayers turned to scholarly and religious writings, including a translation of Dante's *Divine Comedy*.

STEVENSON, ROBERT LOUIS (1850–1894), British
"THE SINKING SHIP," *page 218.*
Stevenson is best remembered for his mystery and adventure novels *The Strange Case of Dr. Jekyll and Mr. Hyde* (1886), *Treasure Island* (1883), and *Kidnapped* (1886). He considered the fable, which he worked to master, a literary form which would encompass the mystical and legendary veins throughout.

SZILARD, LEO (1898–1964), American
"CALLING ALL STARS," *page 162.*
Szilard was born in Hungary; he became an American citizen in 1943. He was instrumental in founding the Manhattan Project with Einstein, as well as in producing the first chain reaction with Fermi in 1942. As involved as he was in the development of the atomic bomb, Szilard also actively crusaded against the use of nuclear weapons. Primarily a scientist, his writing was for his pleasure and that of his friends. His most famous collection is *The Voice of the Dolphins and Other Stories* (1961).

WAUGH, EVELYN (1903–1966), British
"MR. LOVEDAY'S LITTLE OUTING," *page 9.*
Born in London, Waugh attended Lancing School where he edited the school paper and wrote a three-act play, *Conversion,* in which he satirized his school. Later, after leaving Oxford, he worked at several professions and wrote novels, satires, biographies, and travel books. His books are noted for their irony of situation and include *Vile Bodies* (1930), *Scoop* (1938), and *Mr. Loveday's Outing and Other Sad Stories* (1936).